Secret Journey

GOLDEN HINDE

Copyright © Philip Davies 2023
Published by Enlighten Me Publishers

First edition

Paperback ISBN-13: 978-1-7398591-2-1
eBook ISBN-13: 978-1-7398591-3-8
Hardback ISBN-13: 978-1-7398591-4-5

Cover Design by Charles Davies
in conjunction with Spiffing Covers
Typesetting by Spiffing Covers

A CIP Catalogue is available from the British Library

Secret Journeys of the
GOLDEN HINDE

by Philip Davies

ACKNOWLEDGEMENTS

Considerable thanks to my youngest son Charles, who with my wife Ann encouraged me between Christmas and New Year to write about The Secret Journeys of the Golden Hinde. Otherwise there would be no novel !

Further appreciation and thanks to my eldest son Paul who read and commented and encouraged together with Lesley Jones 'Perfect The Word' who needed to be very patient with my drafting.

Cover design by Charles Davies. Really good.

Thank you all for your time and efforts. Enjoy the book !

CONTENTS

CHAPTER 1

The City

Monday to Friday

An alarm sounded.

It was dark.

Someone stirred and moaned.

The alarm sounded again.

'Turn that off.'

'Yeah, I'm trying to.'

Peter stretched his hand out from under the covers, trying to feel something familiar, searching for the 'off' button. In his sleepy clumsiness he nudged a glass of water standing on the bedside cabinet towards the edge, and it dropped over the side of the bed with a crash.

'Shit.'

'Just turn the light on. I'm awake now anyway.'

Peter's search was eventually successful and he pressed 'off'.

The clock read 05.51.

Peter sat on the edge of the bed for a moment to gauge his whereabouts. He reached for his glasses from on top of his book on the bedside cabinet and slowly stood up.

'See you later,' he whispered and stretched across the bed to kiss Sally. She rolled the other way as he kissed her.

'Mmm.'

Peter left her to sleep and tried to open the bedroom door quietly. It squeaked as he turned the handle, and then again on opening, as did the floorboard as he stepped out onto the landing.

'I'm awake – don't bother trying to be quiet,' came a sharp, cross voice.

He closed the door behind him; it squeaked again. On the

landing he stripped off his pyjamas, threw them onto the linen basket, and went into the bathroom for a shower. Before turning the shower on, he made sure that the controls were not on 'power shower' mode, otherwise he would be in the doghouse.

He enjoyed the refreshing feeling of a cold shower first thing in the morning. It woke the senses even though he would rather have remained in bed. He brushed his teeth and shaved whilst in the shower and tried not to sing too loudly – as he was prone to on a Monday morning. He didn't want to disturb anyone any further.

He dried himself with a large white towel they had bought when they visited the Blue Lagoon, Iceland. He roughed up his hair with his hands in front of the mirror, noticing a few grey hairs in his sideburns, caused no doubt by the stress of working in the City. His work clothes were on a chair on the landing. He put on his Harry Potter socks and pants that his parents had brought him for his birthday, his sharply ironed white shirt, royal blue tie, and then his smartly tailored dark grey Savile Row suit with very fine silver pinstripes. In front of the mirror he fumbled with a collar stud and struggled to connect it to one side of his shirt.

Glancing at the clock on the windowsill, he realised that he hadn't enough time to deal with the stud now and would have to leave it till he got in the car. He tiptoed downstairs. There was just about enough light from outside without having to turn a light on and he could see through the circular front window that it was raining outside.

'Brolly. Must remember the brolly,' he said quietly to himself. He put his shoes and overcoat on in the porch, grabbed his briefcase and car keys from the rack and left the house, locking the front door behind him. There was still another hour or so before Sally would get up to go to work.

Seventeen minutes to the station, traffic permitting, and the train left in twenty. 'Should be okay,' he said to himself, breathing a sigh of relief as he got into his car, turned on the engine and drove off.

The narrow lane for the first hundred yards meant being careful with oncoming traffic, but at this hour of the day he only had to watch out for a badger scampering across the road in front of him.

With an annual season ticket he was able to proceed through the barriers quickly.

'Morning, sir,' said the ticket collector at the gate. 'A little late today, are we?' He laughed.

'Yeah, made it, but no paper today,' Peter replied, waving his annual season ticket at the station attendant and running towards the platform. He managed to get on the train just as the automatic doors were closing.

Catching the 06.38 meant that there was always a seat, and he slumped down and stared out of the window for a while as the train pulled out of the station. He slowly caught his breath. What should he do now? Rest or work. He and Sally had been down to the Hamble near Southampton for a sailing weekend with some friends who had come over from the States. They had met up with them on Friday evening and set sail early the following morning for a trip around the Isle of Wight. They had glorious sunshine for both days, all their faces reflecting the strength of the sun. Unfortunately, Peter had miscalculated the time of the tide and they were three hours later than planned. So they decided to travel home late last night rather than stay over, which meant a tiring drive and getting to bed after midnight.

'Work,' Peter said to himself.

He opened his briefcase and pulled out his laptop. It whirred itself into action and started to run its security checks. Security measures in his line of business were seriously important – he could be dealing with tens of millions of pounds or dollars in a single transaction.

Eighteen emails over the weekend that apparently need 'urgent' attention, he thought. *And another forty-three of secondary importance. I'm glad I don't do the weekend shift any more, or the night shifts for that matter. Very disrupting to lifestyle.*

He briefly reflected on the time he worked on the Far East futures team. That was a long eighteen months. He had to stay in London as the markets in Hong Kong opened at one thirty in the morning, trading until 8 a.m., UK time. Knackering. For the first few weeks it was fun and a bit of a joke, as he would go off in the morning and play a round of golf at the club; fine when he was younger, but very disruptive trying to grab sleep at three in the afternoon. *Been there, done that, got the T-shirt,* he thought.

Having scrolled through his emails that needed attention he sat back. Team meeting at seven forty-five. That should be good – always interesting on a Monday and a chance to catch up with everyone. He was responsible for thirty-seven traders and had introduced these meetings as soon as he was given promotion. His previous boss had been asked to leave the company at rather short notice, apparently following an inappropriate meeting with a female trader … on the trading floor. That was the final straw for the COO. His boss had been losing money for the company for months, but they gave him the benefit of the doubt, believing he would turn it around. But his luck ran out and things went from bad to worse for him, and having been in the 'red trading account' for the business for three consecutive months, they were looking for any excuse to get rid of him. Shame, Peter thought, because he was actually pretty good at man – and woman, for that matter – management. It was just that he started interfering with the trading and he wasn't up to date with the latest analytics.

Peter had studied at Bath University and got his Masters in mathematics at twenty-two. After being chased by what felt like hundreds of recruitment agencies he decided to join Goldson's after approaching them directly. Before starting, though, he took a three-month holiday travelling to the Far East and Asia. That was a long enough time in his eyes before starting work.

He had worked his way up in the firm from tea boy – well that was what it felt like at times – photocopying, printing, arithmetical checking and making the tea and coffee. But, with additional study in his own time, and after seven years, he had been promoted to team manager, the youngest in the company.

The train juddered to a halt. A red light just before his final stop. He scrolled further down his emails and saw one from … His phone rang

'Hi.'

'Hi. love, sorry I was grumpy this morning, just not enough sleep.'

'No, problem … Sorry I woke you.'

'Just thought I'd remind you that my mum and dad are over for a meal this evening, and we're going to need some food … I'm tied up at school till six thirty today – we've got a parents evening coming up – and—'

'That's fine, Sally, what do you want me to get in?' The train started up again. A train pulled past them, making the ear-piercing noise of metal wheels on metal rails. The platform was now free.

'See what they've got, but you know – three veg, cauliflower, broccoli and carrots, and we've got chicken breasts in the freezer.'

'Yeah, okay. I've got to go now, honey.'

'Okay, see you this evening. Love you.' The call ended as abruptly as it started.

Sally was a lovely girl and the girl for him. He had met her while travelling after university, surfing in Bali, his last stop before coming back to London to start his job.

He had been travelling from island to island staying in hostels close to the coast and moving around from beach to beach with a number of other Brits. One evening, the two of them started chatting at a bar overlooking the surf rolling in, and, with a beautiful sunset as a backdrop, found they had a lot in common – their values about life and nature. Despite the fact that she was American, from Kentucky, she was aiming to be a primary school teacher in the UK. They got to know each other very well, particularly when at different times they went down with a local tummy bug and looked after each other. After their stay in Bali, Sally decided to follow Peter back to the UK, staying initially with him at his parents' house in Surrey, and then moving with him into a two up, two down closer to London. They married four years later.

The train came to a stuttering stop at Waterloo station. He had been daydreaming. Peter remembered he needed to connect his collar stud and then quickly put his laptop away and left the train with his coat over his arm. Through the barriers at platform 12, he headed across the concourse down a series of steps towards the Underground train set up to take passengers directly to Bank Station in the City of London. Not the most glamorous of journeys, in old carriages swaying about from side to side, but very reliable, when it was working. It was today and Peter joined the queue to board. Seats at this time of day were rare but standing for a few minutes was fine by him.

He skipped up the stairs at Bank Station and then made his way across the road junction towards Goldson's offices.

'Morning, Jan.'

'How are you this morning? Did you have a nice weekend?'

'Thanks, Peter, yes, how about you?'

'Could have been longer. See you later.' He walked swiftly towards the lift lobby.

The lift doors opened and he entered. The lift took him smoothly and efficiently straight up to the sixth floor, where it gently came to a halt and the doors slid silently open. He stepped out.

'Morning, Pete.'

'Morning, Jim. Morning, Giles. 'How are you guys doing, good weekends?'

'Great, thanks. We're just getting a coffee. See you in meeting room three in a few moments,' replied Giles, a short, rounded and balding family man of about forty with four children and a very patient wife Peter remembered from the office Christmas party as she tried to drag him away to catch the last train home.

'Okay, I'll see you there in about ten minutes.' Peter headed in the direction of his office.

Promotion for Peter a few months ago had meant his own office slightly away from his team. It had wood panelling on one side and a big leather-topped table, a TV, coffee table and sofa with an oak drinks cabinet in the corner – not that he needed it. He wouldn't drink in the office, but apparently it was in case clients visited and there was at least the offer of a drink available. Peter didn't like his separate office; he preferred to be on the trading floor with the team. That way he knew exactly what was going on and was seen to be part of the solution when problems arose. He also felt he was giving them personal support instead of just sitting in a high office pushing tabs on his keyboard to keep the accountants happy. He hung up his coat and then realised he had left his umbrella on the train. 'Bugger,' he said out loud. *That's another one sent to join the thousands of others in the lost property department of British Transport, and that was Sally's. She'll be cross – it was a good one.*

On opening his briefcase he pulled out his laptop, placed it on his desk and plugged in the cables. There was a knock on the door and the team's secretary, Isabelle, walked into his office. She was a loud and lively lady, slim, with her brown hair tied back in a bun today. Made a change, thought Peter, made her look a lot younger. She was probably in her mid-thirties, with a very strong personality – which she needed in a mostly male environment. She could swear as well as any of them. She was also very good at her job.

'Peter. Morning. Nice weekend?'

'Yeah. Thanks. Yours, Isabelle?'

'Well, how long have you got? It started okay on Friday evening when we went down to the Market Tavern to celebrate Friday as well as Jim's birthday. Steve – you know, my boyfriend – turned up and some of us went for a Chinese, and guess what? On the way home the car had a flat tyre so we spent most of Saturday morning with …'

Peter had heard enough. He recognised someone walking past his door. 'Martin,' he called out. 'Thanks, Isabelle. Sorry, we'll catch up a bit later.'

She turned and left the room.

'Morning, Peter,' replied Giles as he passed Isabelle and walked into Peter's office.

'Giles, what's it been like in Hong Kong?'

'At the moment the markets appear to be treading water, waiting for the announcement regarding trading tariffs.'

'Make sure we're covered both ways – you know the routine.'

'Yeah, sure, Peter.' Giles returned hastily to his workstation.

Peter set up his laptop and took a sip of the coffee that Isabelle had quietly brought in and placed on his desk. 'Yuk,' he said out loud after taking a sip. 'She's put sugar in there again.' He put the cup back on his desk, picked up his pen and notepad and wrote 'Monday 16 June 07.45'. Peter was a well-organised person and any matters, either business or social, he would note down and then put a line through when the item was cleared; this left room in his head for family commitments.

'The View' was otherwise known as meeting room three. The room was plush but inaptly named because it overlooked the wall of a badly maintained building, the blackened backend of an office block. The building looked great from the front and sides, but the City of London Corporation hadn't quite got round to repairing it. The facade still wore the scars of war damage from the 1940s.

Peter was standing in the centre of the meeting room watching the people entering. He preferred to stand because in his experience it ensured meetings ran to time. 'Okay, you guys, settle down now.'

'We've got another rather busy week ahead with a number of key things happening. First and probably the most sensitive is the announcement on Chinese trade tariffs with the US ... Martin, 'Bigsey', is addressing this, so speak to him if you have any questions. Also, Bigsey, make sure that any news gets to the team straight away.'

Martin gave a slight wave of acknowledgement to Peter.

'Do you know the timing yet, Martin?'

'We've been told there's to be an announcement by the Chinese late this morning, but we must keep an eye on the American reaction across the pond, you know what the media is like, and the news may break early.'

'Okay, who's covering the States?'

'That's me, Peter,' a high-pitched voice screeched from the back of the room, followed by a raised hand holding papers flapping in the air. Stuart, although sounding like a mouse, was far from it. He was a semi-professional wrestler until he tore, or somebody tore for him the cruciate ligaments in his right knee, and he still walked with a heavy limp.

'Okay, Stuart, thank you, the same applies to you. And a reminder to you all – keep us all informed of what's happening outside these four walls. You know that if we're ahead by just a couple of seconds it can make us good money. We've also got the European bank announcement on interest rates.'

'I've got that covered, Peter.'

'Thanks, Mike. Right, anyone got anything else to bring to the table? We've got the London market opening in ten minutes.'

'We've got a new carbon emissions trader starting on Wednesday,' said Isabelle. 'She's replaced Alan, and comes with good references, worked here before about three years ago upstairs on the eighth with old-man Jacobs, but she'll still need briefing and so on.'

'Thanks, Isabelle.' Peter paused and looked around the room. He couldn't see Jonathan. *I wonder what's happened to him.* No one said anything. 'Has anyone seen Jonathan this morning? He's not here.'

A voice called out, 'He called to say he's running a bit late. Sue's going to cover his work until he gets in, he said around ten-ish.'

'Okay, thank you, Bernard. Enjoy your week, everyone, and oh yes, I've got a board meeting at ten and you know they can last half an hour or all day.' There was a chuckle from a few members of the team. 'I'll try and catch up with each of you later today or at worst tomorrow morning. Oh yes, and Friday, mustn't forget Friday. If we have a good week, it's team two's outing and we'll meet at three thirty at the Old Bank of England. Have a good one, everyone.' The team acknowledged and responded to Peter positively in various ways.

Peter reflected on Jonathan being late again. *I'll have to get Isabelle to get a 121 organised … not good for morale for one sour grape to take advantage. I don't think he's been to the last two meetings. Mmm.*

'Mike, Jay,' he called out. 'Could you hang on please? As we're here, we need to double-check the dashboard board report following last Friday's events, in particular the sudden rise in Brent Crude, rather odd for this time of year. Thank you.'

Peter's board reports covered his team's investment portfolio, ranging from income, expenditure, turnover, profit, staff performance and levels. One of Peter's key skills was addressing risk in relation to the daily buying and selling of stocks and shares. He had suggested a new investment risk sensitivity analysis, which he had worked up with Mike's and Jay's assistance into a good management tool. The board liked the idea of this when he presented the draft-for-discussion document last month. He now had to deliver.

This would be Peter's fourth monthly report. Mike called the team's dashboard report up on his computer. Jay pointed out the latest version of the proposed sensitivity analysis of risk, using a slight enhancement to the Monte Carlo algorithms, seemed to be working, but suggested waiting until after the meeting to formally present because they still needed to verify the Python coding. Peter decided that he would show what he, Martin and Jay had been working on as 'work in progress', to help the board better understand the deviations from the current risk analysis that the company undertook. He looked up at the clock.

'Okay, you guys, thanks for your help. I'd better head off in case I get called in early. See you later – that's assuming I survive the grilling.'

'Good luck, Peter,' said Mike. 'You can always give us a call if there's anything we can help with and we'll come up to the boardroom.'

'Cheers. I should be okay – and Mike, can you check with Sue to make sure that Jonathan's positions are covered? I'm a little concerned that he's not as committed as he should be. What's his client's base?'

Mike said, 'Yeah, sure, Pete … he's got the Gresham Amy B account, Solomon's and Attina pensions … so that's gonna be around the twenty to thirty mill.'

'We play around with all this financial sensitivity stuff with our investments and you know what, it's the reliability of people that's the biggest risk. What do you say to bringing on AI?' They all chuckled.

'Thanks, guys.'

'You're welcome,' said Jay.

Peter unplugged his laptop and made his way back to his office. On the way, he stopped to see how Sue was getting on, covering Jonathan's work. She was a reliable girl, he thought as he made his way over to her, and might actually be better placed to do Jonathan's job full time. She provided Peter with the right responses to his questions and he left her watching the two screens on her workstation. He returned to his office, put on his jacket, and took a deep breath. 'Here we go again,' he said to himself, looking at a mirror on the wall, and went off to the board meeting.

At 4.45, Peter was still sitting outside the boardroom. They had either forgotten or had had some heavy discussions to get through. He managed to get Isabelle to get him a sandwich for lunch and had realised by mid-afternoon that he was not going to be back with the team for the end-of-day review, so he had called Giles and asked him to deal with it and summarise it for him in an email later.

He had presented his dashboard report mid-morning and it had been warmly received and accepted. He was sure that the extensive questioning he was put under whilst presenting was because he was young and new in the job, and not just because there were a number of sectors in the company that were in the red at the end of the month and trying to show a better report, he looked again at his watch 4.50, he was still waiting to be called in to make his second presentation about reviewing the way in which the firm dealt with risk reporting. The board's review of each team's dashboard reports, he thought to himself, could also be much better organised. It was however, still early days in his position, to propose a reorganisation.

The door to the boardroom suddenly opened, and Sir John Greenhill walked past reception puffing and blowing as he put on his coat and left. He was followed by two other board members with glum looks on their faces, speaking to each other. They ignored him. Sir John's secretary followed them out of the room and came straight over to Peter and apologised. The board had had an extended conference call with head office in the States and his risk presentation would have to wait until next month. *Oh well*, thought Peter, *at least it will be ready for them by then*.

He went back to his office and decided not to interrupt and disrupt the team's end-of-day review, so he picked up his coat and bag and headed home. Not a very satisfactory day, he thought as he walked out of the building towards Bank Underground station, but there was some consolation in that at least he would be home in time for the in-laws. There had been many times that he had arrived home mid-meal, and that had been embarrassing. Although Sally accepted his job and new position he knew that she got frustrated with the lack of respect to home life, not just by him but generally by people working in the City. At times working in the City became 24/7; it was almost like being on a drug – you kept wanting more and more. But, give Sally her due, she made sure they were busy at weekends, and that ensured that Peter did not get sucked into the City way of life.

Out of the fine rain that had descended on the City in the late afternoon, he descended the steps into Bank Underground station. He grabbed one of the free newspapers before the ticket barrier and followed the throng of people down a long, steeply sloping ramp, and on to the train to Waterloo.

The train was packed and the closeness of people standing felt very unhygienic. One sneeze and everyone could catch whatever bug was doing the rounds. It was also hot and sticky, but Peter had managed to slip his damp coat off before the train moved.

The train juddered for some reason just before Waterloo, then moved slowly forward for a short while as if taking a breather, and then came to another juddering halt. A rather burly, unshaven man with greying hair over his shirt collar and wearing a green parka jacket with fur edging to the hood, barged into Peter as the train stopped. The man breathed heavily with a rushing of air through his nose and mouth. *He must be a connoisseur of garlic – it's fine if you've eaten it yourself.* Peter turned his face away from the man. He and the other passengers waited patiently and quietly for the train to move off, listening out for a train to pass from the opposite direction, knowing that that was the signal for the train to get going again and into Waterloo. A sudden jolting movement of the carriage forward and the man in the parka jacket leant into him again. Peter turned slightly and looked at the man briefly. He had light blue-grey eyes and a wry smile. Peter turned away again and shook his head.

'Mind you read the adverts section in the paper, page twenty-one,' the man said to Peter as they got off the train.

Peter heard the man's comment but ignored it and didn't reply. There were some weird people from time to time on the Underground, but although it was rather early; he decided that this man was one of them and quickly walked towards Platform 13 for his train home. Just before the ticket barrier he remembered that he needed to buy food for the evening meal, so he headed back up onto the concourse and into M&S. It was always good quality but a bit on the expensive side, *But that's perhaps what you end up paying for,* he thought.

Peter managed to get a seat on the train, which he was thankful for, because he could check on the trading carried out by his team during the day as well as some of his own investments. With his laptop suitably up and running, it showed the FTSE down fifty-eight points, Nasdaq composite down 120 points in early trading, Dow Jones Industrial … Standard and Poor 500 … *Mm,* he thought, looking out of the window as the train pulled out of the station, *and no announcement about trading tariffs. I wonder how the team has reacted. Still no email from Giles.*

His own investments were the next he needed to check. Discussions with Sally, when they had decided to go green, addressed their beliefs and values towards nature and sustainability and had made the decision-making process of the type of companies to invest in much easier. He scrolled down the screen of his laptop. Satsev UK Wind Systems 1231 … Green Roof 141 … NJP 42 and Pure Green & Clean 884 (partly) for electric cars. Scrolling down the screen further he came to Canadian

Renewables Pure, SunLight Energy Corp, Greenfields Renewables, and finally checked his portfolio summary. *They look generally okay,* he thought, *but at the end of the day, it's all down to market sentiment.*

His train journey home was uneventful. The email he was expecting from Giles arrived in his mailbox as the train was coming to a stop in his station. He quickly glanced at it and spotted the words 'failure' and 'drop in market' … 'Jonathan still not in'. This concerned him. 'We can't have this,' Peter said out loud in the carriage. The lady sitting opposite looked up at him and winked, as she pointed out an advert in the newspaper she was holding. Peter gave a fake smile back. He hadn't time to read the paper or the full message on his phone; it would have to wait till later. He rushed to get off the train and left his newspaper on the seat, which made him cross; as he and Sally enjoyed doing the Sudoku challenges in bed before going to sleep.

Peter had only met his in-laws a handful of times before this evening – at the wedding in the States and then for a few days after their two-week honeymoon driving around the west coast of Canada. They had accepted Peter with open arms. Sally was the youngest of four girls and the one that her parents had most difficulty communicating with and seeing eye to eye with on worldly matters. This was primarily because she believed that everyone had a responsibility to be carbon neutral and should not ignore the environment for their own betterment. Sally's parents had wanted her to become a doctor or at the very least join the medical profession in some way, but Sally considered that it was up to her to decide what to do rather than be dictated to, just because her sisters were doctors and nurses. But teaching children required empathy and understanding as well as fun and enjoyment, so she followed a career in teaching.

Sally's parents, having retired the previous year, had decided that to celebrate the occasion they would make the most of an extended holiday. They had arrived in London last month and were planning to tour Europe, starting with the UK. They had popped in to see them for a night in their hired motorhome after they had arrived, and had been travelling around the UK for some five weeks. They were stopping over before catching the ferry over to Spain from Southampton. They would drive south through Spain to the Algarve and then along the Mediterranean coast as far as Italy, north through the Alps, dropping down into Germany then up as far as Estonia, west through the Baltic states and Scandinavian countries and then finally catch the boat from Esbjerg in Denmark back to England. They worked out that the loop would take about ten weeks without rushing their travels.

CHAPTER 2

The In-Laws

When Peter arrived home, the big white motorhome was parked outside the house. They had apparently arrived earlier in the afternoon and were sitting in their kitchen area with a hot drink and watching television when Peter knocked on their door. Peter greeted them and they followed him into the house.

He sent a text to Sally, telling her that her parents had already arrived so that she wouldn't worry about them, and that he had bought the food for the evening meal. He changed and joined his in-laws downstairs in the lounge. They talked about where they had been, how narrow the roads were, and agreed that they would leave the detail until later when Sally got back from school, otherwise they would be repeating themselves. Peter sorted out drinks for his guests and, even though Sally had still not made it back from school and she liked to be in charge of the kitchen, he decided to prepare the vegetables. Sally could take over when she got back. As he opened the larder door, Edith, Sally's mum appeared, asking if Peter needed any help. He knew from the last time they stayed that it was pointless arguing with her and understood where Sally got her need to be in charge of the kitchen from. She took over from Peter, so he left her to it and joined Ed in the garden.

Ed was very interested in Peter's work, particularly as he had quite a large portfolio of shares, and was pleased to hear that with promotion they now had the opportunity to move to a bigger house. Although they had two bedrooms, only one was usable as a bedroom; the other was geared up to home working for Peter, and also housed a large TV screen on one wall and on another his floor-to-ceiling library of computer games. His in-laws would be sleeping in their 'home on wheels' again. Peter wasn't overly worried about that, although Sally felt a bit mean about it.

Peter's phone beeped. Text from Sally, home in ten. This was followed by another beep from his phone. Text from Bigsey: 'Thought you would like to know that Jonathan has handed in his notice and also that his investments are heavily down today. Could be as much as six figures. See you in the morning. B.'

Nothing like leaving us to sort out his mess, thought Peter, although to be fair it wasn't quite like that, at least he hoped it wouldn't be. He had been in that sort of situation before – investments out of control and the trader has lost or is losing money. A sudden drop or devaluation of a currency had caught him out in the past, but his new risk management reporting was geared up to minimise that problem. He would just have to do what he could to recover the situation in the morning.

'Anything wrong?' asked Ed.

'No, it's fine, Ed. Thank you. You know, just work. Nothing I can't deal with in the morning.' Peter was hoping that was the case – a six-figure loss was sackable on the spot.

Peter heard the front door open and then close with a slam, followed by Sally's voice.

'Hi, everyone, I'm back.' Sally's bunch of keys landed shortly after on the kitchen table. 'Hi, Mom, good to see you. You look well. Where's Dad?' She gave her mother a big hug.

'He's outside walking around the garden.'

'Hi, darling, how are you?'

'I'm fine thanks, Sal. How was your day?'

Sally didn't respond to Peter but looked at her mother. 'Let me sort this out, Mom. I'll be quicker.'

'No,no Sally, you've been working all day. You and Peter go outside and join Dad. Go on and say hi and then come back and we can get dinner together.' Edith pushed her daughter's arm away from the worksurface. Sally and Peter walked out into the garden.

A further text had landed on Peter's phone. It read: 'What's this I hear of the huge losses on the Soloman and Greens contracts? I want you in first thing in the morning to properly explain yourself or you are out of a job. 08.30 my office.' It was Peter's immediate boss.

'Shit,' he said under his breath. *It must be a big six-figure number.*

'Hi, Dad, how you been?'

'You've grown, Sally,' said Ed chuckling and fondly embracing his youngest daughter, 'or have I shrunk? Your mother's preparing the meal.'

'Yeah, Dad. I'll leave her to it. You know what she's like when she's in the kitchen. Shall we sit outside and eat? It's such a lovely evening – you've brought the good weather with you, Dad.'

'Yeah, good idea,' Peter said, needing to read more fully the text messages he had received. 'I'll go and get the table mats and cutlery whilst you two catch up. I was just telling your dad about my promotion, Sally.' Peter read his text messages, and followed them out onto the patio with the tray of cutlery and listened to what the two of them were saying as he started to lay the table for dinner.

'Yeh, it's really good and we've started looking for a bigger house up in the Surrey Hills with a bigger garden so that we can have some ducks and chickens. That's one thing I miss about home, Dad, the farm and everything.'

'Peter and I were chatting earlier about his work and then he had a couple of texts that seemed to concern him.' Peter looked across at Ed and lifted his eyebrows and smiled back at him.

'Don't you worry yourself, Dad, you're on holiday. Peter's always getting them. It's mostly people just wanting to share an investment problem or pass the buck. But he's good at trying to solve their problems and he's also good at protecting the people that work for him. That's probably why he gets on with most people and why he got a promotion.'

'Oh yes, I forgot. Your mum said it will be about five minutes and if we could sit up she'll bring it out. Ed, what would you like to drink?'

'Just water please, Peter. Thank you.'

'Sally?'

'I'll have a glass of the white wine in the fridge if there's any left from the weekend.'

Peter returned to the house and a few moments later brought out the drinks for the four of them. He was followed closely by Edith with the tray of food. The chicken breasts and salads for Ed and Edith, vegetarian dishes for Peter and Sally.

'Cheers and good health, everyone – lovely to see you both again,' said Ed and Edith, clinking their glasses with everyone at the table.

'And you too,' said Peter and Sally in unison. 'Glad you made it around the UK in one piece,' Peter added.

'Well, we did have a minor dent on the side of the RV, but I put that down to others not paying attention and not my judgement,' said Ed.

'Your father drives very well over here, Sally,' said Edith, gently slapping Ed's thigh.

'Tell us about your travels around the UK. We've been longing to hear how you got on, haven't we, Peter,' said Sally, and tucked into her food. Peter, with a mouthful of food, nodded in reply.

Ed and Edith entertained Peter and Sally for the whole evening with stories of pirates and Cornish cider, the swimming pool on top of the building in Bath, visiting William Shakespeare, or not quite, in Stratford upon Avon.

'Did you know, honey,' Edith looked questioningly at Sally, 'that Shakespeare was born the same day as you?'

'Well I never. No, I didn't, Mom,' Sally replied.

'Twenty-sixth of April 1564,' said her father, then sipped his water.

'Yes, well, that was a little before my time,' said Sally with an impish smile. They all laughed.

'Scotland was one of my favourite spots,' said Ed, 'but the roads are so narrow up there even compared to here. Driving through Glencoe was fabulous and we visited some of the islands off the coast, leaving the RV on the mainland and doing some bed and breakfasts. I tell you I don't like haggis – it's so slippery and—'

'What a glorious sunset,' said Edith pointing through the gaps in the trees at the back of the garden.

'Yea, we're lucky here,' replied Peter. 'We don't get overlooked too much and the garden facing south gives us sunshine, when it's out, for most of the day.'

'On that note, I'll go and fetch the desert.'

Peter returned with a jug of cream and four dessert bowls of fruit salad that Sally had prepared before she went to work that morning. They continued catching up with Ed and Edith's adventures as they finished their meal and tidied up.

Peter and Sally looked at each other, not saying much. Sally's parents had so much to say.

'You do realise it's almost ten,' said Sally.

'Wow, the time has gone so quickly,' Edith said sadly.

'I'll be here in the morning,' said Sally, 'till about nine.'

Peter said, 'I'll be up and away early, I'm afraid, so I won't see you until you return from Europe in a couple of months. Make sure you keep us posted with pictures of where you are. I'm particularly fascinated by Seville Cathedral – if you get there. I have always wanted to visit to see the grave of Christopher Columbus.'

'Well, we'll see what we can do about that. Good to see you again, Peter, and well done again on getting that promotion.' Ed shook Peter's hand vigorously.

'Yes, well done,' added Edith, 'and Sally, make sure you look after him – he works so hard.'

'Yea, I know, Mom. We do try to keep the weekends free of work issues. You go up, Peter. I know you need to get some sleep. I'll sort Mom and Dad out down here.'

'Okay, honey. Thanks. Bye, Ed, bye, Edith – good to see you both and take care driving in Europe. Remember, it's the other side of the road.'

'Heck, I'm used to that – it will be easy,' replied Ed. 'They drive on the right side of the road, unlike the crazy drivers here.' They all laughed.

Peter left the three of them talking downstairs. Ed was right; he was concerned about the email and text from Bigsey and then the text from his boss. *First time I've been called into the office so early ... must be a big, big figure.* Peter sat on the edge of his bed reading the email from Bigsey again, and after a short while of contemplation, saw how the problem arose. He was in his pyjamas scrolling through and rereading his emails when Sally came into the room.

'Are you still at it?'

'I've just finished. It can wait till tomorrow now.'

'Any problem, I'm sure you'll be able to sort it out. Night, love.'

'Night, Sal.'

Peter was up and out early; he couldn't afford to be late. The birds could normally read the time by his punctuality, but today he was ahead of them. He carefully closed the front door so that the lock just clicked, squeezed himself past the RV in the front drive, still with the curtains drawn, and, as quietly as he could, drove off, leaving the slamming of the driver's door until he got to the end of the road.

There was no denying it, he thought, he was a bit worried about this. *What if it's the top end of a six-figure number and I lose my job, we won't be able to move house?*

'Morning,' he said to Jan as he walked through reception.

'Morning, Peter. Martin has just got in if you wanted to know.'

'Thanks. That's a relief. I need to run through the figures with him. Thank you. Catch you later.'

The lift up to the sixth floor was empty, except for his thoughts. The doors of the lift opened and he was met by his boss.

'Ah, Peter. I was just looking for you. Could you come up straight away – I've other business to attend to.'

'I'll just drop off my coat and bag and be with you.'

'Make that two minutes. Got that?'

'Yes, sir.'

Shit. This is not good, not good at all. Got to find Bigsey – and quick.

'Morning, Peter.'

'Isabelle. Hi, have you seen Bigsey?'

'He was headed in that direction just a second ago.'

The men's toilets. Peter stalled in his decision for no more than a few seconds. He didn't like it, but it had to be done, he told himself.

The toilets were quiet, no one else was around. Maybe he wasn't in here.

'Bigsey? Bigsey, are you there?' There was no response. 'Bigsey, you there? I've got to speak to you – it's urgent. Old Barrel Face wants to see me now and we need to go through Jonathan's investments with—'

A cubicle door opened.

'As you kindly put it, Peter, Old Barrel Face is already here. I will see you in my office. Now.'

Peter closed his eyes, momentarily wishing he was on another planet, and made to follow his boss out of the WCs. As he did so Bigsey emerged from one of the cubicles and shrugged his shoulders, unable to help his boss.

CHAPTER 3

Old Barrel Face

'Close the door,' said Old Barrel Face without looking around. He sat down behind his deep oak desk in a large brown leather swivel chair. Peter had only been in his office once before and that was when he got promoted. Happy days.

'Sit down,' bawled Old Barrel Face. 'What do you mean by allowing this to happen on my watch? Never in my experience have we lost this amount of money in one day.'

He threw the bundle of spreadsheets onto the table in front of Peter. It was the first time Peter had seen the papers and he needed to have time to absorb and understand the figures. *I've got to try to buy some time,* he thought.

'Well? What have you got to say for yourself?'

Peter cast his eyes over the myriad figures. Why were the sheets printed in such small text? He looked at the bottom line for each of the investments.

'Apologies for my calling out your name in the toilets, sir, but—'

'But you didn't, Peter, did you? I know … we all know you have nicknames for all the suits, as you call us …'

Peter stopped listening. Old Barrel Face carried on. Peter had bought some time. He needed to analyse the figures in front of him, quickly scanning down and across.

'You're not listening, are you, Peter?' came a stern, sarcastic voice. 'Got better things to think about? Well?'

'Sir. Yes. I have been and I apologise. It's just that I-I—'

'You haven't studied yesterday's trades, have you? Have you? Happy taking the good money we pay you since your promotion and not putting in the effort, and the result is a fucking great mess – which is, from what I've seen, all down to you. Do you realise that there are three positions here of 300% leverage? And I suppose you've been trying to recover from Friday's losses and now ... and now... made the positions even worse. What do you think you're doing?' He paused to take a breath through his expanded nostrils and stood up, gesticulating. 'I was always against you getting a promotion. Well? What do you have to say, boy?'

'Sir. I have seen the figures and the spreadsheets.' Peter had seen them about two minutes ago. 'Sir, and yes, they add up to the printout, but there appear to be a number of anomalies.'

'What do you mean anomalies?' This gave Peter a little more time; he hadn't fully got to grips with what the papers were showing. They couldn't be right. They just couldn't. He started to sweat. He had checked Jonathan's positions on Friday evening in the car on the way down the A3 ... and yes, they were exposed, but nowhere near to what Old Barrel Face was showing him. They just couldn't be right.

'These are the standard computer printouts all team managers and directors receive daily, and you are saying they are wrong?' He was now pacing around Peter.

'It does happen, sir.' He just needed a few more minutes ... he was sure there must be a simple explanation.

'Well, it may have happened in your previous jobs but not at this company ...' Old Barrel Face was shouting now, his face turning bright red, forehead down, and he had lost his composure, what there was of it. He moved towards Peter, his fist raised, and thumped the table, the teacup turning in the saucer and spilling the contents onto the table. Old Barrel had really lost it. Peter had been at this company for the last seven years – in fact, his whole working life. *This could be the end of my career. How do I tell Sally and how are we gonna pay the mortgage? Shit.*

'We pride ourselves in accurate reporting and management at Goldson's. You realise this is a sackable offence.' Old Barrel Face was now breathing deeply and pacing around the perimeter of his office. 'I understand that Jonathan wasn't in at all yesterday, so how did you cover his positions, *if* in fact you did? Well? Answer me. What have you got to say for yourself?'

'Er, that's correct, sir.' Peter was still stalling but was now relieved because he had seen the problem. Top-left-hand corner of the page in very small light text were the initials DK. Peter sat back slightly in his chair, his shoulders now relaxed. He breathed deeply, the stress of the conversation, if it could be called that, the stress of listening, slowly releasing. He decided he didn't want to reply straight away and let Old Barrel Face vent his spleen.

Peter wasn't listening any more – there was little opportunity to respond; he was surprised that his boss hadn't collapsed through lack of air in his lungs. He smiled to himself, but it probably showed on his face, because Old Barrel Face was getting redder and redder.

'Well? Well?' he shouted, thumping the table again and flailing his arms from side to side.

I wish I had recorded this, Peter thought; *nobody will believe me.* He felt he had better say something. He tried to get a word in. 'Sir.'

'Quiet. I've had enough of your inexperienced insolence … you're fired. I'm going to HR now and they will escort you out of the building. Go back to your desk, pack your things and remain there till they arrive.'

'Sir.'

Old Barrel Face ignored Peter and snatched the spreadsheets from his hands.

Peter tried again to get a few words in as his boss stormed out of his office. 'Sir,' he called out, 'top-left corner, the initials DK mean …' Peter wasn't able to complete the sentence as the door slammed shut.

Oh well, he thought … *just hope it dawns on him before he gets to HR.*

Peter followed him out of the office in a much calmer and more confident frame of mind than when he had arrived, intending to go back to his desk. The lift stopped on the sixth floor; the doors opened. Peter didn't get out. He stayed in, got out of the lift at the ground floor and left the building.

He sent a text to Martin and told him that the spreadsheet

from finance for Jonathan's trades was in Danish Krone and not sterling … hence the ten-fold difference from yesterday. Peter asked Martin to keep the team's heads down this morning because as soon as Old Barrel Face realised he would be steaming and looking for blood. He asked him to make sure Sue covered for Jonathan if he still wasn't in, and told him he was getting coffee from the corner café and would be back shortly.

Peter sat down in the café with his drink and contemplated the morning's events. He was ordering a second coffee when Martin walked into the coffee shop and over to Peter.

'What would you like to drink, Martin?'

'A cappuccino toffee latte and one sugar. Thanks.'

Peter shook his head, lifted his eyebrows and smiled back at Martin, wondering how he managed to drink it so sweet.

They sat on a couple of stools together looking out onto the busy street. Peter explained what had happened with Old Barrel Face in his office and they laughed about the incident in the men's washroom. Martin updated Peter on the morning's team meeting and said that Old Barrel Face came charging onto the floor shortly after Martin had received Peter's text. He was searching for Peter, puffing and blowing, and saw Jonathan sitting at his desk with Sue next to him. He was about to charge over to them when for some reason he just stopped in his stride and turned and stormed out, face like thunder.

Peter laughed out loud; he couldn't help it.

'It was about time Old Barrel Face had something to do. All he enjoyed doing was parading around the office like a stuck-up cockerel, trying to catch staff out and pigging himself with so-called client lunches starting at eleven thirty and finishing whenever he wants to go home.'

'Yea. When I spotted the DK at the top of the spreadsheet it all fitted into place. Jonathan had been investing in a number of Scandinavian companies and it looks like the printout given to Old Barrel Face by Finance was all in Danish Krone. He hadn't read it properly and lost his rag. I realised this after about ten minutes of listening to him stomping around, ranting and raving in his office, and I thought I would let it run its course.'

'Someone in Finance is going to get a big rollicking.'

'Well, maybe not,' said Peter, thinking about the situation. 'It will depend on who else is aware. But knowing Old Barrel Face, he would have told all the bigwigs in order to protect his arse.'

Martin and Peter were good friends as well as work colleagues. They had joined Goldson's at the same time and although they had taken slightly different career paths within the company they had remained in contact, and when the opportunity arose for Martin to return to Peter's team he took it. His three years overseas had been good experience but more than enough for him and his young family. He and his wife had decided that they wanted to educate their children in Britain rather than Hong Kong with all the changes taking place there.

'Okay. I suppose we'd better get back,' said Peter. 'Got a proper day's work ahead of us now. Let's see if we can recover Jonathan's positions. Was he in on time this morning?'

'Yes, just about. He got in just before Barrel Face walked the floor. But shortly before he arrived we had a call from someone who said she was his mother and that he had an appointment with the doctor – chest pains, apparently.'

'Oh, that's not good, and he has still come in?'

'Maybe to save his job.'

They made their way back up the road to Goldson's offices.

'Can I suggest when we get back that we both talk with him about his health, if need be get HR in, and we can discuss his positions. He should take some time off until he has seen the doctor – he probably needs a break. When did he last take a holiday? Must have been before or over the Christmas period so probably four or five months ago. That's not good. He's obviously got stressed about his work recently.'

Peter and Martin returned to the office. Jay met them at the entrance to Peter's office and said that Old Barrel Face had already been around again, twice, and was hovering and looking for both of them … but he seemed a lot calmer.

'Good,' said Peter. 'Let's hope the rest of the day isn't like the last hour. I'll be working in my office this morning to have a closer look at what Jonathan's been doing. He's bright, but maybe we haven't given him enough support, or perhaps he has his own private positions that are causing him financial problems. Either way, it's not good when someone gets so stressed out.'

Jay and Martin left him in his room and Peter sat down at his desk, the door to his office remaining open; he didn't want to close the team out.

No sooner had he sat down than Peter's desk phone rang.

It was Isabelle. 'Hi, Peter, glad it's all sorted – well, sort of. I had a call from someone saying they wanted to speak with you.'

'Oh, Jonathan's mother?'

'I don't think so. It was a man and he didn't say what it was about.'

Peter's mobile rang. 'Sorry, Isabelle, I'll call you back.'

He answered the phone. 'Hello, Peter speaking.' He smiled, relieved. 'Hi, darling, how are you?'

'I've survived this morning's debacle. What a waste of people's energy, but all sorted now. Thanks for asking though.'

'I just thought I'd tell you that Mom and Dad have just left on their travels and they wanted to say cheerio. They enjoyed last night and gave us some money. Told us to use it so we could take a break somewhere. The place they stayed at in Stratford upon Avon was called the Shakespeare Hotel, with beamed ceilings and sloping floors ... They said it was fantastic, sixteenth or seventeenth century. So old, so I thought we could give that a go in a couple of weekends' time. I've got to dash now, honey. I'm already later than I expected to get to school.'

'Yup ...' Peter hesitated with his response. 'That would be ... er ... good, honey.'

'You're not really listening, are you?'

Peter was looking at one of the two screens on his desk and checking the timing of trades and volumes made by Jonathan.

'Sorry, honey, we can organise that later when I get back, but if you want to book it that's fine by me.'

'Okay, see you later. Have a good day. Love you.'

'You too.'

Peter was also looking at the team's trades over the last week. He could see that Jonathan was trying to cover a default position, and that hadn't worked, and that he had actually made things worse. *He shouldn't have leveraged on the second cover, particularly by so much. The devaluation of the Krone has also enhanced the dip*, he thought. *And those company announcements, out of the blue.*

He sat back in his chair then swivelled around to look at the rear elevation of the bomb-damaged wall. Interesting in its own little way that something from such a long time ago was still here. Quite a pertinent reminder. *Perhaps they should list the patches of blackened brickwork.*

He heard someone enter his office and close the door behind them.

'Peter. Good morning to you.' Peter swivelled back around. It was Sir John Greenhill. Peter didn't have enough time to stand up as he came in. He sat down in the chair opposite.

'Oh. Good morning, Sir John. Apologies. My mind was elsewhere, contemplative, and when I turned, I thought it would be someone else.'

'No harm in a bit of reflective time, Peter. This change of Risk Protection that you are proposing. How confident are you that it will improve our current systems?'

Peter was slightly taken aback by the question; he was expecting a discussion about the current losses on Jonathan's account. He regained his composure.

'Sir. I felt that in the first instance we would run the programmes in parallel with our existing procedures and thereby cause no disruption to daily business. We could then track the results over the next four weeks before the next board meeting and show the results on the dashboard reports.'

'Good. That's settled then. Do that, please.' He got up to leave. 'Oh, and I heard something this morning about the little tête à tête you had with …'

'Yes, sir.'

'Well, don't worry about him, his heart's in the right place. He's just a bit stubborn and bombastic at times, set in his ways, and usually jumps in with both feet. But he spotted an anomaly in the company printouts and we've had a word with finance so that it doesn't happen again. Can cause many a director to have heart failure.'

Sir John left the room. Peter shook his head. 'The old devil,' he said to himself, 'taking the credit.' *Well, that's just taking the piss after all I've been through this morning.*

The door to Peter's office opened again. 'Peter,' said Isabelle.

'Yeah.'

'I think I've got the same guy on the phone that rang earlier …'

'Bloody salespeople … no calls please, Isabelle, unless it's the team … or my wife, or Sir John. Thank you.'

It wasn't often that Peter stayed in his office, but the events earlier in the day had unsettled him. Later in the morning he relayed Sir John's request to Martin, who Peter often called Bigsey because of his huge hands, and Jay. They reviewed the proposed risk methodology and after a few minor tweaks decided it was good enough to trial within the team.

Peter stayed late for the next three days to make sure that he was fully aware of each set of trades and that he was prepared for any further challenges by senior staff. They had actually recovered a lot of the ground lost on Jonathan's trading account, which meant that Friday's team lunch would take place as planned.

Three thirty arrived, not soon enough for Peter. It had been a long week, and he left the office and met the team at the Old Bank of England pub. There were no tables available, so they ended up having a standing lunch next to the bar. Only eleven of the team joined them, because there was a bit of a panic about commodities rising, which Peter didn't mind; it was heading in the right direction for their current investment strategy. He would take those currently at their desks out next week. Peter wasn't a heavy drinker by any means, and just a pint of Adnams was enough for him. He had a twenty-minute drive once he got off the train. Peter checked in with Martin at four o'clock.

'Everything's good, Peter, I'll send you the summary sheet later.

Enjoy the weekend.'

'You too, Bigsey.'

Peter said his goodbyes to those still in the pub and headed home, relieved that the stormy week had now blown away.

He skipped down the steps three at a time into Bank Tube station, ran down the ramp to the station and fumbled for his ticket. He arrived on the platform as the train came to a halt. He was leading the front of the Friday afternoon rush to get home, so he got on the train and slumped himself onto a spare seat. People comfortably filled the remainder of the carriage, but the train was not as packed as it would be later. The train slowly moved off with a series of screeches.

He picked up his paper, looking initially at the back page for the weekend programme of football. *Oh dear,* he thought. *Spurs are going to have a tough time away on Sunday, but as long as the best two strikers in Europe are playing we're in with a shout.* His newspaper rustled in front of him, and then again as a person squeezed past in the carriage. He closed it to see what the problem was and then opened it up again. The page opposite the one he was reading was slowly being marked in a circle around a particular advert, he assumed from the other side. He watched it, both fascinated and stunned at what he was seeing. When the marker had stopped he folded his paper to see who or what had done it. There was nothing, nobody there. He opened the paper again and looked at what the marker was indicating. The highlighted marking was around a job advertisement.

'WANTED.

Young senior executive about the age of 29, preferably married.

Excruciatingly brilliant salary.

Office location, mostly in and around Victoria and the West End.

Some travel at short notice, all mod (and old) cons provided.

Must have a Master's degree in Maths, excel with computers (e.g. Python)

If you don't have any of the above, well then, don't waste our time and don't bother applying.

Call 0207 983 1234 any time and arrange your appointment.
Good prospects and nice people to work with.
Look forward to seeing you.
Bye for now!'

Peter laughed with bewilderment. What a strange way to end an advert. 'I'm okay where I am, thank you very much,' he said to himself and turned to the finance pages.

The rest of his journey home was uneventful. Emails from Jay and Isabelle but no apology from Old Barrel Face. *Maybe that's how he got where he is. Very sneaky.* After picking up his car at the station he drove towards the garden centre to pick up the ten bags of compost and four large shrubs for the garden that Sally had ordered. They had organised the weekend to focus on tidying up their garden. Whilst paying at the checkout at the garden centre he thought he caught a glimpse of a man in a green parka jacket. He kept looking for him, but he didn't appear again. Strange guy, that one.

There was someone next to his car wearing a Parka jacket loading up their car ... the person turned as Peter approached. It was a lady in a green coat, no fur, just grey hair. Peter's apprehension disappeared and he loaded up his car, the rear tyres looking like they were suffering under the weight of the compost. He moved a few bags to the passenger seat. The car next to him then moved away; both the passenger and the driver were wearing parka jackets and grinning at him.

When Peter got home, Sally was already back and they offloaded the bags of compost and plants. He mentioned his rather strange experience with the newspaper advertisement to Sally. They shrugged and laughed about it. Someone just having a joke, Sally said.

Later in the evening he pulled the newspaper out from his briefcase whilst they were eating their Indian takeaway. He opened the paper at the page. The red marking around the advert had gone, but the text was still there. Sally read the advert. 'Looks right down your street, honey – quite clever the way they get your attention by telling you to go away if it's not for you. You should go for it.'

'But I'm happy where I am.'

'Well, you only need another episode like the one on Tuesday and you might be out.'

'I've had bigger problems than that to worry about in the past, Sal.' He pushed the paper to the other side of the table and they continued eating and talking, mostly about the garden and the opportunity to move house. Peter was thinking about the guy in the parka jacket on the train last week; he had actually told him to apply. *Was I imagining it or what?*

Sally said, 'I went over to Parker and Parker, you know, the estate agents down in town by the station, and picked up a handful of details about houses for sale. There's two really good ones, Peter, down Pine Walk. You remember, we walked down there and often thought it would be the ideal road to move to when we could. The big detached houses set back off the road, in-and-out drives, large gardens out the back.'

'Sal, I don't think we can afford a house up there.'

'Well, at least let's go and take a look – it won't cost us anything. Anyhow, if they are out of our price range then we can look elsewhere. It's a lovely evening – how about we take a walk up there, and see if we like the feel of the road?' They drove up to Pine Walk and walked up and down, passing the two houses that were up for sale. It was very quiet and didn't look as if it was a rat run for commuters.

Peter reluctantly gave in. Sally organised the visits. They agreed that they would focus on getting the garden sorted as best they could this weekend as planned and then think about the house. Sally would be in charge of the estate agents and putting their house on the market. They both realised that they were going to need a big tidy-up in the house, especially Peter's stuff in the second bedroom, and get it boxed up and into the loft.

They visited the local estate agent that Sally had contacted early Saturday morning and managed to organise the two viewings for next week, both early evening. Of greater concern for Peter was the cost; he felt that it was a waste of time. The agent they saw, spotty and young, couldn't have been long out of nappies. He worked out that with the estimated value of their house, their mortgage would sit at a staggering £675k, assuming the asking price for the Pine Walk house was the agreed sale price. Peter had whistled out loud when he said that. The agent, without batting an eyelid, said that despite interest rates going up a little they are still reasonably low, and that they wouldn't need to worry about it. But both houses were beyond what they could afford even with Peter's increase in salary and bonuses. 'You never know, some vendors might accept a lower offer. See what you think,' he was told. They returned home with work to do.

CHAPTER 4

The Green Eye

Monday came around quicker than either Peter or Sally had wished. The work in the garden on both Saturday and Sunday had left both of them physically exhausted. They had achieved what they had set out to complete, finishing around eight thirty on each of the evenings, tired but contented. They chilled out on Sunday with a late breakfast and a couple of local walks, one up to Pine Walk.

Peter had diligently checked his work emails and messages over the weekend because he didn't want to be caught out on the wrong foot so soon after the episode with Old Barrel Face last week. But all was quiet.

It was almost as if nothing had happened in his meeting later with Sir John Greenhill. Peter was focused on the demands from his boss.

I wonder how Jonathan is, thought Peter as his train caressed the buffers at Waterloo, Platform 13.

As Peter passed through the ticket barriers, a man walked into him.

'Sorry, mate,' he said and turned and walked quickly away. Peter checked he still had his wallet, which he did, and carried on walking.

He got a seat on the train next to a mother sitting with a child on her knee. A heavily built man then sat clumsily on the seat on the other side of him.

'Very tight seating on these trains, isn't it?' he said in a slight countryfied accent.

'Yes, just a bit,' replied Peter, moving his arm away and opening up his paper. He tried to ignore the guy and settled down to read.

'You've got something of my mate's in your pocket.'

'What?' said Peter, taken aback.

'In your pocket, it belongs to my mate.'

'No, I haven't. Why should I? I don't even know your mate.'

'Oh, you do.' A broad smile grew on his face. He moved his head and pointed towards a passenger sitting opposite. Peter recognised the parka jacket.

'Your right pocket.'

Peter could smell garlic just like last time. He obliged rather than cause a scene, and he pulled out what felt like a small box, but it was heavy – weighing like a stone in his pocket. 'I've never seen this before. I don't even know what it is.'

'There you are, I told you you had it. Now be a good man and pass it to my mate,' he said, smiling and showing the flicker of a gold tooth.

The other man got up and stepped towards the two of them as the train moved off, a heavy smell of dampness preceding him across the carriage. He opened his hand and Peter placed the small box in the palm of his hand. The man opened it. He carefully lifted out the contents, which were wrapped in fine paper, and unwrapped it to reveal what looked like a green stone, then took off his dark-tinted glasses revealing one deep black socket and one normal eye. He threw the green stone into the air, caught it again and showed Peter.

'This is what I've been looking for, young lad. Thank you.' He smiled at him showing yellowed teeth, then lifted the stone towards his face and put it into the depths of his eye socket. Peter looked away. The other passengers appeared not to have noticed; it had all happened so quickly, one might say 'in the blink of an eye'.

The man looked down at Peter and thanked him again, one green eye glowing and winking at him and the other blue. He put his sunglasses back on. Peter was flabbergasted. The train had now completed its journey to Bank Station, and the man next to him got up to leave the train, but as he did so, he pointed at an advert in the paper which was open on Peter's lap. As passengers for the return journey started to pile onto the train, Peter managed to get off and sat briefly on a platform bench wondering what had happened. Last night's red wine was good, but he didn't overdo it.

Later that morning after the team meeting and a number of impromptu discussions with his team, he retired to his office, where he found some peace and quiet to reflect on this morning's journey to the office. He closed the door, which he rarely did, but it was shortly opened by Isabelle who sheepishly pushed her head around the door and asked if everything was okay. Peter responded in a nonchalant manner that he just needed to resolve a few personal issues and that there was nothing to worry about. 'No problem, Peter,' she said, retreating and closing the door behind her.

Peter pulled out the newspaper from his briefcase and reread the advert, which was now circled with a red highlighter. 'Wanted. Aged 29. Maths …Python …'

It all points to me, but why? Why me?

There was a knock on the door and Bigsey poked his head round. 'Peter. Hi, sorry to disturb you, but I thought you should know that Old Barrel Face is on the prowl.'

'Thanks,' replied Peter. No sooner had the door closed than it opened again. Old Barrel Face walked in unannounced and stood opposite him.

'I thought I would speak to you about the episode last week and apologise. How is Jonathan?'

'He's fine, thank you, sir. We've had a 121 with him and he's taking some well-earned rest, but he's back on board with vacation organised,' said Peter.

'Oh good, and … er … yes. About that other matter … we'll see.'

He can't say it, can he, thought Peter, looking him straight in the eyes. He couldn't look back at Peter and apologise for taking the credit for something Peter had spotted – and that he had caused so much grief. *We'll see what?* he thought.

Old Barrel Face said nothing. He eventually turned and walked out of the office and slammed the door.

How can people like him get into senior positions? It's ridiculous. No wonder companies are forever struggling to make a buck when they're so top heavy. He swivelled in his chair and looked at the newspaper. He picked up his mobile.

'Hi, it's me.'

'Can you call me back later, honey? I'm in the middle of an art class with thirty-five children.'

'I just thought I'd let you know I'm going to call about that advert – the one I pointed out.'

'Oh good,' Sally said matter-of-factly. 'See you later.' The call ended.

He swung back in his chair and decided he needed a drink. He hadn't opened his drinks cabinet before and glanced at the bottles. *A short, that's what I need. Nice. A small vodka. Oh hell, let's do it. Come on, Peter, pluck up the courage.* He sat down at his desk again with the newspaper open at the advertisement.

He rang the number.

'Hello, is that Peter? We've been waiting for your call. What took you so long?'

'I … well, I …'

'Don't worry about that. Your interview is arranged for eleven o'clock tomorrow.'

'But I haven't looked at my diary to see if I'm available.'

'You will be.'

Peter hesitated. 'Where do I have to—'

'Number 21 Great Smith Street, third floor. See you tomorrow. Bye for now.'

The line went dead. Peter was still holding his phone away from his ear, gazing out of the window. 'Yikes. Well, I've gone and done it now,' he said to himself.

Isabelle's head appeared again around the door. 'How was it? I thought you still had someone in here.'

'What do you mean?'

'With Old Barrel Face,' said Isabelle, giving Peter a shake of the head.

'Oh … yes, that was fine thanks, Isabelle. I'm sorry if I've been out of sorts lately. We've had a lot on with Jonathan, the risk management tool and everything else.'

'Jonathan's here and would like to see you. I thought that Martin should be here with you, because of all the HR stuff.'

'Yeah. Thanks, Isabelle, that's fine, good thinking. Let's do it now. And could you put me out of the office tomorrow from late morning. I should be back in the afternoon. I've got a mortgage interview at eleven.'

'Ok … but remember you've set aside the afternoon for Martin, Giles, Sue, Malcolm and Jay to go over the risk profiles in the Far East markets.'

'Thanks, Izzy. I don't know what we'd do without you.'

After the meeting with Jonathan and Bigsey, at which they reassured Jonathan that everything had been sorted with his trading position and that it and the teams were now fully in the green. Peter told Jonathan he could take some time off and that Sue would hold his clients for him until he returned. The rest of the day was as normal as he could expect and there were no untoward interruptions to his journey home. Thank goodness.

Peter told Sally about his telephone call to arrange the interview over their evening meal. She was content with him changing jobs as long as he was happy, and they could still plan to buy a new house; it was all fine with her.

The following morning, Peter felt both guilty and embarrassed all the way to the office and then whilst talking with his friends and colleagues, knowing that later he was going for an interview. The unknown. What exactly would he be doing? It was only the second time he had had an interview – and then would there have to be a second or third one? The advert said 'Good salary, prospects and stable job.' He sighed. *Oh well. Just have to see how it goes.*

CHAPTER 5

Interview – The Special One

Peter didn't want to be rushed and wanted to collect his thoughts before the interview, so he left the office much earlier than he needed to.

Walking out of the office building, he felt a cool breeze across his face mixed with the dreadful smell of exhaust fumes. His stomach was turning with apprehension about the interview, he felt like a naughty schoolboy. Or was he excited? He couldn't decide. He walked towards the river; he had decided to pick up the Thames Clipper river bus at Tower Millenium Pier. It was a sunny morning but still a bit chilly for May. Tourists of all shapes and sizes were already milling around at the ticket concourse with their maps and cameras, waving them around aimlessly and pointing, almost knocking out a city worker or two.

The river bus set off, Tower Bridge looming above him to his left. It really was magnificent. Such a huge and truly amazing structure to have been built over a hundred years ago. The Tower of London now behind him, dwarfed by larger buildings, but it must have been daunting when originally constructed. The White Tower, constructed by William the Conqueror in 1078, was still standing after over nine hundred years. Peter thought about its phenomenal history and terrible bloodthirsty past. On the left he could see Shakespeare's Globe. As he got closer the feeling of being immersed in history got more intense. He considered the astonishing programme for the theatre's reconstruction and recognition of the past. Onward to Blackfriars and their foreboding darkened towers. The boat continued steadily, Peter now relaxing and glad he had decided to take the river bus; it was a nice feeling being on the water again and for a short time it took his mind off the interview. He glanced at his mobile and then turned it off and put it back in his coat pocket. Past the old Parliament buildings. Under Waterloo, then Hungerford Bridge, arriving at Westminster Millennium Pier. He disembarked, drawn along with the flow of tourists eager to see the modern-day Houses of Parliament, up the steps and ramps and onto the wide riverside pavements of the embankment.

He was early, and calmly made his way past the Parliament buildings, Westminster Abbey and into Great Smith Street. He spotted the building from the other side of the road. It looked to him as if it used to be an old school, with its black cast-iron railings, feature brick elevations and tall sash windows. He looked up at the stone parapets; a buddleia was growing from the roof. *They get everywhere.* Paint was peeling off the window frames; the windows were dark as if there were no lights on, or perhaps they were blackened. The front door, however, looked very substantial and new, painted a shiny black gloss with two small obscure bevelled glass panes with a brightly polished brass plaque reading 'CPS'. So, the Crown Prosecution Service. *Mmmm.* There wasn't a coffee house near the building, so he walked around the block and past the entrance to number 21 three times until his phone showed 10.55. He hadn't seen anyone enter or leave.

'Oh well, here goes,' he said out loud and pressed the brass doorbell.

The lock opened almost immediately.

He pushed open the door whilst the buzzer was still going to find a polished stone floor lobby and a pair of glazed doors opposite, which he pushed open. A woman was sitting behind the reception desk. She didn't look up.

'Good morning, Peter,' she said as he came through the second set of doors and up a number of steps.

'Err … good morning. I'm a little early. I have an interview at eleven o'clock with … I'm not sure who?'

The woman was spectacled and dressed as if she was from the 1950s and going to a rock and roll concert.

'Oh yes, that's right. Take the last lift on the left-hand side.' She still didn't look up but pointed with her left hand.

'Thank you.' Peter reached the lift and asked which floor he had to go to.

'Just press the lift button.'

As he did so, the lift doors opened and he was greeted by a short, portly, middle-aged man, smartly dressed in a brown suit and tie, wearing brown-rimmed glasses. He had a round face and a rapidly receding hairline.

'Morning, Peter. Good to see you. I'm Julian, Julian Smithers.'

'Nice to meet you,' replied Peter. They shook hands.

The lift doors closed behind him.

The lift didn't move. But the lift doors behind Mr Smithers did. They opened with a creak and Peter stepped out behind his escort.

They immediately entered a light and reasonably modern open-plan office, at least on first appearances, thought Peter, and quite a contrast to the entrance.

'This is one of our recently refurbished open-plan offices. As you can see, we're trying to keep up with modern technology.' He laughed.

Peter wondered if it was Smithers who had drafted the advert. As they were walking through the office he glanced at the equipment used by various staff. Yes, a computer or two, not very modern, but … he recognised a word processor and desk phones with a cable on the handset on every desk. *I wouldn't call that modern,* he thought , *maybe back in the 1990s.*

'We'll show you around a bit later, Peter. I appreciate that there's a lot to take in when starting a new job. I'll take you straight to the meeting room where the senior people are waiting to greet you.'

Starting a new job? I haven't had the interview yet and I don't even know what they do or if I want it.

They walked past forty or fifty desks and a mixture of men and women. Some looked up and smiled and nodded at him as he walked past; others were busy on the phone or at their 'modern' computers. Then up a couple of flights of stairs and along a wide corridor with what looked like a series of offices on either side with glazed partitions and vertical cream-coloured blinds.

Mr Smithers opened one of the doors on the right.

'Here we are. This way, Peter.' He closed the door behind him, leaving Peter by himself. Strange man, Peter thought.

The room was empty, except for a single chair in front of a large solid wooden desk with a water jug and a set of glasses on a tray. On the other side of the desk were five chairs. A fanlight above a door let some additional light into the room.

Oh well, I'm here now. This place does feel very old fashioned and odd. Peter put his laptop bag down by the single seat, hung his coat on the metal coat stand in the corner behind the door and walked around the room. The small clock above the door read 11.07. Behind the five chairs was a large window looking onto an internal courtyard and nothing but a blank white-painted brick wall, but at least it brought a bit of natural daylight into the room. Just the one picture on the wall, a picture of Her Majesty Queen Elizabeth II. *She must have been in her early twenties when they took this picture.* Peter went and had a closer look. *She looks so very young.*

The door opened abruptly and in walked a tall man, probably in his late forties, wearing a dark suit, yellow shirt, green patterned tie and red braces, with a pile of folders and papers under his left arm. He appeared rather flustered as he shuffled across the room towards the desk.

'Sorry we're running late, Peter, bit of a flap on. You know what it's like. Nice to meet you.' He shook Peter's hand vigorously after plonking the papers he was carrying onto the desk.

'Err, yes. And you,' Peter replied, rather taken aback.

'I'm Jon, by the way, without an *h*. Good to meet you. And this is Ann and … and Mary … they were here behind me a second ago. Where could they have gone?' He turned back to the door and looked down the corridor. 'Ah, here they come. Always chatting, those two. Come on, you two, hurry up. This is Peter.' They hurried into the room. 'Where have the others got to?' said Jon, disappearing up the corridor.

'Hello,' said Peter.

'Nice to meet you, Peter. I'm Ann and this is Mary.'

'How do you do.' He shook their hands. The two ladies went to sit at the desk. Peter turned and went to sit on the single chair in front of the desk.

'No, not there, Peter,' said Ann. 'You're over this side with us.'

Peter didn't reply. He was even more taken aback.

'Yes, you're better over here. We'll look after you,' added Mary, leading him around.

Peter sat in the middle seat of the five chairs, Ann and Mary either side of him.

'Just waiting for the others,' said Jon, coming back into the room and sounding like he was starting to get a bit impatient. He moved his files and papers to one end of the desk.

'Would you like some water, Peter?'

'Thank you, yes, that would be good.'

The door burst open as Jon poured water into the glasses. Two men came in; Peter recognised them immediately – the man with the green eye and parka jacket man.

'Sorry we're late, sir, slight delay, you know.' So Jon was their boss, Peter thought.

'That's fine. Now, sit down, both of you, and let's get the admin out of the way. This is your first meeting regarding the—'

Ann interrupted him. 'Sir, excuse me for interrupting, but this is Peter's interview.'

'Yes, yes, Ann, of course. Thank you.' Jon was becoming more flustered and moving papers around on the table. 'Indeed. Peter … let's get that out of the way first then, I suppose. I apologise – I get over enthusiastic at times, can't help it. Life's exciting, isn't it?'

Peter looked back nonplussed and wondered what on earth had made him ring up in the first place.

'This is Ann and Mary, who you have met, and here are Tom and Will, who – yes – you would have been introduced to them as well. You replied to our advertisement.'

'Yes. Sort of.' Peter looked over his shoulder towards Tom, alias Parka man, and Will, who Peter had nicknamed Green Eye, who winked back at him with his good eye.

'Good, well, that's the introductions out of the way and … what else do you need to know?'

Peter didn't reply. He was expecting one of the ladies to give Jon a prompt. He looked around and realised that they were all looking at him and decided that he was the one who needed to reply.

'Well. Well, to start with, if I might ask. What will I be doing? What are my hours? Salary, pension, holiday entitlement and that sort of thing. I've been told nothing so far other than the words in the advertisement, if you could call it that, and to turn up here. It feels as if even this interview has been prearranged with my secretary.'

Jon had been walking around the room while Peter was speaking, and now sat down again. 'You will eventually be leading a team of about forty, not straight away, of course, and that will depend on circumstances. It might increase or reduce to nothing. Let us all hope not, of course, otherwise most of us will be without a job.' Jon laughed, as did the other four.

'And?' said Peter, slightly impatient with his interviewer.

Jon stood up again. He definitely had ants in his pants, thought Peter.

'You will be training and learning about your work. History, language, that sort of thing.'

'Where does my maths come into all this?'

'Oh. We just thought,' Tom replied, 'that—'

'That will be finance and currency,' said Mary, interrupting Parka man.

'Oh yes, of course. Yes, that's right, there will be some of that,' said Jon, perking up.

'What exactly will I be doing?' asked Peter very directly, and looked Jon straight into his eyes.

'You will be in charge of a team and, yes – we've all been through the training business. You will have an annual season ticket paid for by the firm and a salary and bonus that is better than your existing by fifty per cent. We don't like to talk about exact figures. You start next Monday at nine sharp. Everything is organised and your desk is ready for you.'

'I haven't accepted yet.'

Jon was quiet, as were the others, who were all looking at each other.

Following the prolonged silence, Peter continued, 'I only replied to the advert because I was forced to and I've come to the interview to see what this is all about, that's all.'

Jon sat down again and leant across the table. 'Peter, listen to me. You have been chosen. You were chosen some twenty-nine years ago when our boss met your mother and father. Your father worked for us and as you know he's now retired.'

Peter reflected on the word *retired*; his father was still working as a joiner. But he remembered his dad being away a lot when he was younger and then being injured doing something at work. He was then at home convalescing.

He realised he hadn't been listening to what Jon had been saying and was therefore surprised at Jon's next comment.

'You will be starting this coming Monday.'

'Sorry?'

'You will be starting this coming Monday.'

'But I haven't—'

Jon put his hand up. 'Quiet please, Peter. Now listen.' He paused. 'Peter, you are starting Monday twenty-seventh. There are no ifs or buts about it.'

'But I have to inform my existing employers and I'm on a three-month notice period.'

'They already know you are leaving. They have been informed. Your team has not been advised but they know you will be having a party on Friday this week.'

'I'm not sure that this is right. I haven't—'

'Peter. Perhaps I haven't made myself clear. There are no issues here, no ifs or buts. You are the man for the job, there is no one else, and the opportunity doesn't come along very often. See you here on Monday.' Jon stood up, leant across the table to shake Peter's hand and walked out of the room.

Parka man and Green Eye did the same, leaning across Ann and Mary respectively, and followed Jon out of the room. Jon returned shortly after they left the room for his papers, which were still on the desk, looked at Peter without saying a word, and left, closing the door behind him.

'I'm … I'm … I just don't know what to say. I can't just …' Peter was shocked that he was where he was and had been given no option but to accept.

'We've all been through it, Peter, at some time,' said Ann. 'It's all been sorted for you, Peter. You've nothing to worry about. We'll look after you, won't we, Mary?' She put her hand on Peter's forearm. Peter said he had had enough and was leaving. Ann led him out of the office, into the lift and through to the reception.

'That was a quick interview,' said the receptionist, not even looking up in Peter's direction. 'Got the job then?'

'I, er …'

'Course you did. And I know because there's been no one else that's come in. It's only you. Lucky man.' She lifted her head and grinned towards him, taking a bite of food.

'Nice to meet you, Peter. See you Monday. If there's anything you need to know before then just call the number and ask for me or Mary. Bye,' said Ann.

Peter just wanted to escape as quickly as he could and did not reply.

Outside, Peter put his coat on and started to walk, he wasn't sure in which direction. He felt like he was in a dream. *Those two guys, they knew all along. What do I say to the team when I get back? They already know something's up. And Sally. Sally. I always talk through big decisions with her. What if it doesn't work out? We have a mortgage to pay for. She's going to go mad. Oh my god. Maybe she's in on all this? Or Dad?*

He walked past the Houses of Parliament and then along the embankment in the direction of the City of London, contemplating everything he had experienced, not just the last two hours.

He pulled his mobile out of his coat pocket and turned it on. *Let's see what's been happening in my absence back in the real world of the City.* He continued walking and watched to see what came up on his screen. There were no emails for him at all, just a text from Bigsey telling him that he was stopping for lunch at one fifteen and if he wanted to join him he would be at Ye Olde Mitre just off Hatton Garden.

Peter had been there before. It was one of Bigsey's favourite alehouses, as he called them, and it was sort of on the way back. 'Yeah, go on,' he said to himself whilst crossing Waterloo Bridge Road. After a few more minutes looking at the boats he headed away from the river and up towards Holborn. He called his dad and told him where he had been for interview. They discussed the craziness of the people and the interview itself. His dad concluded the conversation with, 'Go with the flow and take it. I had to. There's no option and I did enjoy it for the brief time I was there.' Peter finished the call and reached Holborn Circus; the pub was just a minute or so's walk from there. He walked down the narrow blackened-brick alleyway; there was hardly room for two people to walk past one another. A sign read 'Est. 1546'.

'Crikey, I've not noticed that before,' he said to himself as he pushed open the swing door to the public bar.

Ye Olde Mitre was very small inside with low beamed ceilings and yellowing paint, adding to its quaintness. There were not too many customers and he soon found Bigsey sitting on a chair reading a paper; he had saved the seat next to him for Peter. He had already drunk half his pint of beer and there was another full pint sitting on the table. Bigsey indicated that it was for Peter. He joined Bigsey at the table after squeezing past a group of people standing around the serving hatch.

'Thanks, Bigsey. Appreciated.'

'It's Seafarers.'

'Thanks.' Peter took a big gulp of beer and then another and relaxed as he put his glass back down on the table. 'This pub goes back a long way.'

'Yep, Elizabethan times. That's why I come here. Happy memories.'

Peter enquired how the morning session in the office had gone and Bigsey said, 'Positive territory, up one point three per cent.' So the team were in a good place, thought Peter, and he felt confident enough to leave them to trade for the rest of the afternoon.

Peter took another mouthful of beer.

'You must be thirsty, how was the interview?'

'What? What do you mean?' Peter tensed up and put his drink down on the table.

'You know, the interview. Isabelle told me that you had some interview, with a mortgage guy, and—'

'Oh yeah.' Peter relaxed. 'Yea, me and Sally are thinking of moving now with the promotion and everything.' Peter was struggling within himself about his actual interview. Should he tell Bigsey? He was a close friend as well as a work colleague. *He's going to have to be told soon, very soon.* He took another sip of beer. But he wanted to tell Sally first. Maybe Bigsey had noticed a change in his approach at work, particularly because he had been sitting in his office more frequently. Peter plucked up courage and asked Bigsey what his reaction would be to being offered a job with a salary fifty per cent higher than he was currently on. Bigsey's initial reply was that there was probably a catch.

'We're on a pretty good arrangement at the moment, but don't get me wrong, it sounds very attractive – and bonuses on top. I would seriously think about it.'

In a funny sort of way that provided some reassurance, but in Peter's case there was no option. He was starting his new job next week. Neither had eaten and they decided to order food as well as another beer. Peter needed some Dutch courage.

Bigsey returned from the serving hatch having ordered the food and gave Peter his beer. 'Cheers, Peter.' They clinked glasses. 'So where are you thinking of moving to?'

'Sally wants us to stay local, near where we are at the moment. She needs to be close to the school. Possibly up towards Pine Walk. We've had some details through from an agent – d'you know it?'

'Ay. I've heard it's quiet up there and spooky at night. There's no street lights, and the gardens are supposed to be pretty big out the back.' Bigsey had been brought up in the area and lived a few miles away so he knew the roads reasonably well.

After a gulp of beer Peter spoke. 'I've been offered a job.'

'Ah, I was wondering where the conversation was leading to.' Bigsey's eyebrows lifted.

'It's over towards Victoria.'

'Good for you.'

Peter was disappointed with Bigsey's response; he thought maybe he was upset or would complain about the work that he would now have to do.

'Start next week.'

'Auch that explains the celebration on Friday for you that Isabelle has organised.'

'She's been keeping it quiet.' *God*, thought Peter, *the guy at the interview said that it had been organised, but how?*

'Well done, Peter. I'm pleased for you. Really I am.'

'Thanks.'

Their glasses met again and Bigsey toasted Peter's success, which was followed by their toasted cheese and tomato sandwiches arriving with a flurry of salad on the side.

'Thanks, Jackie,' said Bigsey.

'You're welcome.'

The noise in the bar had become increasingly loud so they ate their lunch in silence. Peter contemplated how he was going to approach the people at work. Whilst eating he decided he would get Isabelle to organise a one to one with each person and then have a team gathering on Friday morning before the leaving do. *That's the way to deal with it.* So he sent Isabelle a text telling her that he would not be back today and asked her to organise the one to ones from eight thirty tomorrow, leaving Giles till last on Thursday afternoon.

'That was good,' said Bigsey. 'I needed that. Well, I've got to get back. I've a session with Patricia in HR at three thirty regarding Jonathan.' He finished off the beer at the bottom of his glass. 'Okay, Peter, that's me done. I'll see you in the morning.' Bigsey got up, gave him a thumbs up and patted him on the shoulder before leaving Peter to finish off his beer.

Peter sat looking around at the people enjoying themselves and chatting to each other. He observed the social interaction. A man by himself on a single-seat sofa was doing a crossword. Someone asked if they could use the spare seat at his table and they sat down with their glass of red wine, having moved the chair to face slightly away from him. There seemed to be no let-up in the number of people coming in and out. He thought he recognised a face, but they were blocked out by someone else and the face was gone. Looking down at his phone he saw it was already 4.05 and there were no messages or texts.

On a Tuesday evening, he and Sally often had a Chinese takeaway to break up the week, but he hadn't had a text from Sal yet to confirm. He stood and left the pub and decided to walk to the station.

On route home, a text from Sally arrived confirming that she wanted a takeaway, and he ordered her usual. By the time he drove through the village from the station the restaurant was open, so he picked up the meal on the way through.

Sally wasn't at home when he got back so he decided to get some relaxation time and went upstairs to play *Call of Duty: Ghosts* on the big screen. No sooner had he started his first game than his phone bleeped. It was the office. 'One to ones all sorted. See you tomorrow. Isabelle.' The phone bleeped again. 'Hi, me here, home in ten mins.' That was perfect. It gave him enough time to complete a game.

When Sally got home he was still playing on the Xbox – he had started another game. She called up to him and he joined her in the kitchen.

She told him she had received a call from the agent that a house called Two Cherries in Pine Walk had come onto the market. It was a four-bedroomed, two-bathroom property needing some modernising and there was no chain. The elderly owner had recently been widowed and was moving to her daughter's in the Shetland Isles and was therefore keen for a quick sale.

'We've also got someone coming over at the weekend to look at our house. The agent said they are first-timers, so no chain. Isn't that good?' When Sally was excited she talked non-stop and Peter couldn't get a word in.

When she eventually stopped for a breath, he told her that he had been offered the job at an increased salary and that his first day would be on Monday. Sally let out a scream of excitement and jumped at Peter to hug him, almost knocking him over.

'That's wonderful, we should be able to afford the house. Look,' she said, pointing at the house details that she had pulled out of her bag, her fingers covering the price of the property. 'It's perfect for us, and see the pictures of the garden – and its south facing, Peter. I'm getting the old bottle of Malbec out, you know from the case for celebrations. I know we don't normally drink during the week, but I need one and this is a special occasion. Mom and Dad will be so pleased to hear your news when we speak to them later – and we can move house. Well? Aren't you pleased?'

Peter had a closer look at the agent's details and saw the price. It was way over what they could afford.

'Well. Yeah, honey, I am, but …'

'But what? You don't seem to be.'

Sally struggled with the bottle. The cork came out abruptly with a pop and Sally instantly poured the wine into their glasses. Yes, it tasted very nice on the palate but perhaps a little longer to air, but refreshingly pleasant. Peter relaxed a little. Did he have to tell Sally that he didn't even know what he was going to be doing.

'I gave my dad a call earlier, honey.'

'Great, and what did he say?'

'Well. I got a bit of a surprise, and his reply was far from what I had expected to hear. Apparently, when I was very young he worked for the same organisation for about three years, and …'

'No. Really. That's amazing. Well, it must be alright then.'

The phone rang. Sally's parents were somewhere high up in the Swiss Alps and they conversed with them for over an hour in between the various courses of Chinese food.

The following morning. Peter started to work through his one to ones at the office. There were a few people that expressed surprise about him leaving so soon after getting promotion and a number of other more senior people that just shrugged their shoulders as if it was the norm, but it did mean that the whole process was easier for Peter than he had thought it might be. There was going to be a senior guy from the fifth floor taking over Peter's role, so he briefed him on the procedures and positions with Giles and Jay present because they would be preparing the monthly dashboard report. He seemed quite happy until Jay mentioned he would have to present to the board the new risk analysis template.

Midway through Friday morning Sir John came to see Peter. He said he was sorry to see him go and wished him all the best, saying that it was going to happen some time. Peter couldn't quite work out what he meant. He added, 'We can't always hold on to our best people,' which Peter was quite flattered about and rendered speechless.

Even Old Barrel Face moved his butt from his office in the sky to say his goodbyes. 'I know we've had our differences, Peter, but I do wish you all the best. Just be careful of the nicknames you give people, and when to say them out loud.'

At the leaving presentation, his team gave him a high quality and by the look of them expensive pair of gold-coloured standard lamps. How he was going to get them home on the train he didn't know, let alone in the car, but they knew he was planning to move house. 'Something to remember us by,' said Isabelle with a tear in her eye.

He took the two standard lamps, with some help from Mike, to his leaving drinks do in the Old Bank of England restaurant. Bigsey said he would help carry them to the station later in the evening. Peter's brief leaving speech was well received and a number of the senior members of staff patted him on the back and shook his hand before they made their excuses.

Bigsey and Monica from accounts helped him get to the train at Waterloo. He must have made a strange sight with two standard lamps in the carriage lying partially horizontally across two sets of seats. Sally met him at the station with her car, a mini, because it had an electric sunroof. After a difficult few minutes in the station car park squeezing the lamp bases into the car, they set off home. It reminded them of bringing home last year's Christmas tree which was much too big for the lounge and they'd had to cut it shorter, much to their disappointment. Sally drove. With no room in the passenger seat, Peter sat in the back, laughing most of the way home. His laughter was only partly from too much beer. He was happy.

Sally had the weekend planned for them. A late breakfast on Saturday morning, partly because Peter had a headache and didn't want to get up. After breakfast they tidied up the house because the viewing was at 2.00 p.m. It was all hands to the deck ... clothes, vacuum, dishwasher, dusting, throwing out old newspapers and magazines and putting some flowers in vases around the house. The study/second bedroom would have to wait until later, although they did manage to put most of Peter's computer games up on the shelves. The people viewing were a couple of a similar age with a young child and they seemed keen.

The house that they had arranged to see was available for viewing early Sunday afternoon and they duly met the agent at the house as planned. It was perfect in Sally's eyes, and even Peter nodded with approval as they walked around, but there was a lot to be done – some of the rooms were stuck in a 1960s time warp. There was ample space out the back for ducks or chickens or both and a pool if they wanted one. The garden was south facing with a small pond towards the back as the land dipped away from the main lawns and flower beds. They both agreed that it was wonderful. The only problem still nagging at Peter was the price tag.

'Sal, do you realise that this is still quite a bit over our budget.'

'Yea, but Peter, you've got a pay rise in your new job.'

'Yes, but even with that,' said Peter. 'The agent hadn't realised that we had a loan as well as a mortgage on our existing house when he did the calculations.' This put a damper on their conversation and Sally went quiet.

They sat in Peter's car after the viewing, looking at the house and the details again and pondering what to do. Later that morning the agent for their house sale called to say that the young couple had put an offer in slightly below the asking price and that they should accept it. Peter and Sally decided that they would call the agent for the house they had viewed and put in an offer. It was the best they could do without stretching themselves beyond sensible, but it still sat way below the asking price.

'I don't think your offer will even be considered, let alone accepted. I will get back to you after I have spoken with the vendor,' said the agent, 'but as you know, there's already quite a lot of interest in this house because of its location, plus the benefit of a double garage, wine cellar and space in the attic for another room as well as the large garden.'

They were both slightly subdued following the agent's comments and decided to take a walk to discuss it further, concerned about the amount of work they would have to do to the house if they got it and the cost; they may well have to look elsewhere and not set their requirements so high. They visited the supermarket to get the week's food supplies in before driving home for Sunday roast. This was prepared by Peter most weekends when they weren't away – it was his speciality.

Peter's phone rang whilst he was preparing the Yorkshire puddings. He couldn't pick it up so Sally brought it to his ear. She put it on loudspeaker because it was the estate agent. 'Sorry to call you so late on a Sunday, but the vendors asked me to give you a call. The house is yours at the price you have offered, as long as you complete the purchase within six weeks, otherwise the price goes back up to the asking price.'

'Well,' said Peter, 'there's an incentive.' Sally was jumping for joy and hugged him enthusiastically, despite the flour on his hands. Peter thought about the position on their house and decided that he would try to incentivise the people buying theirs: if they completed within the six weeks they could have seven and a half per cent off the asking price. They informed the agents.

The conversation over the evening meal was very much house talk and Sally's excitement spilled over to Peter. She rang her parents who, having arrived at Santander, were now driving south on their way to visit Madrid. With the discussions about the house talking over the weekend, Peter had completely forgotten about starting his new job until he was getting his clothes out ready for the first morning. The change of jobs had happened so quickly.

CHAPTER 6
First Month Or Two

Peter was greeted by the receptionist on his first morning in the same way as he had been when he went to the interview. In fact, it was the same every morning. She would say her morning greeting without even looking up from the computer screen. Most mornings she would be holding some form of bread roll, sandwich, or crisps, in her left hand. She must over time have developed the skill to be able to type and eat at the same time, because her right hand was constantly busy tapping away on the keyboard. As he walked past her desk on the first morning he was aware that the only problem she had seemed to be when the phone rang. When deciding what to do, she became agitated and indecisive and her orangey-ginger coloured hair shook from side to side.

Peter's first day dragged; in fact, the first few weeks dragged. Compared to the hectic and sometimes frenetic atmosphere at Goldson's this was so quiet, but it wasn't boring – everything was new to him.

Ann and Mary were looking after and mentoring him in the first few weeks. They introduced him to so many people that he found it difficult to remember all their names. A few people stood out, like Julian, who had escorted him to the interview room. He was an strange character who would suddenly appear at the oddest times, mostly when Peter was going to the canteen. Ann and Mary set him up at his desk in a small office, close to one of the large open-plan office areas on the fourth floor where the only access was a narrow staircase, the final flight being a pair of spiral stairs, one up and the other down.

His office had no windows, just a skylight above the desk. The carpet colour varied from light to dark green depending on level of usage. The room was clean but tired and could have done with a coat of paint. A picture of Hampton Court hanging, or leaning, on one wall gave the room some life. He straightened it up and decided that a few plants would help – greenery was lacking throughout the offices. With the help of an elderly bespectacled man from the IT department, Ann and Mary took him through the IT security protocols and training programmes respectively and finally issued him with a mobile phone. *What a cool number,* he thought: 01110 010203. The phone was already set up with a direct-dial button to reception as well as one to Jon, which Ann said should not be used except for dire emergencies. All three of them reiterated to him at different times that the work phone must only be used in connection with work matters because of security issues and breaches in the past, and that his personal phone must be kept for personal matters only with no discussion about work or any of the people in any form on his personal line.

The HR department was probably the most challenging for Peter. Although he thought they were very efficient, they were so boring. If only they could view life with a little more energy and enthusiasm. Maybe it was the form filling that was frustrating him. They asked him about his medical history and illnesses, which was to be expected, plus what vaccinations he had had. Some of the injections they mentioned he had never heard of, but he presumed that his parents had arranged them; he would have to check with his doctor and then probably with his parents. HR had also arranged for him to have a full medical examination at Guys and St Thomas's Hospital the following week. Fortunately, Ann had warned him that he would be having some injections. The reason HR said that he had to go through all this process was to see if he needed to go on any fitness training as well as to check his general health and well-being. He was glad to see the back of HR.

The training programme was the opposite of the rigours of HR, IT, medical and admin matters, and he was hoping it would be interesting and give him some idea what he had got himself into. However, the programme gave Peter the impression that he was going back to school. Why so many subjects and so diverse? And exams! There was so much to take in. *Perhaps that's why Dad was so good at history and facts about the past.* Most of the subjects he had hated at school were now being thrown at him.

God, why did I take this job? He reflected that he had had no option. He sat at his desk reading down the list of training he had been given on a sheet of paper.

Most of the training sessions appeared to be online, which, from past experience, would be monotonous and tiresome.

'The history of the kings and queens of England since 1066.' *I've really only ever known of Queen Elizabeth II, and now Charles III, and the Battle of Hastings with William the Conqueror.*

"Understanding and applying self-defence strategies since mediaeval times." What a subject – and why?' he said out loud, shaking his head and looking around the room for some form of explanation.

'The history of secret societies.' *Oh, that should be enlightening, and might help me understand what's going on in this place.*

The skills of levitation and its use in modern society.

ESP training, practice and putting to work.

Techniques in meditation, thought control and management and when to apply.

'The development of the English language.' *Oh god, no. I was terrible at English at school. I hope this isn't going to be too much torture.*

'Food and drink availability and diet over the last millennium.' *Perhaps a little more interesting.*

'Herbal history, recipes and cures.' *Sounds like a witches' convention, this one. I wonder who will be taking us for these lessons?*

'Economics, finance and currency to the present day.' *At last. Thank goodness, subjects I know something about.*

'Health issues and protection.' *Sounds like I've just started my first day at school and advice about the birds and bees.* He laughed to himself.

'"Theatre and acting." Why?' he said out loud and leaned

back on his chair away from the screen. 'Well at least this one is practical and not online.'

'Fashion through the ages.' *Really? Me? Sal will enjoy this anyway.*

The text on the sheet of paper continued. Each module, once completed, in the training programme required a series of questions to be answered.

In the first module he got caught out; he was so intent on reading he had forgotten that there would be a test. He had to achieve a hundred per cent before he could move on to the next module. If he got a question wrong, he would have to repeat the whole module. What made it doubly difficult was that the questions varied each time on the retake. Ann explained that it was something that 'we all go through'. She said it so matter-of-factly. *Well, I suppose she would if she has passed all the tests.* But to be fair, as he went through each module for each subject she helped and reminded him that it was all important with personal development.

At home at the end of each day there was a revision test. Sally would ask questions and some of the facts that he had learnt were both interesting and intriguing.

'Did you know,' Peter told Sally, 'that England has had six queens?'

'No, I didn't.'

'Neither did I. There was Mary, Elizabeth, Anne and Victoria.'

'That's only four, Peter.'

'There were two Marys and two Elizabeths, and Elizabeth the first reigned for forty-five years ... and you know that was unheard of in those times. If you think about it, only basic provisions were available to them and she lived to the grand old age of seventy.'

'Yeah,' Sally replied, 'but don't forget that she was the elite of society in those days and would get the best food, the biggest roof over her head and transport.'

'Yeah, I suppose so, but still pretty amazing.'

The conversations at home, though, quickly moved on to house matters. They now had a moving-in date set for 11th July, which was within the stipulated period for them to buy the house at the discounted amount.

'I spoke to Mom and Dad again on a Zoom call earlier and guess what – they've made it to Seville and are gonna send you some snaps of Christopher Columbus's grave.'

After the end of the fourth week, Peter had had his visit to St Thomas's Hospital, and five injections later, varying from cholera to smallpox boosts, his arm felt like a pincushion. He was also called to see Jon. He hadn't seen him since the interview and, although he sounded bright and breezy when they met, his face looked strained.

Jon's office was on the ground floor, on the other side of the reception hall, which Peter discovered was to enable him to come in and out of the office when he pleased. He also had his own front door onto the street, which from the street looked like an old bricked-up door.

'Peter, good to see you, make yourself comfortable. Take one of the seats by the fire and I will join you in a few moments.' The fire was roaring. Peter sat down and looked around the room which was steeped in historic artefacts, bookshelves with rows of ancient books and a wall of pictures ceiling high. Jon was sitting at his solid oak desk working through paperwork of some sort or other.

'How are you getting on with your training? One thing I remember is to make sure you pay attention to the online stuff – you never know when it's going to come in useful, or that's what they told me. We've all had to go through it, Peter. But Ann and Mary have probably already told you this.' Peter sat waiting for Jon to join him, looking around the room in amazement. It was like he had stepped back in time – the rugs on the floor covering the boards, old portraits, pictures, and maybe even a grand master on the walls, the dark heavy oak wall unit and sideboard, candles lit on the table and even the open fireplace with the homely smell of burning. Thick heavy curtains hung either side of the solitary arched leaded light window.

'The training has been going fine, thank you, Jon, but to be honest, it's a little boring at times. Ann and Mary have looked after me.'

'Have they taken you over to the local hostelry yet?' Peter shook his head. 'Goodness. Well, let's organise that for lunch today. Shall we say two o'clock? I like to get the business side of the day out of the way before I have any ale. I'll see you in reception just before two and we can walk over to the alehouse.' Jon returned to his desk, head down again and busy with his paperwork. So, after a few minutes of silence Peter stood up and left the warmth and comfort of Jon's office.

The walk over to the Westminster Arms was quiet, Jon deep in thought. He said little.

'I'm told from the feedback I have from both Ann and Mary that so far your progress is … as expected, but as I said earlier, remember to pay attention to detail. It's all useful information and you never know when it will be important.'

'Why is it important?'

'It is, you just have to take my word for it for the time being. It's important to you and to all of us. At the CPS we rely on each other for support when needed.'

'I must admit that I never expected the Crown Prosecution Service to require this type of training.'

They crossed a road carefully. 'Well, Peter, it does, and, er … and it doesn't.' Jon skipped up the kerb in front of him.

'You mentioned that I would have a team and a specific purpose or plan of work.'

'You do. All in good time, Peter. All in good time. What you are undertaking now are the foundations for your work ahead. You've got the basics for your team and it's building up slowly.'

'Where? Who are they?'

'You will find out. You've met most of them already. Here we are.' They had reached the pub. 'I suggest we keep our conversation to aspects of life other than work.' Jon pushed the door open. 'Lovely little alehouse, this one. One of my favourites. Oh, and by the way, if you can't find me in the office on a Friday afternoon, you don't need to ask anyone – you know where I am.'

Jon obviously liked the pub, and his beer. The staff talked to him on first-name terms. Their table was upstairs and set on its own in a recess overlooking the square. Jon enquired about Peter's house purchase and was pleased to hear that it was going to plan – pleased for Peter and Sally, as well as for himself, because he had helped with the 'acquisition' arrangements, as he put it. Peter found out that Jon only lived about eight miles from where Sally and Peter were going to live, which he said was very convenient if he needed a lift home of an evening. That of course assumed that Peter wasn't drinking with him. Jon also suggested to Peter that he grow his hair a bit longer; he said there was no need for a short back and sides anymore and not to worry about shaving some mornings. 'Relax, Peter, don't take life so seriously.' He handed Peter the menu and ordered two pints of the finest ale.

Peter looked across the seating area towards the bar. Raucous laughter was coming from downstairs, but they were the only ones left upstairs. The clock was about to touch four fifteen, and they were still at the Westminster Arms with beer to drink. Having eaten a three-course lunch and working his way through his third pint of real ale, Peter sent Sally a text to say that he would need picking up from the station at around six fifteen, explaining that his boss had taken him out to lunch, that he had had to keep up with his drinking in order to socialise, and to keep the takeaway order small this evening.

Week five began much as the previous week and Peter was starting to get used to the routine. Training sessions throughout the week consisted of the seven prime subjects, as they were referred to, and then a selection of others that were not mandatory. For the prime subjects he had to complete three hours of study in the morning and three in the afternoon, between the times of nine and five thirty, until he completed each module for each subject. He had planned to take the Friday off because the solicitors had advised that they would be completing. Any spare time at the office and in the evenings was involved in organising the move and packing. The trickiest part of the move was the removal of boxes from the loft. Sally, after they had got married, had her belongings crated and shipped over from the States, and some crates hadn't been opened after six years of storage in the loft. Peter was glad that in their new house, there was a dedicated stair to the loft space. They might not even need to store anything up there, because they would have so much room in the new house.

The move on Friday went smoothly, with Peter's parents helping at the new house. Before they knew it, Sunday evening had arrived and Peter had the roast to cook, but for once the responsibility was handed over to his mother, who knew how to cook on an Aga. That was one thing that they had not fully appreciated when they bought the house. His mother summarised very succinctly. 'This one on the left is hot, this one simmers, and the same with the two ovens – top is hot and the lower, warm.' Peter did not pay much attention. He plunged himself onto a sofa in the lounge and was exhausted, they all were, after the packing, lifting, moving and now unpacking.

The following week, Jon asked Peter if he could come over and visit the house. He duly did on Wednesday evening. Walking around with a cup of tea he was almost in a dream, chatting away to himself.

'Good. Yes. This is what I expected. Just perfect and ... yes. I do like the cellar at the back of the house, most convenient,' he concluded after Peter had shown him around the inside of the house. Sally and Peter watched him from the kitchen window wandering around outside in the garden, still chatting to himself.

Eventually he returned to the house with an empty cup. 'Right, I must go. See you tomorrow, Peter. And Sally, lovely to meet you.' He lifted her hand and kissed it. Sally gave an embarrassed laugh and brought her hand up to her mouth.

'You must both come over to ours some time.'

'Yes, we'd love that, wouldn't we, Peter?'

'Yeah, great, Jon, thank you for coming over. See you tomorrow.' They waved him goodbye from their front porch on the sweep-around drive. He drove away in an old Jaguar.

'Strange man, your boss.'

'Yeah. I suppose so, but he seems alright. I've only really had a few conversations with him.' They went back into the house.

Peter didn't see Jon the following day, but he knew he must have been around because when he went out for his lunch he saw the door from Jon's office onto the street closing.

Peter wasn't looking forward to the training arranged for the afternoon. 'Theatre and Acting' – and this couldn't be carried out online. He joined about twenty other people in a small theatre-cum-hall. At one end of the room was the stage with the curtains open, the seating in front arranged haphazardly. Looking around, he worked out that there was a split of roughly fifty-fifty male to female members of staff, some of whom Ann and Mary had already introduced him to. He found a spare seat near the back, and noticed a man whose face he thought he recognised. *Ah yes, of course,* Peter thought, *he was from the pub – Ye Olde Mitre.* Well, maybe not as he took a closer look. Peter had always been good at faces but struggled with names. *That's right, he was there, up at the bar talking to a group of people when I met up with Bigsey. Wow, that seems like a long time ago.*

'Peter, Peter.' The loud bellowing voice came from in front of him. 'Are you going to join us or are you on Planet Zog?'

Peter had been daydreaming and the lecturer had noticed. She was right up close in front of his face. 'Peter. Were you listening?'

'Er, yeah, of course.'

'Well, you are here to learn. It's for your benefit. You're in the first group, so go and join the others, go on and take your shoes off. And by the way, my name is Avril.'

Peter did as he was told.

'Your group has the instructions for this first session, the second group will then perform.'

Perform. Perform what? thought Peter. God, he wished he had turned up a bit earlier and paid attention. A number of those in group two still sitting down had heard his conversation with Avril and looked at him, smirking. Avril pointed towards the rest of his group, who were going through a doorway that led behind the stage. He joined them. Some of them he vaguely recognised from the canteen and a couple he had been introduced to briefly, and gave them a nod, but he had little knowledge of what they did.

Chairs were spaced evenly across the stage in two rows of ten. The curtains between the stage and the hall were pulled across and closed.

'This is the first of your series of six lectures and practicals in Theatre and Acting,' said Avril loudly from the other side of the curtains. 'The aim of these sessions is to boost your self-confidence and calmness in stressful situations. I can't teach you everything, but you will learn from some key experiences over the next six weeks. Deidre. Could you please close and lock the door at the back. Thank you.'

Behind the stage, Deidre, who seemed to be Avril's assistant, was taking charge of proceedings. She was tall, slim, slightly tanned, with just a touch of make-up and probably in her late thirties with brown hair in a ponytail. He vaguely recognised her from the open-plan office on the second floor.

'Right, all up on the stage please, choose a chair please and sit on it, men at the back please. This is all about confidence and ability in yourself. All please look ahead at the curtains.'

Deidre then blindfolded each of them in turn. Peter couldn't see anything other than a glimpse of his socks at the bottom of the blind.

'Okay, is everyone ready?' came Avril's voice from the front.

This was followed by the sound of the curtains opening up in front of them.

'Right. Would you now please all stand up. Would each of you take your shirts and tops off.' *Why?* thought Peter. *Just as well I had a shower this morning.*

'Now your trousers or skirts.' There was no comment from the people on stage, just a rustling of clothing, zips and buttons, and clothing landing on the floor. 'When you reflect on this later, it will boost your self-confidence. If you are not happy with this then put your hand up and Deidre will deal with you. Now, lift your arms up high. Now carefully touch your toes. Slowly now, we don't want anyone falling over. How does that feel?'

'Fine' and 'Good' said a number of female voices in front and to the side of him. There were no male voices.

'Feeling more confident, are we?' Avril's voice. A few more *fine* and *good* could be heard from the females in the group together with a few giggles. 'Now, remove your underwear.' The bubble of voices on stage stopped. There was silence for a few minutes. But slowly there were sounds of the slow removal of clothing and snapping noises. Peter could see out of the bottom of his blind perfectly and saw a pair of perfectly formed ankles.

'Well,' said Avril, 'come on, where's that confidence in yourself that we've heard about? Deidre, how's it looking up there?'

'Full house, Avril,' shouted Deidre from somewhere behind him at the back of the stage.

'How does that feel to everyone?' Avril said from the front. There were no replies from the stage. 'Now, get dressed, keep your blinds on to protect others' modesty, and then return to your seats at the front.' There was an immediate sound of shuffling and rummaging for clothes and the curtains closing.

Peter heard Deidre moving around behind them all. She must have enjoyed watching from a distance from the back of the stage.

'Deidre, can you go and get group two now from the anteroom and take them up on stage once everyone from group one is back in their seats in the hall? Thank you.'

The same procedure followed with group two. Peter's heart was still pounding with the adrenaline of standing up naked on the stage with goodness knows how many people looking at him. He looked around and there were a few flushed faces from those in group one.

Avril went through the same routine for group two, except that the curtains didn't open. There was just a sound as if they were opening and a few giggles. He had the advantage, as did the rest of group one, of seeing the deception.

'Tomorrow we are here again for a two o'clock start. Make sure you have your outfits with you … and think about the production. Remember, it's the roaring twenties and we want to see dance, fun, excitement from you. Play your part. You should have learnt your words by now.' *God,* thought Peter, *I must have missed something here, outfits and learning words? Shit, I'd better check my emails.*

The evening meal with Sally was full of discussion about the stage experience and what he had gone through.

'How do you know that no one was looking?' asked Sally with a big smile on her face.

'Because we saw group two going through the same routine as us.'

Sally continued to tease Peter. 'I never realised that I had married one of the Chippendales.'

Although Sally's questioning did bring some doubt into his mind, he felt pretty calm about it. 'What I can tell you is that the experience up on stage did bring the people together. We all had that same terrifying feeling and experience, but at the same time we fought that feeling with the satisfaction of achieving something exciting.'

The following morning, Peter and the rest of his group were given a script, and each had to learn lines and choose costumes for a 'theatrical' performance. This was a surprise for all of them. Peter felt himself immediately becoming apprehensive that there would be more trickery from Avril in the afternoon. But no. Jon, and a few other senior people that he had seen at the interview, Parka man and Green Eye, came to watch their performance on stage-a roaring twenties party at an imaginary stately home.

The following day was the start of the Self-defence and Firearms classes, which Peter had been looking forward to. He had never fired a gun other than at country fairs, trying to knock cans off a shelf for a cuddly toy. Other than that, the closest he got to shooting was when he played his *Call of Duty* Xbox games. Sally said that she couldn't understand why this was needed for his work at CPS. But apparently, Peter had been told, it was because there had been an increase in the number of instances when people who were being interviewed or arrested had tried to break bail or their friends with firearms had tried to release them.

'Self-defence and Firearms.' Peter was in his office reading the text on the screen of his computer, hoping there would be no surprises. He was fortunate, because when he was at junior school his dad had made him join the after-school Judo classes. His father would come to watch whenever he could. Peter did well with the classes and passed all the Kyu grades. He progressed to his Rokyu test and passed, which enabled him to move forward with his black belt, until the early years of secondary school, when team sports, in particular rugby, took over. Peter was quick and powerful for someone quite slight in build, and he was put on the wing, and the skills he learnt in Judo helped him with his upper-body strength and quick movement. So when it came to the training at CPS, he gave the instructors a run for their money.

'Peter. You've done this before, haven't you?' said Bernard, who had a black belt around his waist.

'It was a long time ago.'

'Well, grab hold of this.' Bernard threw a pole about half the length of a garden rake at Peter and they started sparring. Peter got a whack on the shoulder.

'Now try this.' And he gave Peter a knife.

'Are you sure?'

'Come on, make a dive for me. Don't worry, I will avoid it,' said Bernard confidently. Peter thrust his dagger forward, and for his trouble, got Bernard's dagger thumped into his chest. Peter's adrenaline pumped … Bernard pulled the retractable dagger away.

'My only suggestion or criticism of you, Peter, is to make sure that you keep yourself fully focused at all times, particularly during the knife exercise and baseball bat exercise. You saw how easily I got past your defences. These are both key attributes and skills and are the essence of self-defence.'

The following day there was a repeat of the self-defence exercises with Bernard, and Peter markedly improved, much to the instructor's satisfaction. Peter's past Judo experience meant that he could calmly work through these lessons and was able to go to the shooting range more often than the rest of the group and learn about firearms.

The shooting range was down in the basement, level minus five. Pistols, machine guns … it was all there, locked in cabinets for safety reasons. There was even a musket labelled 'original'. He had never used or even held a firearm before. But he concluded that they were noisy, immediate and violent. What particularly interested him was the intricacies of the musket – the loading of the muzzle and setting of the flintlock. He must have tried to load and fire the musket a dozen times before the 1623 snaphance flintlock actually fired. The musket ball shot out, and with it an extremely loud noise, leaving a strong smell of burnt gunpowder. The blast sent his ears ringing even with the defenders on. After a few more attempts, Peter was able to ensure that the musket fired every time, by ensuring that the setting was right and making sure that the powder was dry. According to Paul, his instructor, that was the main cause of deaths – firing at the enemy only to find that the powder failed and you had to run, be shot at, or be stabbed to death.

Paul was blunt with his instructions, to say the least, and Peter soon learnt that his priority was safety in all aspects of firearm use, at all times. From walking through the door to the range to leaving, there was a routine and strictness.

'We've invested a lot in you guys and the last thing we want is an accident.'

Peter discovered that Paul had had spells with the British Forces and United Nations throughout the world for over a thirty-year period and had a safety mentality ingrained in him as well as the priority of looking after number one. What Peter enjoyed about Paul was the extent of his knowledge about firearms and that he was so keen on muskets as the 'basic firearm', as he called it, 'invented' some five hundred years ago. He would bring in all sorts of types, shapes and sizes of firearms to show Peter, some of which they managed to get to fire a shot, and some other weapons that should probably have remained as museum pieces rather than being risked with a novice like him.

More often than not, after the 'Self-defence and Firearms' lectures and practicals was 'Food and Technology'. Peter considered this to be the most fun. The lessons required practical skills rather than just online training and putting into action what he had learnt online. Basic foods eaten even only a hundred years ago were interesting, but the extent of knowledge about herbs and spices intrigued him and when he returned home from one of these lessons, conversations with Sally were challenging – as she was the head chef in the house.

One of the biggest issues in the past, other than getting the raw ingredients, was how to store and heat food. Preparation techniques were easy with a knife, but other utensils were rather cumbersome and in certain instances almost prehistoric. Which was why many meals, stews, soups and the like were cooked on a cauldron over a fire. The trainees were allowed to take home the food they cooked, much to Sally's amusement. Peter and Sally concluded that she should remain master of the kitchen and Peter the chief washer-upper.

CHAPTER 7
The Summer Party

The invitation promised by Jon earlier in the month duly arrived one Friday morning. Jon burst into Peter's office and threw an envelope across the room like a frisbee, Peter catching it just before it whizzed past his ear.

'See you there. Follow the directions to the house and you'll find it easily. Anyway, it's all in the invitation.' Jon left Peter's office closing the door as abruptly as he had opened it. *Obviously on a mission to deliver his invites,* Peter thought. The door to his office burst open again moments later and Jon's head appeared around the door.

'Oh, and by the way, you play golf, don't you?'

'Yes,' said Peter.

'What's your handicap?'

'I'm a three, why?'

'Well, we'll perhaps manage a game whilst you're over. And by the way, I'm a minus one.' He smiled then his head disappeared out of Peter's office and the door closed again.

Crikey, Peter thought, he must have acres of land. He decided he would open the envelope when he got home because it was addressed to both him and Sally. He continued with his final series of training in how to start a fire without matches, watching it online and then, with a number of colleagues with whom he had become more social after the acting and theatre experience, gave it a go in the courtyard out the back, with mixed results.

At home, Peter discussed his day with Sally over their evening meal, and he remembered the invitation. He left the table mid-meal, pulled out various papers from his briefcase, found it and gave it to Sally. The envelope was decorated with a wonderful picture of a house and garden, and the invitation was handwritten, with a quill by the look of it, Sally said, and showed Peter.

'What does it say, come on,' she said with excitement.

'Hold on, hold on, I'm about to read it,' Peter said. Sally stretched across the table trying to read the invitation. Peter lifted it away from her hand and read it out loud.

'Dearest Peter and Sally,'

'Nice picture at the front … is that their house I wonder? Wow, that's seriously impressive – they must have a huge garden,' said Sally.

'My family and I cordially invite you to join us at our early summer garden party at Regal Heights, Abinger, in the Surrey Hills.'

'Goodness what a name for a house,' said Sally.

'Be here, from twelve noon (don't be late and it shouldn't end late either!).' *That's odd*, thought Peter, *the wording has a humour similar to the job advertisement. It must have been Jon who drafted the text.*

'Dress (ladies and gentlemen) 16th century please, no excuses. If you haven't got any outfits, check out the costumes department at work. If you have a problem we'll sort you out here, but before noon.

'Unshaven (gentlemen) unless you already have a beard!

'Ladies either plain or dolled up, nothing in between. A make-up artist will be here if you need assistance. Again arrive early, before noon please. Lunch will be served at 1.00 p.m. and finish at 2.30 p.m. sharp. You may wish to enjoy a stroll in our gardens, at your leisure, and if you would like to have a swim, bring a costume.

'If you are going to bring a bottle make sure it's either a port or Madeira … pre-1990 would be most desirable because most of the stuff since then is undrinkable (my opinion only, of course), preferably from the Douro Valley, Oporto, Portugal, SW Europe.

'Parking in the field opposite the metal entrance gates (mind the cow pats!).

'Unless I hear from you by this afternoon, we will assume you are attending.'

'When is it?' asked Sally

Peter showed her the invitation.

'The 13th? That's tomorrow,' said Sally with a shocked look on her face.

'And today is the twelfth,' replied Peter. 'He gave me the invitation this morning.'

'Oh, and by the way, this invitation is compulsory, no excuses for absence.'

'Yours, Jon and Jemima.'

'Well,' said Sally, taking the invitation card from Peter. 'Looks like we're out all day tomorrow.

'I think I'm going to give Dad a call. I know it's late but it's good to be prepared.' They finished their meal and whilst Sally loaded the dishwasher, Peter rang his father.

'Dad. Hi. Sorry it's rather late.'

'That's fine, you know I'm always here. How's Sally?'

'She's fine, thanks.'

'And the house?'

'Yes, plenty to do – there's so much space we really are at a loss for furniture to fill the house.'

'Don't worry about that, it will come, and your mother and I can always help if you need us – and you've already got me down to do the fitted wardrobes.'

'Thanks, Dad, appreciated. I won't keep you long, Dad, I know it's late, but it's about work, actually.'

'Oh, is there anything wrong?'

'Well, it's just … it's just that we've had an invitation from Jon at work …'

'Oh, one of those. Yes, I remember my first invitation many years ago. It poured with rain all day – your mother and I got drenched – but it was good fun.'

'You've been to one?'

'Yes, of course, quite a number, you know I worked at the CPS for a few years and my career overlapped with Jon's for a short while, but I came out the other end in one piece.'

'Yeah, I only vaguely remember – I was still quite young and I only have a few fleeting memories. I do remember a garden party and running around the gardens playing hide and seek with other children. It seemed like hours of fun.'

'Yes, you'll enjoy it, I'm sure. They were happy days.'

'Okay thanks, Dad. You know we've been asked to dress up?'

'Oh good. What's the theme?'

'Sixteenth century.'

'Ah yes, exciting times, the sixteenth century, but watch out for creepy crawlies and keep your wits about you.'

'What do you mean?'

'How can I put it? You'll be meeting different people, some more friendly than others, but we can catch up after your party.'

'Okay, thanks. Night, Dad, and night to Mum.'

'Night, Peter.'

Peter put his phone down on the kitchen table and reflected on what his father had said. He felt sort of reassured. Sally said that Peter was overthinking it all, and that it was a work party with Jon's family and friends and they had been invited to get to know the people better and that she was going to enjoy it even if he didn't. 'Come on, Peter, I always like dressing up.'

'So what are you going as? Plain or dolled-up colourful?'

'I do too much plain at work so I'm going to enjoy putting my make-up on and dressing up. It's not often we have an invitation to a themed fancy-dress party in the summer – it's usually at Christmas when it's cold. Anyhow, the invitation says if you haven't got clothes or make-up then turn up early. So I think I'll do my own make-up and then choose an outfit when we get there.'

'Yeah, good idea, Sal. I haven't shaved for a few days and yeah, let's go early and see what they've got for us to put on.'

On Saturday morning, Sally, excited about what the day would hold, was up and out of bed early and off for her five-kilometre run, followed by a half hour of yoga online and a shower before breakfast. Peter slept in; he had been struggling to sleep these last few weeks, thinking about the size of the house and garden and why he should need to learn unarmed combat skills and the intricate development of the English language mixed with people observation, surveillance and negotiation skills.

Sally spent over an hour in the bathroom after breakfast, appearing downstairs with a towel wrapped around her body and hair pulled up in a tall bun as far as Peter could make out. Her face was well and truly made up.

'Crikey. You've really gone to town, Sal.'

She spun around and smiled widely. 'Yeah, as I said yesterday, it's nice occasionally and a bit of fun.' She kissed and hugged Peter, swallowed a mouthful of coffee and then ran upstairs to get dressed. Peter was ready to go – he was going to find a costume when he got to the party and the make-up team could get to work on him if they wanted to.

'What are the golf clubs doing in the back of the car?' asked Sally.

'Jon said that he played and that we might manage a game.'

'Oh,' was the sullen reply from Sally.

They took Sally's silver-grey mini convertible. It was about a twenty five-minute drive south-west to the Surrey Hills. Peter wanted to take the roof down on the car because it was such a sunny day, but decided against it as it would mess up Sally's hair. She already looked a little like Marge Simpson with her hair so high on her head. He preferred the Marge look rather than the classic Bridget Jones.

They set off from Ashtead just after ten thirty, driving out towards Dorking, then out and through Westcott and Wooton on the A25, up Coasthill Road for a few miles until they reached the village of Abinger.

'Okay, Peter, looking at the map I think we're almost here – it's coming up on the left – here, Peter, just here.' Sally was pointing frantically at the junction. 'And then after about seven hundred and fifty yards, a left and then a right and sort of slightly back on ourselves,' she said, glancing between the road and the map on her mobile.

They drove carefully up a steep hill and finally round to the right saw the imposing gated entrance and a direction sign on a pole pointing to the car park in the field opposite.

'Phew – we made it without getting lost and plenty of time to get changed.'

'Wow, what a place! My parents would be over the moon to see this,' said Sally, looking around and towards the spectacular building.

There were already cars in the car park – a deep blue Bentley, a red Porsche, Land Rovers and a sprinkling of commuter vehicles. Peter counted at least twelve vehicles. *Mm,* he thought, *that's a nice enough number not to feel crowded.* They walked out of the field, crossed the road and went through the huge metal-gated entrance. Peter spotted security recognition cameras as they went in. Ahead stood a stunning mansion with tall sash windows. The gravel driveway crunching beneath their feet accompanied by the smell of neatly mown lawns led them to a huge projecting porch with a balcony over it.

The music they had heard from the car park became louder and more distinct as they got closer to the house. They approached the arched oak front door protected by the porch. The door opened as they were about to knock and a lady dressed in pink stepped out, greeting them with a beaming smile. She was slight, with gentle bouncy brown hair. Her hands stretched out towards them.

'Peter, isn't it? Hello, and this must be Sally. Lovely to meet you both. I've heard so much about you both from Jon. Oh yes, and I'm Jemima, Jon's partner in crime.' She giggled and moved to kiss Sally on both cheeks and shook Peter's hand.

'You're nice and early, so you'll have plenty of time to get ready. Jon's out in the garden somewhere. You look wonderful, Sally. I do like your hair – it …' Peter knew what she was going to say but like him she decided not to mention it. 'Let me take you both through to the barn, where you can change into your costumes. You will have plenty of time to choose. Jane is there, Peter, from the make-up department. You'll recognise her and Wendy from costumes.' Other guests were walking up the drive towards the entrance and Jemima led Peter and Sally quickly to the barn.

Chatting amicably with Jemima as they walked, they reached the barn and their host opened the big wooden door. There was a lady sitting at a table to the left as they walked in. She was stunningly dressed.

'Names, please.'

Peter recognised her voice immediately and had to hold back his laughter. 'I'm surprised you needed to ask,' he said. She looked up, tapped a number of keys on her computer with one hand, holding a crisp in the other.

'You will know Marilyn from the office,' said Jemima.

'Yes, we've sort of met. How do you do,' replied Peter, hardly able to believe his eyes at the transformation that had taken place.

'Jane. Wendy?' called Marilyn. 'Two more customers for you … and be kind with them. They're first-timers.'

'I'll see you both when you're ready,' said Jemima, pointing to a door at the back. 'That will take you through to the garden. Oh, and will you be wanting a swim? Well, you can decide later – see how you feel, you don't have to decide now. You've got plenty of other things to think about.' She excused herself and left the two of them in the barn to attend to another group of guests.

On the left side of the barn were racks of brightly coloured women's outfits, and in the far corner Jane was finishing off a lady's make-up. She beckoned them over to her.

'Jane. Hi, this is Sally, my wife.'

'Hi, Sally. I'm Jane from the office. Looks like you've beaten me to it with your make-up – you look stunning.'

'Thank you. I just thought it would be fun to dress up and …'

'Wendy, Wendy,' called Jemima, who was with another group of guests. 'Peter and his wife Sally are here, can you sort out their outfits? Thanks.'

'Peter, I'll sort your make-up once you've got your clothes. There's no point in me making you up as a ruffian if you're dressed as a gent … have you decided what you're going to be?'

'No, I've no idea, really.'

'We'll let Wendy sort you both out then.'

Peter was led up a set of rickety wooden steps that took him up to a balcony running the length of the barn and overlooking the central main area.

'This is where the men's costumes are kept, Peter. Why don't you take a look and try what you want on? The changing rooms are at the end. I'll sort a dress for Sally. When you've chosen, just come down when you're ready and I'll do your make-up.'

Peter was left to his own devices.

Sally was attended to by Wendy. She tried a variety of dresses on and decided on a light green flowing dress and cream-tied bodice with the top frilled at the edges and sleeves. Sally swirled in front of a long mirror and gleefully made her way to Jane in make-up.

'Well, as I said earlier, Sally, I don't think there's anything left for me to do. You've done a brilliant job. Where did you learn to do that?'

'Drama school back in the States when I was in my teens and then at college.'

'I think there's only a few minor bits that I would add or slightly alter.' Jane asked Sally to sit still as she added black eyeliner and planted a small black beauty heart on her left bosom and a beauty spot on her top lip.

'Now, I think we'll just drop the hair a touch. Wow, look at you.'

Sally stood up and looked at herself in a mirror and was stunned by the change.

'Peter's going to get a shock when he sees me.'

Peter had already chosen his outfit and joined Sally and Jane.

'Has anyone seen my wife?' Sally turned and laughed. 'Wow, you look fantastic, Sal. Mine is a bit basic by comparison.'

'Sit down here, Peter,' said Jane, 'and I'll deal with your make-up.'

Sally stood in front of the mirror admiring herself and turning her shoulders from side to side. Peter had chosen a rich merchant's outfit and Jane decided that he needed a tanned face browned by the sun. She showed her artistic flare again adding an arrow-shaped scar below his right eye.

'You'll do.'

Sally came up to have a closer look at him. 'You look more like a rich pirate,' she said, laughing.

'Thank you, Wendy,' said Peter, looking at the mirror. He stood up and joined Sally.

'I suppose that was the fun bit. Now we have to meet the crowds,' he said apprehensively.

'Oh, come on, Peter. It's just a bit of fun.' She tickled him as they left the barn. Glancing behind Peter could see others struggling to get into their outfits.

The door from the barn opened into glorious sunshine and stunning gardens laid mainly to lawn with forested hills in the distance. An ornamental pond was next to the terrace, which ran along the back of the house. Arches cut through yew and laurel led to other parts of the garden. A small thatched garden building caught Peter's eye. He could see someone of Jon's height and build serving drinks. He was in his element, thought Peter.

'Sally, you look amazing,' said Jemima as she approached the two of them. 'Doesn't she, Peter?'

'Yes, I must admit she looks pretty good without make-up as well.' Peter gave her an impish smile.

'What a lovely compliment,' said Jemima. 'Now let me take you over to see Jon who will sort you out a drink for you both, and then I'll introduce you to some of our guests. You should know some of them already, although you might find they are difficult to see under their disguises.'

'Peter, Sally, how wonderful to see you both. I would shake your hands, but no kisses or I'll mess up the make-up. You do scrub up well, Peter. Now, what can I get you to drink?'

Peter said they had brought him a little something.

'Peter, how kind ... how very kind. Now let me see.' He felt the bottle through the wrapping. 'I can feel the indent and the motif on the glass ... it's definitely a port.' Jon didn't hold the suspense any longer and opened the present.

'How very kind of you both – a 1966 port. That's a good year – it must have set you back a bit, Peter. Well, I'm sure we can enjoy a sample a little later. Sally, what can I get you?'

'A margarita, please.'

'And you, Peter?'

'Just a lager, please.'

'Surely not. Do you not want to try some of my home-made ale? It's a special. Let me get you one.'

'Oh dear,' said Sally to Peter. 'Looks like I'm driving home then.' Jon disappeared behind the bar and they heard the sound of beer leaving a barrel. He reappeared a few moments later with a tankard full of beer frothing over the top.

'Try this, Peter. Surrey's best.'

'Ah, that's good.' Peter wiped his lips with his sleeve.

'Sally, this is my daughter Josephine, Josie for short. She'll sort out your drink and look after you. A margarita please, Josie, for Sally. I need to introduce Peter to a few people whilst I remember and then we will be back to collect you.'

Peter looked at Josephine. She was slight and tall, and looked like a younger version of her mother. She had hazel eyes, big eyelashes and floaty mouse-coloured hair, very high cheekbones and bright orange painted lips, although this all might have been due to her make-up. Peter moved away with Jon, chatting. They walked towards a group of people sitting on a Lutyens bench on the terrace.

'What a fabulous house,' said Sally to Josephine while she was making up her drink.

'Yes, it's what you can't see that's truly amazing,' she replied mysteriously.

The rear elevation of the house comprised a series of four timber-framed sash bay windows onto the extensive stone patio, with wild flowers and moss growing through the cracks. The walls of the house, a mixture of local Leith Hill stone and brick, were tile-hung at first-floor level with a mixture of plain and diamond-shaped leaded-light windows and two shallow, elongated eye windows across the roof at attic level.

'I've lived here all my life and there's always something that fascinates me. A view, or a piece of furniture. We've got just over six acres here, and other than the cutting of the grass and the croquet lawn, which we get people in to maintain, Mum and Dad sort out the rest of the garden. Oh yes, and the pool, or pools. Let me show you – no one else seems to need a drink at the moment and they can always help themselves. That's what Dad usually ends up saying anyway.'

Behind the thatched bar was a thick laurel hedge screening the pool behind. The opening in the hedge was an archway into a dark tunnel and out the other side to the pool area and glorious views across the Surrey countryside. The pools were on three levels following the slope of the ground away from the house. A jacuzzi at the top spilled over in a small waterfall like an infinity pool into the pool below, which in turn spilled over into the larger pool with a diving board at one end.

'That's where I learnt how to dive and swim for Wales.'

'This is to die for,' said Sally. 'It's fantastic. I just can't take it all in – and the views across the valley, and no houses overlooking … and all so peaceful.' Sally was awestruck.

'We do get a few planes every now and again but so do most people. Well, hopefully you will be able to do wonderful things to your house and garden. Dad described it to me and showed me the agent's details. Nicely secluded and plenty of space for a pool and croquet lawn.'

Sally wondered how Josie and indeed Jon knew so much about their house. 'How come you know so much about our house? And why croquet?'

'Dad's really good at croquet … golf croquet – you've heard of it? He's a minus-one handicap.'

Sally chuckled to herself. *Wait till Peter finds out – he'll be in stitches.*

'Dad took us over to look at the house when it came on the market and felt that it might suit you both.'

'But … how?'

'Sally, Josie. Come on back, we're serving lunch shortly.' Jemima's voice came from the other side of the hedge.

Making their way back to the house, Josie explained that Jon always tried to help with house hunting for new employees – it was a perk of the job in his eyes. Sometimes he would try to help things along with a purchase or discreetly advise that the property was not for them. She added that the one Sally had chosen and persuaded Peter to go for was more than perfect.

Emerging through the laurel tunnel, Sally could see Peter and Jon speaking with a group of people standing on the terrace by the house.

Peter beckoned Sally over. 'Paul, Jason, Brenda, Sue this is my wife, Sally.'

Pleasantries over, a loud brass gong was heard, followed by Jon's voice calling, 'Lunch is served, everybody. Please follow me.'

Jon was quite a showman. He led the procession into the house whilst playing a penny whistle. Everyone followed him through the lounge and into the drawing room. The room was laid as a banquet. *Jemima must have gone to a lot of trouble.* Each person's seat was tagged with a name card. There were candelabra running down the centre of the ornately plastered ceiling over the table, napkins fashioned like birds, harpsichord music playing gently in the background, and a fire roaring even though it was summer.

It took a while for Sally and Peter to find where they had been allocated seating, which had been arranged with men and women alternately placed. The ends of the long table were rounded so that guests could speak to each other more comfortably. They found their name tags and fortunately they were next to each other; Sally breathed a sigh of relief. Standing behind their tall oak carved chairs they waited, chatting amongst themselves and introducing themselves to the guests sitting next to them. Jon banged a spoon against the rim of a tall cut-glass wine glass and called out, 'Thank you, Lord and Guardians. We are grateful for this sustenance that you have provided for us. Please be seated, everyone, and enjoy!'

The men pulled out the chairs for the ladies to sit and then the men joined them at the table.

'This is a fantastic place, Peter. Did you see the pool and the croquet lawn? I had a lovely chat with Josie. She's very nice.'

'Yeah, it's very impressive.'

'Did you know Jon is a minus-one handicap player?'

'Yeah, he told me. That's why I brought my clubs – he said that we might—'

Sally promptly interrupted him. 'Yea, Peter, but at golf croquet, not golf golf.'

Peter's hand came up to his mouth and he laughed out loud.

Jon must have seen the two of them laughing with each other because he called out across the table, 'Peter, there's obviously something making you laugh. Can you share your secret with us?'

Sally looked at Peter to her right and gave him an impish grin.

'I was just catching up with Sally. Josie showed her around your lovely gardens and she mentioned the croquet lawn.'

'Ah, yes, good, we'll be able to play later, time permitting.'

'I've brought—'

'Excellent, your mallet. Well, I'm looking forward to it. The lawn is running fast at the moment because we haven't had much rain, but I'm sure you're used to playing on different lawns. Each one can be so different. You may start, everyone.'

Sally and Peter laughed together some more as the chatter of people increased when the food arrived.

Jon's wife Jemima and their daughters served the starters and laid them on the table in front of the guests: sliced boiled egg and mustard with a sprig of watercress.

Sitting to the left of Sally was a man called Quintin dressed as a court jester.

'Great outfit,' said Peter leaning across Sally as he spoke. He thought he recognised him from the accounts department but couldn't quite tell with all the make-up. To the right of Peter was Susan dressed in an outfit similar to Sally's, but it didn't quite fit her top half. Sally nudged Peter in the ribs; he was staring rather too long at the lady and not really listening to her conversation. There was a choice of wine. Peter and Sally chose red, which was poured into the tall cut glass. The food was served as a buffet, which suited everyone, with roast pork and chicken, boiled potatoes and salads for those not feeling up to a roast on a hot summer afternoon. This allowed Jemima to relax a little and join them.

'I hope there's enough choice for you both,' she said with slight concern in her voice as she passed them in the queue.

'There's ample, thank you, just deciding what to have. It's so wonderfully presented,' Sally said, looking amazed at the spread on the table.

'Oh, that's good, you can always come back for more, depending on whether your dress can cope, and don't forget there will be pudding afterwards,' she said. 'That's the problem I always have dressing up like this – it does make you wonder how they coped with it years ago, stuffing themselves with food and then somehow managing to maintain their poise.'

'Back in the States they would love to see the house and gardens and the banquet laid out like this. It's really fantastic. Thank you for inviting us, Jemima.'

'I hope Josie showed you around the grounds.'

'Yes, they are lovely, and I'm tempted to go for a swim later if that's alright.'

'Of course you can, darling. I'm sure there will be others that will want to join you. Now, Peter, how are you enjoying working with Jon?' Jemima touching him on the arm.

'Oh yes, it's good, thank you. So much different from my previous job. Although I don't see much of Jon.'

'Oh yes, he's busy, quite a responsible position – and he has to do a lot of travelling. Did you know that he and your father used to work together, until his … accident?'

'Yea, Dad told me but he's never really said much about it.'

'Well, Peter, he was very brave and he deserved the medal they gave him.' This took Peter's breath away. *Dad, a medal? I never knew.*

'I must mingle now, both of you, but if you're lacking in anything please find me or one of the girls. They will help you out.'

Peter and Sally returned to their places. Peter muttered under his breath, 'Dad, a medal? What was that for, I wonder.' Peter's plate was full. When they sat down, the conversation with Quintin and Susan either side of them was mainly around work, their new house, and how Peter was finding his job.

Sally excused herself and left the table to find a dessert. She returned with a small dish of fruit salad with a dash of cream. 'I just want to make sure that I enjoy my swim later, as well as not burst out of my dress,' she said, pulling up the top of the dress as she sat down. Peter had remained at the table talking to Susan, who seemed to be deeply interested in the theatre and the acting course they had taken together. Peter was finishing his main course when a hand was placed on his shoulder. Peter turned; it was Jon.

'Peter, I hope you and Sally are enjoying yourselves, and haven't had too much red wine. Remember, we have important things to tackle this afternoon after lunch, not the least of which is our game of croquet.' Peter, with a mouthful of food, stumbled with his reply but was saved by Sally.

'Sally, you've chosen well. I understand that you will be partaking in some exercise later in the pool. Good not to swim on too full a stomach.'

'Don't worry, Jon, thank you. I'll leave it a while before I go in. I'm sure there will be a few others who will have to wait as well. You have a lovely place here.'

'Yes, we do, thank you. I inherited the house from my father over fifty years ago. He died very young, he was only twenty-three. I never knew him.'

'Gee, I'm sorry to hear that,' said Sally.

'I didn't know you worked with my dad,' said Peter.

'Oh yes, he was good fun and a great man to have around. Career cut short. Way too early for my liking with his skill and intuition. Now, finish off your meal and we will be meeting in the library at two thirty sharp please, Peter. Sally, Josie will look after you again whilst we have our … er … work meeting.'

'Yea, that's fine, thank you, Jon. Your daughter is a very lovely girl.'

'Thank you,' added Peter. Jon walked off, talking to others with a hand on their shoulders as he made his way around the table. *They must also be joining the meeting,* thought Peter. *Must be important if we're having to discuss work, today of all days.* He decided not to finish off the remainder of the wine in his glass.

Just before two thirty, those at the table who had been invited to the gathering started to make their way to the library. There were both men and women walking towards what looked to Peter like a secret sliding door set in the wood panelling at the far end of the room.

Peter entered the room; it was outrageous, so spacious, it must have reached up two storeys, with exposed beams in the ceiling, full-height dark-wood panelling and crests and shields on the walls shelves of ancient books and paintings of various monarchs hanging around the room. A thick patterned rug lay on the wide wooden floorboards and standing on this was another long wide table set with candelabra at either end of the table and nothing else. The central area of the table was clear. Name cards were laid at positions around the table.

'Your first time, isn't it?' said a man dressed similar to Peter as a mediaeval merchant. Peter recognised him from the open-plan area back at the office; he was another team leader. He introduced himself as Henry and said that he was to help Peter throughout the … meeting this afternoon. Peter realised too late that he needed to visit the bathroom. He had no time now; it would have to wait. Jon was the last into the room and looked around checking to see if everyone was there. He shut the door with a slam; the key turned with a clunk in the lock. Peter noticed that there were windows in the room, but they had timber shutters and were closed. Only two skylights on the far side of the room let any light into the vast room.

Jon made his way to the centre of the room next to the long table. Everyone was standing at their places at the table – there were no chairs; they were along the sides of the room. Peter looked around the table; there were twelve people including Jon.

'Welcome, everyone. In particular, a warm welcome please to Jadie, Dianne, George, and Peter. This is your first attendance at one of these events and my summer party. I felt that it would be appropriate to introduce you to some of the tasks we have here at CPS because you have excelled in your training. May I remind everyone that this is an observation exercise and there is no action required of any of us.' Jon looked around the room to make sure that everyone was paying attention, as a general would do, inspecting his troops.

'The new attendees each have a buddy, which as you seasoned members know is usual, and he or she is next to you on your right-hand side. If you haven't already introduced yourselves, then please do so. We have just under twenty minutes to prepare ourselves, so will you please place all coins, watches, keys, jewellery and the like on the table in front of you. When you have done that, please go through the doors at the back of the room, ladies to the left and gentlemen to the right. Change if you need to into the clothes on the hangers and return when you are ready.' Jon pointed in each direction. 'Jane and Wendy, whom you met earlier from costumes and make-up, are there to check you over and tidy your make-up so if you need any assistance please ask them. Thank you.'

Peter followed his buddy Henry out of the room still wondering what this was all about.

On their return, Peter saw Jon making his way to a bare area of wall panelling; he turned a key he had taken from his pocket, and slid part of the wall panelling across to reveal another room. He switched on the light to reveal a table, in the middle of which was a deep crimson velvet cloth covering something. Very carefully, he carried it out and placed it in the middle of the main table. Jon returned to the secret side room and Peter could see he was looking at the rows and rows of small drawers on the walls that surrounded the table on three sides. There must have been hundreds of drawers,Peter thought, each with a different number. Jon pulled a drawer out of the wall and returned with it to the main table, meticulously placing two pieces of shaped wooden counters that looked like small gold bars at each person's place at the table and waited for the others to return.

Peter's eyes followed Jon as he inspected each of them in turn and reminded them that any final items of jewellery and so on must be placed in their boxes on the table. Peter was told to remove a copper band around his wrist, and Jadie her engagement ring, which she did reluctantly. Peter noticed that the brightness and colour they had all been wearing for the party had now dulled. The colouring on his own and everyone's faces was duller, and their clothing was now distinctly brown and grey. Shoes had been changed to wood or cork bases with leather uppers and tied or buckled. He remembered wearing these when putting on costumes a few weeks ago. They were awkward to wear and hard on the ankles when walking, with little give.

'You'll get used to them, it's only for a short while,' said Henry, as Peter twisted and turned his ankle in his shoe. When they had left the drawing room each person had been checked for suitable clothing and make-up that suited the occasion.

'You will see in front of you two wooden tokens. They are of ancient yew and the numbers are in gold paint. They are important, in fact, extremely important, and very precious to you. Imagine them as a gold bar with immense value. Put them safe in two different places about your person, and not in the same piece of clothing.'

Peter picked up his two tokens which were slightly narrower than a draught counter. They both read 2023 in a golden script, underscored.

'I tend to put one in my sock and one in my breast pocket,' said Henry, hiding them away. Peter followed his advice and placed one in his right sock. The shoes were painful enough as it was without the extra irritation, but that was what Henry was recommending. The other he placed in a small buttoned pocket in his waistcoat.

'You may have noticed, everyone, that the token I have in my hand is dated 1584,' said Jon, and showed it to everyone. 'Do any of you remember what happened then? Have you been paying attention in your classes? As I have said to you before, you must keep your wits about you at all times. This, may I remind all of you, is an observation visit for the newcomers here today. There will be no interaction unless it's a life-or-death situation.'

On hearing this, Peter was questioning to himself the reason for Jon referring to 1584 and wished he had kept his Swiss penknife with him that was attached to his keyring.

Jon carefully pulled away the cloth covering from the object in the middle of the table. He revealed a wooden ship. It must have been at least three or four feet across and the same in height. There was a pulsating intensity about the ship that Peter couldn't quite put his finger on. It was spectacular in detail.

Jon went on to explain. 'For those of you that don't know, this is the *Golden Hinde*.'

'Wow, what a brilliant model,' Peter whispered to himself.

'For those of you that do not know,' repeated Jon, looking towards Peter,

'Crikey, he must have heard me,' Peter whispered again.

'Listen up,' said Henry, 'and you will learn something.'

'The ship you see in front of you now is not a model but is the original of the *Golden Hinde*. It was commissioned by Christopher Hatton in advance of construction of the full-size ship. This construction is exactly the same in every detail. You may have seen a replica in London located near the Globe Theatre on the South Bank.'

'Or perhaps the ship down in Brixham in Devon,' added Henry. 'That's my favourite spot for our meetings and visits.'

'The ones at the Globe and in Brixham give you a flavour,' Jon walked around the table, 'but this ...' Jon paused, looking at the ship. 'This is a wonder and a joy to behold.' They all gazed for a few more moments at the ship.

'Would everyone please gently put the index finger of your right hand onto the ship and keep it there. Do not take it away under any circumstances. Put your left hand now onto the shoulder of the person to your left.'

Jon waited until they had all done this, then he lifted a long pencil shaped piece of wood, which he called the whipstaff, from the *Golden Hinde* and put it safely away in his waistcoat pocket. He placed the token with the date 1584 into a slot on the front of the ship.

Immediately he did so, there was a roar like the wind in

the room and a rushing and swirling motion around the ship. Everything, the people around the table and the ship, merged into a blur in front of Peter's eyes.

CHAPTER 8

The Virgin Queen

The blur and shaking and noise suddenly stopped.

Peter opened his eyes. His head was spinning. He still had his left hand on Henry's shoulder to his left as did Jane on his to his right. His heart was pounding with adrenalin. The smell. Where they were was unpleasantly stale, to say the least. The ceiling was low and he brushed his head on a beam. The floor was moving slightly under his feet, the room from side to side with a gentle rocking and an occasional jolt. His head felt vaguely numb. The dim lighting in the room made the intensity of light through the low windows on three sides very harsh.

'Good,' came a distant voice. Peter recognised it and made him calmer. 'How is everyone?' said Jon in a jolly voice.

'Jadie? Dianne? George? Peter, how is it for you all?'

Peter looked across at Dianne and then towards Jadie, just as her legs gave way from under her and she dropped to the floor. 'Help her up please, Henry and you Peter.'

'I'm fine, thank you, Henry. I just haven't got my sea legs yet. They'll return. I've not been on a boat for a while.'

Peter looked out of one of the small low-level windows and could see the sea.

'Dianne. George. How are you both feeling?'

'A little like Jadie's legs,' replied George. 'Just a bit of a leg wobble or two, but otherwise okay.'

'That's good, and Peter, what about you, how are you feeling?'

'I don't rightly know. My feet feel weird but sort of okay now although they are rather heavy, as if they have run a marathon. But where are we?'

Jon smiled back at Peter and looked around the room. 'Those

new to CPS, you may have all already guessed and you may have guessed right. We have used the ship's portal, created when the original ship was built, and we are in fact on the *Golden Hinde*, the captain's quarters, docked at Plymouth in 1584.'

'My god,' said Peter out loud, astonished by where he was as he looked in more detail around the cabin. Henry nudged Peter's arm and nodded for Peter to look out of the window towards the quayside. Peter looked across and then moved towards the window. Jadie and Dianna squealed with delight and rushed towards a window.

Jon asked them not to go too close. 'We don't want to draw any unwanted attention to ourselves. Step away now.'

'Jon,' Jadie asked, 'can we go out?'

'No. As I said a few moments ago, this is an observation journey for you and the intention is for the four of you to remain here. The rest of us who are more experienced have a little research and work to undertake. You are with us today to experience your first journey and to stay here as observers. Maybe, if circumstances allow, we might come and collect you to join us. As I said, it depends on how things progress.'

'How did you know we would arrive here?' asked George.

A very reasonable question, thought Peter.

'It's very simple. The portal takes us to within fifty metres of the Crown. In this instance, Queen Elizabeth I.'

'My god,' said Jadie, stooping to look out of the window. 'Is that her there now? On the quayside … it must be.' She moved away from the window to allow Dianne and George to view the spectacle.

'Yes. She is very pale with her white make-up, but radiant in the backdrop of the poverty surrounding her. Keep away from the windows now please. Do as I ask.' Jon's and Henry's arms moved swiftly in front of Dianne and Jadie and pulled them back into the centre of the cabin. 'You must all remember what I have said, otherwise it will put you and others in jeopardy.' Jon sounded both stern and concerned that they may have exposed themselves.

'Listen. Let me remind you. The four of you newcomers will

be staying here and minding your own business. Have you got that? The rest of you, we have limited time here this afternoon. Henry, you will take Stephen, Mary and Jackie whilst I will take Sam, Louise and Patrick. Henry, make your way with your team to the rear of the procession on the quay and I'll take my team up towards the front and the market area. Remember that we are at all times to keep our eyes and ears open for potential enemies of the Queen, be they religious, Scottish, French or Spanish, remember the Crown has many enemies. The rest of you, please please stay back from the windows and lock the door when we leave. You will know that we have returned because I will give a series of three knocks on the door. Let's go, everyone. We should return within the hour because I have an important game of croquet this afternoon,' said Jon, smiling towards Peter.

The two groups of people left the cabin and George locked the door behind them. For a brief moment they heard cheering and gaiety from the crowds.

Peter looked out of the windows, but kept well back, and could just see Jon and his team mingling with the crowd, and there was Henry at the back of the procession. It appeared that the Queen was being protected by a guard of soldiers and that she was inspecting members of the crew and the contents of crates and sacking strewn along the quayside. There was a series of stallholders ahead of the Queen's route in a market area slightly up from the quayside and an argument seemed to have developed between a number of them. A man was being hauled away by two soldiers. The description of this by Peter led to the others in the cabin wanting to see what the commotion was.

A loud knocking on the door startled them. The door handle turned and then rattled back and forth when the door didn't open. A voice called out. 'Open up, you lubbers, this is the first mate. We knows you're in 'ere.' More thumping on the door.

'Shit,' said George. 'What do we do?'

'Keep quiet,' said Jadie, 'and they might go away.' Panic rapidly spread across their faces as they stood motionless.

'Open up in there or I'll knock the door down.'

They stood still in fear, glancing at each other, hoping that the man would go away. Peter took another look out of the window; he could see Jon in the crowd. Another thumping on the door and a murmuring of voices outside the cabin. Then nothing.

'They're going away,' whispered Jadie.

Soon after, there were two heavy blows against the door. It collapsed into the cabin sending dust up off the floor and floating through the air. In stepped a broad bristled man with a huge pink birth mark on the side of his face, waving a cutlass in front of him. He was joined by two other men, both with blades drawn ready for a fight.

'Oh my god,' said George. Jadie and Dianne raised their hands to their mouths, both giving muted screams behind their hands and cowering together. Peter tried to remain calm.

'Got yeah. What do ye think yer doin' in the captain's quarters? Hey?' He strode further into the cabin, leading with his cutlass, which he waved in front of each of them. 'I saw ye at the window.' He prodded his cutlass under George's chin, a drop of blood slowly emerging from his skin onto the blade.

'And what's with all this fancy clothing?' He grabbed Jadie's arm and touched the material on her shoulders.

'I reckon we got ourselves some stowaways, Jake,' said one of the other men.

'Yeah. I reckon we has. I don't think the cap'n will recognise these 'ere people. I don't recognise 'em. You not from these parts?'

None of the four replied.

'Where you from, eh?' He shoved the cutlass under George's chin again.

'London,' stammered George, fear spread over his face.

'Wha' he say?' said Jake to one of his companions.

'Dunno, Jake … summit like lundo.'

'Where's you from, you lubbers?' he said, pointing at Jadie. She didn't speak.

'London – London Town,' replied Dianne in a slightly rural accent.

'Yes, yes that's right, London Town,' Jadie added quickly.

'Ah, now I 'eard you, London Town, eh. I been there many year ago.' He stomped around the wooden floor in the cabin and turned sharply towards George.

'Why didn't ye say in the first place?' He hit George in the side of his stomach and George struggled for breath.

'You not saying anything, matey?' Jake was moving towards Peter. Close up Peter could see his broken yellow teeth, part of his breakfast and the dark brown stain of a birthmark. His skin was riddled with scars on one side of his face and he wore a heavily stained royal blue jacket. He had breath out of a cess pit. Peter turned away and grimaced.

'You got very soft skin.' He gripped Peter's cheek. 'And your breath smells of … of mint. Why's that?' Peter smiled to himself … toothpaste, better than a sewage farm spitting at him. The first mate moved around to the others, stroking Dianne's bare arm up and down; he paused before taking a step towards Jadie and touching her cheek, lingering with intent.

'We are from London,' said Peter quickly, taking Dianne and Jadie's lead with a more West Country accent, and trying to take the first mate's attention away from Jadie.

'Well, why didn't you say so the first time when I asked you?' The mate strutted over to Peter and thumped him heavily across the stomach just below the ribcage the same way he had George. Peter bent double; it was a while before he could breathe properly again. The four of them stood still whilst the first mate continued to parade around them with his chest puffed out like a fighting cockerel ready for the kill, making further inspection of them, picking at their buttons and emptying their pockets, feeling and smelling the ladies' hair. Peter's 2023 token was taken from his pocket, together with a one-pound coin. 'What's this?' said the first mate. He bit into it with his teeth. 'Looks like gold.' Jake snatched it from his hands and put it in his pocket and discarded Peter's token onto the floor of the cabin.

'No weapons on 'em, Jake. No nothing.'

'Strange, very strange,' said the first mate.

'Maybe they's hiding them somewhere or maybe they's the

cap'n's friends bein' in here, but I don't think so. They would have said to us, wouldn't they? I dunno tho.'

'Shut up, let me try to think,' said Jake, rubbing his chin and hair.

'I says we ties 'em up,' said one of the crew, putting his cutlass back and pulling out a bundle of rope from his pocket.

'Yeah. Tie their hands and make it tight. I don't want any of 'em getting away, especially these 'ere ladies.' He stroked Dianne's face again. 'And we'll take them to see the cap'n and see what he says.' He wiped the drool from the side of his mouth with the back of his arm, his lecherous looks continuing back and forth between the ladies.

Jadie and Dianne, George and Peter looked at each other with concern and desperation. The ship continued to creak and sway from side to side.

Jon said we must stay here, but how? thought Peter. *We can't do anything – we're now captives. How are the others going to know where we are?* The ropes were tied harshly around their wrists. Peter realised that they needed to stiffen their hands when the ropes were tightened so that when they relaxed their hands they might have enough space to untie them later. The girls had obviously not considered this – although George seemed to – and Peter could see that their hands were already red, swelling and tightly bound, the first mate stroking Dianne's arm up and down again with dirty stubby fingers. Her eyes were open wide with fear as she stared across the room to Peter.

'You're Frenchies, I reckon, with skin so soft and dressed like you're at a party.' He rubbed the stubble on his flat chin and moved forward to touch the frill on the edge of Jadie's dress and rubbed his hand up and down her exposed forearm again. He suddenly seemed to get cross with himself, perhaps realising that he wasn't in charge and had to report to the captain. 'It's criminal,' he blurted out, pushing Dianne, who stumbled, towards the door.

'Lead 'em out, John, and we'll see what the cap'n's got to say.'

As they were led out of the cabin onto the deck, the brightness made Peter squint, but he could just make out Jon in the market area with Sam. Jon was looking in their direction, so had at least seen what was happening, but Peter could also see that he couldn't get over to them quickly enough. With the commotion on the ship, the Queen's guards were getting restless. Jon would have to keep to a safe distance.

They were frogmarched by Jake and his crew off the deck and down the gangplank from the ship to the quay, hustled and pushed along, but not by their captors – by people in the crowd.

'More Frenchies for the gallows,' came a shout from a man in the crowd, hitting George on the shoulder.

'Aha,' called a few others, hissing sounds and booing. Children poked them with sticks.

'Let 'em hang!' They were spat at by the crowds and a bad egg was thrown, which narrowly missed its target as they were pushed along. Peter wished he had gone to the toilet when he was at Jon's house, an age away. He was thankful when they reached the back of the procession and were taken to a person that looked like a ship's captain.

'Cap'n. Sir. Cap'n, sir. I'm sorry to interrupt ye hereabouts, but I got these people 'ere from the ship and they was in your cabin and before I was to doing anything with 'em, I thought I would ask ye. What's to do wiv 'em? I's never seen 'em before.'

The captain stopped in his tracks and looked at Jake and then at the prisoners. He looked them up and down and felt the quality of their clothing, running the lace trim of Dianne's dress through his fingers. He pondered a while and smiled.

'Mm … As you can see I'm busy now, Jake, and I don't have the time to deal with such matters now. I don't recognise any of them.'

'They says they come from London Town, Cap'n, but I reckons they are Frenchies as they don't speak proper English, you knows.'

'Jake. As I said, you can see I've no time to deal with this now. Just lock 'em up in the town's gaol and I will join you there later when this is finished.'

'Aye aye, Cap'n.' The first mate grabbed Peter by his hair and collar and hauled him away; the others were pushed and shoved along closely behind. The crowds around them slowly subsided and their captors eased their aggression towards them. An alleyway that they were led up from the quay was steep and became narrower, the centre of the path acting as the local sewage system. Women were washing clothes in the street, others relieving themselves up against a wall. Soiled water poured out onto the alleyway, helping to wash whatever was in the middle of the pathway to the next person's house and onwards down to the sea. The squalor was something Peter never thought he would witness. The faces of the men and women were drawn and dirty. *No wonder we're viewed as gentry.* Naked children caked in mud and dirt ran out of their thatched huts and houses either side to see who or what was being taken to the gaol. They threw sticks and poked fun at the captives as they were led up the alley.

How are we going to get out of this? thought Peter. He glanced behind and saw George with a similar questioning expression on his face. Peter slipped and fell on what he thought was mud but on closer inspection saw that it was human excrement. The alleyway turned to the right through a narrow open archway in a wall, and soon opened up into a bright courtyard.

Straight ahead of them they could see where they were being taken – an arched solid wooden door set in stonework. Across the courtyard and to the right of the entrance, they could see a series of stocks with a person, in fact two people's heads and hands fixed, various excuses for food strewn around them. Further round from there, people were attending to something. They realised it was the remains of someone being taken down from the gallows.

'Oh my god,' squealed Dianne.

'Hey, it's okay, we're nowhere near that situation. We'll be fine. Let's make sure we stick together and think it through,' said Peter.

'You Frenchies talking again? I said quiet.' The man thumped Peter across the back of the head with the handle of his cutlass, drawing blood. He made to do the same to Dianne, but held back. The solid blackened timber door to the gaol had metal studs and a small metal grated opening at head height.

The first mate pounded the door with his fist.

'Gaoler. Gaoler. I got some business for you,' he called out, then turned and chuckled to himself.

'You Frenchies are going to wish you had never landed on these shores.'

The gaoler opened the shutter behind the small grate in the door and Jake handed over some coins.

Peter was hoping that Jon had been able to see what was happening from the market area and knew where they were being taken. He had spotted Henry and Sam at a discreet distance off to the left of them as they were being dragged up the alleyway, no doubt discussing when would be the best time to intervene without endangering anyone's life. My god, thought Peter, an hour ago I was eating a meal next to Sal.

The gaoler opened the door after three bolts had been pushed from the other side. The smell from the gaol hit Peter as soon as the door opened. It was something he hadn't expected to ever experience, but resembled a mixture of dead fish and the first mate's breath, made worse by the heat of the day. The gaoler was partially bearded and his face scarred from the ravages of smallpox. He stood at the door looking at Jake, and then glanced at the four of them, his eyes glinting, one grubby hand holding his cutlass and the other hand awaiting further payment from Jake, which he duly made with four coins. The gaol became more oppressive the further they went in.

Peter noted that there was no lock to the main door as they entered, just the three huge bolts presumably to stop people getting in to release prisoners. There was a heated discussion between the gaoler and Jake, followed by the first mate handing over some more coins to the gaoler.

The four were corralled together whilst the door was closed behind them and led along a dark sloping corridor and down a set of stone spiral steps, flickering candles lighting either side of the passageway. Peter noticed a door slightly ajar as they left the lobby area; it must have been the gaoler's office. It had a window. There was a bottle and glasses on the table, and rats were scurrying around on the floor for scraps. Peter's eyes started to water the further in they went into the depths of the gaol, which became a stinging sensation from whatever was hanging in the air. He didn't want to think about it.

At the bottom of the stairs was a locked metal gate and a flickering candle on the wall. The gaoler duly opened the gate with the keys tied to his belt. Beyond the gate seemed to be the dungeons, or what they could see of them through the gloom. The open area was supported by a central column, the ceiling arched both left and right, with cells on either side.

'Take the men to the left, women over there,' said the gaoler, stumbling and slipping on the moist floor.

The gaoler opened a metal-grilled cell door, shouting out to the prisoners inside to keep well back and waving his cutlass. He spat at Peter and George and shoved them both through the opening. They both fell over something on the floor of the cell as they were pushed in and landed on top of each other. No sooner had Peter gathered his senses than the door was clanged shut and locked.

Peter found it difficult to sit up but, having loosened the bindings around his hands, he quickly managed to free them, then helped George do the same. They could see Jadie and Dianne being shoved into their cell opposite in a similar manner by the gaoler.

'Well, at least we're sort of together,' said George wiping whatever his hand had squashed into on his trousers.

'Yeah, but for how long,' replied Peter.

'How the hell are we going to get out?' said George, gripping the bars of the cell.

They soon became more accustomed to the lack of light. Swiping flies away from their faces and turning, Peter saw the squalor lying around and behind them. Maggots crawled on the cell floor. Pairs of bulging eyes looked at them from lice-ridden skulls of people standing, lying down, propped up, or dead around the cell walls and in all the corners, except for one. The corner no one tried to get close to, was piled knee high with human excrement and urine flowing away from the cell. Rats scurrying here and there waited for the next death. There must have been upwards of twenty-five men in the cell.

'Sorry, George, I wish I had gone earlier. I need to relieve myself.' Peter headed for the lavatory corner. His already stinging eyes were now dripping with tears.

'Peter, we have to get out of this now,' said George on Peter's return.

'Tell me about it.' Peter was taking in his surroundings and wondering how on earth they would be able to get out.

George was standing with the back of his hand over his mouth, although Peter wondered what good it would do him. This definitely made him appreciate the sanitation at home.

'Dianne? Jadie? Are you okay?' Peter called out.

'Yea. Yeah,' came the faint replies.

'You Frenchies keep quiet now, otherwise the gaoler here will deal with you. You got that?' shouted the first mate from the other side of the gate into the dungeon.

Peter waited until the voices faded. 'In answer to your question, George, yes. But how do we get out?' he whispered.

He looked at the cell gate, grabbed two of the metal bars and shook them, but the railings held fast. He looked closer at the gate and rubbed his fingers over the accumulated dirt around the hinges, and reluctantly picked at it to expose the connection. He turned to George and was confronted by the fellow occupants of the cell moving slowly towards them.

He spoke to George. 'These cell doors, George. I think they're on lift-off hinges. If we can lift the gate, we should be able to force the lock and it will drop away.'

'And then what?' replied George, who appeared almost hysterical with anxiety.

'We do the same for the women …'

'And?'

'Well, the main door is just bolted. They're not expecting a breakout from the inside … only from outside.'

A number of men in the cell were now almost on top of Peter and George. They stopped talking and looked at each other. A tall, particularly gaunt tanned man dressed in rags stepped forward and spoke up.

'We're up in front of the magistrates tomorrow and that's likely to be it for us five hereabouts.'

'The gallows,' said one of the men standing to the side of him, motioning with his hand around his neck the yank of a rope.

'So if you're minded to get out of this hellhole and got any ideas as to how to escape, we're all for joining yer.'

The stench of the men now standing up close to them was appalling, and stuck in Peter's nostrils. They would have to get used to it.

'We have a vague idea of a plan,' said George.

'But perhaps you can help us? How many guards are there here?' added Peter, now seriously considering their position.

'Only the gaoler, unless a prisoner is being moved in or out. He holds the keys to the cells and the gate at the bottom of the stairs.'

Peter heard voices and keys rattling at the gate into the dungeon.

There were three people, the gaoler locking the gate behind him, with the first mate Jake, and one of his companions from earlier.

'I wonder what they want,' whispered George to Peter. They had their cutlasses drawn and the leader had obviously decided that he wanted to return to the cells before the captain. The three men glanced across at the men's cell but headed straight for the women's.

'You two new uns, come o'er 'ere,' shouted Jake. 'Gaoler, open up.'

Dianne and Jadie did not respond, and edged their way towards the back behind some of the other women.

The first mate shouted out again. 'You two new uns come 'ere, or do we have to come in and fetch ya?'

Timidly, the two women made their way to the front, other women following closely behind them, holding on to their hands and shoulders, desperate to get out, but the gaoler shoved and pushed the other women back in and locked the gate to the cell, much to the groans and complaints from the women left inside, who clung to the cell railings. 'You didn't mind me yesterday, gaoler, did you?' shouted a young woman exposing her chest at the railings. The gaoler put his hand through a gap in the railings and shoved her back.

'You two. We've been thinking, and decided that we should start some of … you know … interrogatin' you before the cap'n comes, so he knows we've been doin' our job, see.' The first mate ogled the women up and down, stroking his beard and feeling the sleeve of Dianne's dress. He paraded the two women past the men's cell.

'Do something, Peter, George, create a disturbance and—' called Jadie desperately in French as flies danced around her head. Dianne was glassy eyed with fear and her arms shook.

Jake grabbed Jadie's hair and pulled her away towards the exit gate, licking his lips with anticipation.

Peter and George approached the metal bars. 'Distract them, or—' Peter couldn't finish his sentence.

'Oi, yous, I already told yous to be quiet.' His fist powered through the gap in the railings and thumped Peter on the side of his face, sending him flailing backwards. George quickly retreated. The gaoler opened the gate out of the dungeon and roughly shoved Jadie and Dianne through, their hands still tied. He locked the gate behind him.

Peter could see the group working their way up the stairs and their flickering shadows disappearing.

'Where do you think they're being taken?' George said to Peter with grave concern in his voice.

'My guess is the gaoler's room at the top of the stairs – Jake was talking about interrogation before the captain arrived.' Peter rubbed the side of his face.

'You probably saw it as you were brought in,' came a croaked voice from behind them.

'George, we have to move fast. Now, let's set to work on this gate,' said Peter. The two of them cleaned off the dirt around the two hinges and tried to lift the gate, but it didn't move. They stood back. The tall man, who had high cheekbones and deeply shadowed eyes, joined them and then others in trying to lift the gate; it still didn't move.

'On my count of three we all heave at the same time. You all got that?'

Others in the cell tried to get a hand on the gate to help but it was getting rather crowded. 'One. Two. Three.'

The gate jerked and clanked up and swung out of the lock. They managed to hold it before it crashed down onto the floor of the dungeon. The men in the cell rushed towards the dungeon gate.

'Hold on, hold on,' said Peter.

The tall man, clearly realising that this was only part of the way to escape, pulled the men back. The next stage of the escape plan was explained to them. On seeing all the commotion in the men's cell the women noticed and raised their voices in dismay. 'What about us what about us?' they called out.

Peter and the tall man left the cell whilst George stayed back, holding the men in the cell.

'I don't know what your name is, but thank ye,' said the tall man.

'We're not out yet, a long way to go. I'm Peter, by the way, and you?'

'Archibald. Call me Archie.' They shook hands.

'We need to quieten the women down for a bit and then get them to make as much noise as they can when we say so, and we'll need to get our cell gate back in place for when the gaoler comes down. Let's hope it's just him.'

Archie seemed to know a few of the women who were calling over to him, desperate to be let out. He rushed over to their cell with Peter.

'Jess, we will give it our best,' he said, touching her hand through the railing. He explained to all of the women what they needed to do, and for now to keep quiet for a while as the plan was to try and get all of them out. Peter told the women that when he and Archie shouted 'now', the women were to make as much noise as they could.

Peter and Archie returned to men's cell and carefully repositioned the gate back into place so it looked like it was still closed. They hid behind the column in the central space in the dungeons between the two cells.

'Alright, here goes.'

Peter nodded to Archie.

'Jess, make as much noise as you can now. As loud as you've ever screamed,' called Archie, turning and smiling back at Peter.

Upstairs in the gaoler's office, the first mate was starting to enjoy his time of being in charge. Dianne realised that she and Jadie would need to buy some time to allow Peter and George to … do something.

'Ladies,' said Jake whilst his companion was pushing the two women to the middle of the room, the gaoler closing the door behind him. Jake put his hand into his jacket pocket and produced a handful of coins, picked out a few and gave them to the gaoler. The gaoler gladly accepted and undid the rope around the women's wrists.

'Gaoler. Will ye be good enough now to build the fire up – we might be having a need for it.'

Jake and the crew member, whom Dianne recognised from earlier, paraded slowly around the perimeter of the room, touching various metal pieces hanging from the walls and making the metal clink together.

'Ladies, I, er, knows that ye will understand that I will call you that and not Frenchies as we don't rightly know that yet, do we?' said Jake, laughing at his own joke and looking towards his companion. 'But I hopes that ye will, er, come to like me, if you knows what I mean.' Jake's companion lifted a pair of thumbscrews off the wall and shook them in front of Dianne.

On entering the room, Dianne had looked at their surroundings and at the walls as they walked through the flickering candlelight. She recognised some of the rusty pieces of metal hanging around the walls. Manacles, thumbscrews, a head restraint and iron pokers.

'Oh god,' said Dianne to Jadie as much to herself.

'Well, let's try to buy some time,' Jadie whispered back.' You know what I mean?'

Dianne started to clap and sing a song that she remembered as possibly being from the Beatles. Dianne was never good at singing and at the Karaoke team-building event she did not feature in the top ten, but this would have to do.

Jadie moved three chairs towards the men and lifted one onto the table. Then she climbed up on the table and swished her dress from side to side showing a little of her bare legs, her body moving to the 'music'. The men were open mouthed and Dianne motioned for them to sit on the chairs.

Jadie bent down from the table and ruffled Jake's hair as he sat down. He tried to make a grab for her arm but she managed to step back on the table.

'Gaoler. Rum. Now.' He threw some coins onto the table. The gaoler duly obliged and placed the bottle on the table with three glasses. Dianne continued to sing out loud, something resembling 'yeah yeah' and mentioning a sergeant, clapping and stamping her feet to a tune of sorts. The men joined in with gusto trying to pick up words and follow the tune with the clapping and stamping, but without much success. Jadie swirled around on the table and almost fell off, but managed to find her balance and composure. She slowly pulled her dress down one side of her shoulder. This was met with a roar of approval from the audience and a spilling of rum whilst drinking.

'These Frenchies know how to entertain a man,' shouted Jake, taking another swill of rum and sitting on his chair rubbing his hands up and down his thighs. He shoved Dianne to join Jadie up on the table. She glanced up at Jadie, who shrugged her shoulders and continued to dance, sing, clap her hands, and stamp her feet, then helped Dianne up onto the table. Jadie bent to pick up Jake's mug of rum, took a mouthful and spat some of it out, grimacing. She wiped her mouth and gave it to Dianne.

Jadie put her leg up onto the chair and slowly brought up her dress, revealing and caressing one of her legs and then the other.

She rolled one of her long socks down her calf and ankle (revealing the M&S on the label) and threw it at Jake, who immediately put it to his nose and mouth to smell; she did the same with the sock on her other leg and threw it between the other man and the gaoler who fought over it. Dianne was still managing to keep the singing going whilst dancing, and drew up her skirt a little and then a little further to reveal her pants. Again, not quite sixteenth century, but the men were goggle-eyed with enjoyment and shouting encouragement.

'Men, they never change, do they?' Jadie said to Dianne. 'They're the same as in the sixteenth century as the twenty-first.'

They continued to dance. Jadie bent down and took another gulp of rum from the tankard, this time without spitting it out. Perhaps they had gone too far, thought Dianne. Jake was becoming impatient and stood up, making his way up to the table to grab Jadie, but Dianne managed to persuade him to sit down and continued to clap and stamp her feet and sing.

'Gaoler, get us some more rum.' The gaoler was goggle eyed and not listening. 'Gaoler. Gaoler, now.' Jake threw some more coins onto the table.

Jadie, now looking anxious, dropped her skirt and started to undo her bodice.

A huge roar and clamouring reached the room and drowned out Dianne's voice. *This must be the signal.* But they had to keep dancing and inviting the men's attention. The gaoler filled the tankards and put the flask on the table.

'Gaoler,' shouted the first mate without moving his eyes off the women. 'Gaoler, go and stop that noise, will ye, I can't hear myself see.' The gaoler was reluctant to go. 'Go. Go on now and quieten 'em down, will ye.'

The gaoler reluctantly turned and opened the door, which brought an even louder flood of noise into the room. He took a final glance behind as the first bow of the bodice was untied.

'Gaoler, go.'

Hidden behind the central column, Peter and Archie waved

encouragement towards the women for them to increase the volume. The noise they managed to produce from such starved and emancipated bodies was deafening. The gaoler turned the key and pushed open the metal gate to the dungeon, pulled out his cutlass and made his way towards the women's cell, calling out at the top of his voice. 'If any of yous continue with this 'ere noise there'll be—'

His sentence was cut short as both Peter and Archie jumped on him. After a brief scuffle, in which Peter used a Judo move to throw the gaoler to the floor, which much impressed Archie, who nodded at him, they disarmed the gaoler. The two of them had him face down and Archie tied his hands behind his back. Seeing this, the men poured out of their cell whilst Peter unlocked the women's cell with the gaoler's keys.

'George. George, we need to be at the front of this mob to make sure we get to Jadie and Dianne. Get there now.' Peter explained to Archie what he wanted him to do before they could get out. The rush to the top of the stairs was averted by Archie and George, and, as best they could, they made their way to freedom, Peter continually waving to them to be quiet as they got near to the top of the ramp. Peter slowly approached the door. He could hear singing and clapping and spied past the gap in the door. Dianne was clapping and singing, and both the men sat gawping at Jadie. 'Oh god,' Jadie said to Dianne, 'not much left now.' She had fully untied her bodice and kicked her dress off the table in the direction of Jake, who caught it and threw it across to his mate.

'Cheeky Frenchies,' shouted Jake, now standing up. Jadie pulled her bodice open revealing a twenty-first-century pink brassiere – not what he would have expected.

'These Frenchies.' He advanced towards Jadie, but Dianne pushed him back onto his seat and told him to wait. Peter realised that he had to act now and pushed the door slowly open. 'It's now or never,' he whispered. George and Archie jumped ahead of him and attacked the two men. Peter held the gaoler's cutlass to Jake's throat, who was now standing up and pleading for mercy.

'Don't move. Don't move, either of you,' shouted Peter.

'You wait till the cap'n hears about this. He'll …' Jake tried to make a move towards Peter but he held the cutlass firm against his neck.

'Shut it or I'll slit your throat,' said Peter with venom, his heart pounding with adrenalin. Jake went quiet. The singing had stopped but was replaced by the increasing level of the prisoners' excitement. Jadie stepped off the table with the help of Dianne and put her dress back on. Archie and George swiftly tied the two captives' hands behind their backs, Archie making sure that the knots were nice and tight. He emptied the pockets of Jake and his mate and ensured that they were suitably relieved of any coins. The released prisoners from the cells were now packed onto the top landing and starting to draw back the bolts on the front door and clamouring to get out.

'Archie,' said Peter in a bit of a panic, 'you've got to stop them getting out until we've got these two locked up downstairs.'

'Good point,' said Archie, who pulled people away from the lobby to the main door and made space on the ramp for Peter and George to take Jake and his mate down to the dungeons.

'Come on, George, let's get these two downstairs quickly with the gaoler,' said Peter. They pushed and shoved the two captives down the stairs, Archie giving Jake a kicking on his way. Peter and George, with the help of a couple of the other prisoners, threw them into the cell with the gaoler and locked the gates behind them.

'Right. Let's get out of here quick before we get locked up again,' said George. At the top of the stairs they met Jadie and Dianne, now fully dressed, standing next to Archie.

There was a knock at the front door to the gaol. 'Open up,' came a shout from outside. 'Open up.' Archie managed to quieten everyone down. Another knock. 'Open up, gaoler.'

The prisoners all backed away from the door and into the gaoler's room, huddled close to each other. Archie slowly drew back the small panel in the door to reveal four soldiers standing outside.

'Open up, gaoler.'

'The gaoler's not here,' replied Archie after a pause.

'Open up, I say—'

'But he's not here, as I say, and I don't have the keys. The gaoler left me in charge until he returns later this afternoon.'

'We've been informed that there's been a lot of noise and disturbance from the gaol this afternoon and we've come to investigate.'

'Well, as you can hear, it's all quiet now, just a small disturbance and all now under control,' replied Archie.

Peter hoped that they would go away and not leave a sentry. The soldiers spoke to one another. 'Well, see to it that the gaoler comes up to the garrison when he's back.'

'Yea, I will, sir, thankee, sir,' replied Archie. He drew the shutter in the door closed and they waited. He looked out through a slight crack in the door. 'I think, I think, yeah, they's gone. There's no sentry but let's leave it a minute or so, so as they'd be away from here.'

The crowd behind Archie was beginning to get restless, and desperate to escape. He slowly drew back the three sets of bolts. As the last bolt clunked across, releasing the door, the crowd surged behind him, the prison door slamming against the wall and the ex-prisoners spilling out of the gaol as fast as their legs could take them, scampering in all directions like rats from the sewers, with their hands up to protect their eyes from the brightness of the afternoon sun.

Peter caught up with Archie standing in the shade in an alcove next to the entrance to the courtyard. He was counting the coins he had recovered. 'Thanks, Archie, good teamwork.' He smiled

'I will remember that trick if I need to, and good luck to you, sir, whoever you be and wherever you are going. Show me how you flattened the gaoler.' Peter duly showed Archie the Judo move. Archie held his hand forward. Peter expected a handshake, but he gave Peter a pile of coins, dropping them into his open hand, nodded, and then he scurried off into the crowds milling down towards the town and quayside.

Getting as far away from the prison as possible was essential now for the four of them. They tried not to run, and to be as inconspicuous as possible, but they walked swiftly.

George needed to relieve himself and the others waited whilst he followed the local custom outside against a wall. He was still holding the gaoler's keys. 'What shall we do with these?'

Jadie took hold of them and ran up to a hay trailer heading away from the town. She stuffed her arm in as far as she could, leaving the keys buried in the trailer heading in whatever direction it was going. She walked back to the others with a skip in her stride.

Their own direction was aimless, keeping clear of anyone who looked to be in authority. They were now lost and searching for some form of assistance; people looked at them as though aware that they were strangers. They passed a smith working at a bench adjacent to the muddy track. He gave them a questioning look for a short while, but continued with his rhythmic tapping. A farm hand with a long length of hazel in his hand yelled and whistled to persuade his cattle to move on.

They needed to find the others quickly. For a few minutes, confusion and panic built up in the group as they realised their situation – lost.

Where are the others, where would they be? Peter thought he recognised an alleyway that led down to the quay and the ship and, as he made to move towards it, a heavy arm landed from behind onto his shoulders. He turned sharply about to attack the person and was ready to warn the others and run.

'Are we glad to see you,' said George with a beaming smile on his face.

It was Henry.

'Thank god,' added Dianne, wiping tears from her eyes.

'This way, all of you … quickly – the others are waiting for us. Come on, quickly now, Jadie, Dianne, before someone realises that you are the group that was taken to prison and have escaped.'

Henry had obviously been to the town before. He knew his way along the alleyways and footpaths, but they still seemed to be going around in circles, twice passing the same bakery until they stopped at a corner building with a bedraggled sign protruding from a wall and swinging in the breeze. 'Ye Goate Alehouse'.

Henry pulled the door open. They were met with a sound of happy voices and a cloud of brewery scents mixed with smoke from a peat fire. Henry let the others go in first, Peter stooping below the door frame and beam as he went in.

This was a warm homely smell which Peter relished compared to the depths of the dungeons – the smell of beer and mead and a pig being roasted over the open fire. Henry motioned and directed them towards an alcove. After readjusting his eyesight and wiping the moisture away from his stinging eyes, Peter recognised Jon and the others sitting around a table. The four of them sighed with relief and made their way over.

Jon stood up and beckoned them over. 'Well, well, well,' he said, 'we have had an adventure, haven't we? We were about to call in the artillery, but your appearance was perfectly timed.' The others greeted them with relief and made space for the four of them on the wooden benches. Peter, Dianne, Jadie and George looked around at the others, smiling and acknowledging each other. Peter noticed that the table was littered with spilled ale and mugs of various shapes and sizes. Those that were unfortunate to have one of the four sitting next to them gave them plenty more space than they really needed. Their smell was too pungent for some of the group of travellers. A large round-faced barmaid with braided hair pushed and barged her way to the table trying to avoid unwanted hands.

'Any more? What will ye be drinking ?'

Jon signalled to her as the noise around them was becoming deafening. 'Four more mugs and ale and mead.' She understood and made ready for battle to fetch the order.

The mugs duly arrived with two large flagons, one of mead and the other of ale, frothing over and spilling onto the table. Jon gave her a coin which she looked at intensely and then smiled back at him through broken and yellowed teeth, tucking the coin safely away under her dress.

'Just you call me over when you want some more,' she shouted out. Henry poured the ale from one of the jugs. The four newly arrived at the table drank their mugs of the watered-down beer. It tasted like anything but beer, but was so refreshing and better than nothing. Peter looked across at Jon and realised now how this was very much his environment, sitting in a Tudor alehouse drinking beer and soaking up the atmosphere.

'Try the other jug,' said Jon, motioning to George and Peter. 'I think you might prefer it.' Henry poured from the second jug into their tankards.

'It smells and tastes sweeter,' said Jadie and Dianne, now recovered from their ordeal.

'Mead to warm you up inside and with a bit of a punch to it,' said Henry.

'Be good to get the recipe for this,' added Peter. They all toasted each other and drank and started to relax.

A female voice rose above the general noise of their conversation and started chanting from a table to the far right of them. The clamour of the alehouse subsided. Jadie and Dianne looked at each other and laughed out loud. Peter realised that he still had his fist clenched around the handful of coins that he'd been given by Archie. He opened his hand. Henry asked where he got the coins from.

'Looks like sovereigns and a few other bits from ...' said Jon from across the table. 'Let me take a closer look. Goodness, and a couple of silver doubloons as well. I've not seen those for many a year, not since ... the coronation. That goes back a while.' He sat back, returning the coins to Peter, and pondered on his thoughts, then stretched across the table and picked out one of the silver coins and held it up, looking closer at the fine detail. 'Astonishing craftsmanship and detail for their time.'

The female singing voice was now more distinct and drifted over to where they were sitting.

'Friends I love, I miss them so. Friends that come, and them that goes.

'Wi'out friends, where would yous be? Like driftwood floating out at sea.

'No purpose. No aim. Which direction to go? Just floating

along with the ebb and the flow.

'Friends guide us and help us steer the ship, cutting through the waves.'

It was pleasant enough, thought Peter, taking another mouthful of mead and then a deep breath. He looked around at the people at the table. *I wonder what would have happened had we not made our escape?* Would Jon, Henry and the others have been able to free them? He looked up from the table and saw the jollity around him, and was thankful that they were back safe and sound.

'They help us when it gets tough, and whether the seas be calm or rough.

'My friends are my rudder, mast and sail, so we can move fast when the winds prevail.

'My friends stay close. They know I'm here, and I respect and love them even though I'm not there.

'My friends I need on this choppy journey to move with the tide and stay afloat.

'Together we watch the waves, as they break, let's ride the crest with courage and zest.

'However rough the sea may be, I will always have my friends to safely anchor me.'

'What lovely words,' said Jadie.

'Yes, beautifully sung,' replied Dianne. 'I must try to remember them and the tune.' The four of them laughed out loud from a mixture of relief and drink.

'We're just waiting for Louise and Sam,' said Jon. 'They've been completing their tasks here whilst waiting for you.'

'Where's Henry?' asked George.

'He's on sentry duty, just outside the entrance in case we have any unwelcome visitors.' Jon filled their mugs with more from the flagons on the table. Peter supped and was quiet and in reflective mode, looking at the wisps of smoke rising from the fire around the cauldron.

A short while later Henry appeared at the entrance looking flustered. He made his way quickly over to speak to Jon.

'They're just coming up the road, Jon, but have two soldiers behind them looking suspiciously interested in them.'

'Everyone. Please could you all retrieve your passports home from wherever you have hidden them and place them in the middle of the table.' The door to the alehouse opened. Sam and Louise spilled in, both gasping for breath, followed by Henry who turned and bolted shut the entrance door. Henry quickly made his way to the table and said that he was anticipating a visit from the soldiers who had been following them. They needed little time to finish their drinks.

There was a thumping on the door followed by shouting from outside the alehouse, just as Henry sat down at the table. The landlord made his way over to the door. The last of the tokens landed in the middle of the table from Sam; she had a handful of herbs under her arm.

'Left hand on the shoulder of the person to your left please, everyone, and right hand on your token in the middle of the table, making sure that your hand is on a token touching another, when I say so.' The door was broken down and the soldiers piled in. 'Now,' said Jon. He placed the whipstaff from the *Golden Hinde* in the middle of the pile of tokens and they were gone.

Peter was first to open his eyes. 'My god' he said out loud, his head moving from side to side in disbelief. 'Was that real or am I in a dream?' He saw Jon and Henry check around the table to ensure everyone was with them both physically and mentally. As soon as they were aware of where they were, Jon instructed them all to leave their date tokens on the table. Henry would collect the tokens and return them to the drawer. Jon retrieved the whipstaff and placed it back on the *Golden Hinde*. Jadie, George and Dianne couldn't stop talking about their experience.

'Now, go and shower, all of you, and make sure that you get any bugs out of your hair. There's bound to be some, particularly those of you who had the joyful experience of the cells. The costume and make-up ladies will find replacement clothing if you need it and tidy you up before you return to the party and your partners. It's coming up to four thirty-five now, so can I suggest you make sure you're outside by five. Thank you, everyone. Very successful. Now hurry up and get yourselves changed and then go and join the party. Remember to speak nothing of this to anyone until after we have reviewed the events and experiences of this afternoon on Monday in my office. Understand?'

'What's happening on Monday?' asked George.

'Lesson learnt. Nine o'clock in my office – don't be late,' snapped Jon. 'Peter,' he called out as Peter was leaving the library, 'once you've showered and changed I'll see you out on the croquet lawn, and we can see what you're like doing something serious.'

Peter acknowledged Jon's request. He had forgotten about the challenge. *How do you play croquet?* he thought. *I'll just have to follow whatever Jon does around the lawn.*

Peter turned to leave the room with the other travellers. As he did so he saw Jon carefully return the *Golden Hinde* to the side room and cover her over with a velvet blanket. Henry collected up the tokens on the table and returned them to the drawer on the wall. Jon slid the door shut and took a deep breath, then unlocked the door to the library and left it slightly ajar, presumably so that once changed they could rejoin the party. Peter left the room and reflected on what Jon had said – a successful trip. He was sure that Jon had said this to give everyone some much needed confidence. Peter wondered whether the excursion had been executed as well as Jon had hoped, and was sure that Jon would carefully review the journey with each of them on Monday. They must have been close to losing key people, which would have been worrying for Jon as well as their partners. Perhaps we were just unlucky, he thought. We could have arrived in the crowd or in an alehouse or in a field.

Peter had a long hot shower followed by a debugging by Freda in make-up, as well as a proper plaster over his wrist where the cutlass had rubbed briefly against his hand whilst throwing the gaoler in the dungeon. 'Hellfire,' he said, 'that was literally out of this world.'

He changed and joined the others leaving the drawing room and out into the brightness of the gardens. The sun was not as high as when they had left at two thirty. They had been away, or 'locked up' as Henry called it, for just over two hours and Peter was still finding it hard to find his balance. He went to the thatched roof bar on the far side of the lawn, grabbed a proper beer from the fridge and looked out towards the house and gardens, grateful for a safe return.

He could hear splashing and screaming from the swimming pool area and decided to investigate and find Sal. Coming out through the tunnel in the laurel hedge he saw a group of people playing volleyball in the lower pool.

He was nudged from behind. 'Hello, sir, an' what can I do for ye today?'

Peter turned round smartly, his heart missing a beat, expecting … he didn't know what. 'Oh, it's you, Jadie. I thought for a moment I was back in—'

'Yes, I thought you might. An amazing out of this world experience.'

'Yes. You did well, Jadie, to distract them. Dianne told me what happened. I must admit, I didn't know where events were going to take us when we were locked in the cells, but with Jon, Henry and the others around, I knew we would be looked after and they would find a way to rescue us.'

'I asked Henry about what they were planning and all he said was that we would have all got back. Then he added, "alive or dead".'

He looked away from Jadie and saw Sally in the distance climbing out of the pool. A beautiful sight in Peter's eyes.

'Anyway, Peter, your wife's coming over and I need to get back to my fiancé. We shouldn't really be talking about all this.'

'Yea, I know, you're right. See you later.'

'Peter. Hi, darling.' Sally gave Peter a hug even though she was wet. 'Are you okay, you look like you've seen a ghost?'

'Sal. Yeah, I'm fine. Thanks. Might be something I've drunk. How are you doing?'

'Fine, what a lovely swim. Are you coming in? Your meeting was a long time. How was it – and why have you changed some of your outfit?'

'Long story, but the meeting was ... how can I say ... interesting.' Peter realised he would have to be careful with his words.

'Jemima and Sophie, Jon's other daughter, have looked after me, and we've just played a fabulous game of volleyball in the pool, four versus four.'

'It's messed up your beautiful hair.' Peter looked at her and stroked her hair.

Sally gave him an enquiring look. 'You okay, Peter?'

'Yeah, never better.'

'Yeah, my hair. I know. Never mind. You know, I've been thinking. We've got the space at home now. What do you think about us putting in a pool?'

'Yes, I think you're right, Sal, that's a great idea. We can have a chat with Jon and Jemima and see who they used.' He felt almost back to normal now and thankful to be back safely with Sally.

'It doesn't have to be a big pool, Peter. This one here is outrageously big, with four of them on different levels draining into one another as you look down the slope. I thought perhaps we put a jacuzzi up on the back first and maybe the pool with steps off the patio could follow next year when we can afford it.'

'We'd need a changing-room-cum-summer-house as well. It all adds up.' Peter gave Sally another long hug.

'What was that for?'

'I just wanted to give you a hug. Appreciating what we have and ... everything.'

Peter looked across to the other side of the upper pool and saw Jon speaking with Jemima. *She must know what he's responsible for and his travels. Perhaps she's been with him,* he thought.

'Peter. Pete. You're daydreaming again, aren't you?' said Sally, tugging at his sleeve.

'No. Not really, Sal. Just thinking about the meeting and all that, and ...'

'You've got to play croquet with Jon shortly, haven't you? I didn't know you could play.'

Peter looked at her and said, 'I can't.' They both chuckled.

Jon made his way over to them, talking briefly to some of the other adventurers on the way.

'Sally, I hope you've been enjoying yourself whilst we've been busy and that I haven't kept Peter away from you for too long?'

'No, it's all been fine, thank you for asking, Jon. You have such a wonderful house and garden and Jemima and your daughters have been looking after me. We've had great fun playing croquet, such a weird game, and then having fun in the pool.'

'Ah, thank you, Sally. That reminds me, Peter, we should have our game before it starts to get dark. Let's just go and see if the lawn is free, shall we?'

They followed Jon up to the lawn but he sped off in front of them, eager to play. By the time they caught up with Jon, he had already got the croquet balls placed in one of the corners. 'Go and choose your mallet – there should be a few spare in the hut if you haven't brought your own with you.' Jon knocked a few balls across the lawn towards a hoop.

Sally laughed out loud and gave Peter a hug and spotted a bruise on his cheek and a plaster on his hand. 'Hey, what have you done to your face and your hand?' she gently touched his face.

'Oh that … I walked into the edge of a door and that … it's just a … papercut.'

Sally gave him one of her enquiring looks, 'Anyhow, I'm going to get dried and changed. Make sure you let him win – he is your boss, you know.'

'I don't think there'll be any problem there, Sal. You've probably already played more games than I have.'

Jon shouted for Peter to hurry up. Peter found a mallet, the first he saw hanging up in the hut, and went to join Jon on the lawn. Jon was talking about the history of the game of croquet and said he couldn't understand why the game wasn't played in the Olympics, and that our old Queen, bless her, had been patron of the Croquet Association for many years. Perhaps, Peter thought, that was why Jon played. Jon tossed a silver coin up and onto the lawn.

'Heads or tails?'

'Tails.'

Jon picked it up. 'Sorry, Peter, it's a head. In fact, it's a 1720 George I half crown picked it up on my travels.' He smiled and winked at Peter.

Peter breathed a sigh of relief. All he had to do now was to follow what Jon did.

'Have you played against Reg or Stephen?'

Peter didn't reply other than a shake of his head.

'John-Paul, Tobi or Rachael?'

'No. None of those,' replied Peter, feeling quite embarrassed now. Peter hit his red croquet ball, sort of in the direction of Jon's. It finished half the distance to where Jon's blue was sitting, in front of the first hoop.

'Looks like you're a bit rusty, Peter. I'll put it down to nerves, shall I?'

Peter and Sally were among the last to leave and Jemima saw them off. She apologised for Jon not saying goodbye – he was still on the croquet lawn practising, despite beating Peter 7-0, 7-0, 7-1. Peter was sure that the one hoop he won was because Jon was being kind to him.

During the car journey home they exchanged their stories of the afternoon. Peter was mindful that he had to keep secret his afternoon 'meeting'. 'I think Jon must have realised that I was a novice as soon as he started talking about how many bisques he was going to give me, you know, extra shots. When I shrugged my shoulders and didn't reply he must have realised that this would be an easy game for him. I must give Dad a ring and catch up with him before Monday – I know he would be interested in Jon's place.'

Peter called his father late the following morning after a much-needed lie-in, his mind wrestling with flashbacks of the experience of yesterday afternoon. The view of the Queen from the ship, the sight of a sailor being dragged along the cobbles by two soldiers, the apprehension about being caught, and the stench of the gaol still stuck in his nostrils. It was outrageous. He didn't have the best night's sleep.

'Dad. Hi. It's Peter here. How you doing?'

'Fine thanks, Peter, and you. You sound excited. How was the party?' Peter looked out of the house towards Sally in the garden.

'It's … how can I say it, er, mind blowing. As you know, we went to Jon's house yesterday for his summer party and met up with Jemima and his daughters. They are all very welcoming and great hosts. I didn't know that you had actually worked with Jon directly. He mentioned your accident and having to be laid off. We also had an awesome meeting'.

'Ah. Yes. The meetings can be, how should I put it, adventurous. I'm surprised that he mentioned that I had worked for CPS, but I suppose as it's in the family I can talk about it. The accident was over twenty-five years ago. You and Simon were toddlers then and you probably didn't notice much, but your mother looked after me after the crash. I was on CPS business and I guess that you have now been briefed as to its purpose.'

'Yea, some information. Jon explained it briefly yesterday and we have a *lessons learnt* on Monday.'

'It was in autumn 1995, and I had only been working there for about two years. Oh, and by the way, your grandfather also worked at CPS although he never knew Jon. In 1995 I was co-piloting a BAe146 into Dyce Airport, Aberdeen. The Queen's Flight and Number 32 Squadron had just merged and there was confusion around flight arrangements from Bensen or RAF Northolt. The late Queen and Prince Philip were on board. They had decided rather last minute to visit Balmoral for the weekend – there was a shoot taking place that they weren't originally going to attend. Anyway, to cut a long story short, we were preparing to land into Dyce and it was a tricky approach off the sea. It was buffeting quite badly when the pilot had a seizure, which as you can understand caused a bit of a stir upfront as well as behind. I took the controls. We aborted the landing and came in a second time. To cap it all, the front tyre burst on landing. I jolted forward, knocked my head, which we later found out caused concussion, and as we came to a stuttering halt, I caught my ankle on the seat support and caused a freak twisting and tearing of the ligaments around my knee. It never got to the papers – they would have made a field day of it. The Queen and all the passengers were fine. I then spent some two to three months convalescing. You know I still have a slight limp. The management decided that having had concussion and a leg injury, it would be too risky to continue in service with CPS. So, with a good pension, I decided to take up carpentry as a trade, which as you know I still enjoy doing today. So is next weekend still okay to start the wardrobes?'

'Wow. Yes, Dad. I'm sorry I didn't ask where your limp came from before …'

'Don't worry, Peter, it's fine. It all had to be kept quiet as you are finding out yourself'.

'Thanks, Dad. I never appreciated it – and working for the CPS as well.'

'Yes, it was a shock to me when I was approached. No one had mentioned it to me before and I had no inkling as to what I was in for with the recession and employment problems in the early 1990s. I was approached by two men when I was playing Sunday morning football for the local pub. I thought I was being scouted and so did the rest of the team, which provided camouflage for their real intentions. Later I found out about your granddad, my father. He was in the RAF, top recruit in his year and recruited by the CPS at the beginning of the Second World War. I shouldn't really be saying much more – perhaps we should wait until you have your briefing with Jon on Monday.'

'Thanks, Dad. That helps me understand – and it's a great feeling to be following in your and granddad's footsteps.'

'No problem, Peter. Anyhow, I've probably kept you long enough already. Have a good week. Your mother and I will see you and Sally next Saturday and we can get going with sorting out those wardrobes of yours.'

'Thanks, Dad, you too.' Peter, reflecting on his conversation with his father. A warm, proud feeling sent a shiver down his spine.

'That was a long call with your dad. Is everything okay?' Sally called from the garden where she was sitting with her feet up on a chair and enjoying the late morning sunshine.

'Yeah, all good. Absolutely fine.' He gave Sally a kiss on the forehead and sat down. 'All okay for them coming over next Saturday. Dad's keen to get going with the wardrobes for us.'

'Did you tell him about the changing rooms and summer house?'

'No. I thought we would see how he gets on with the wardrobes first. I don't want to impose on him too much, even though I know he doesn't mind. Mum might.'

'Yeah, sure, darling. I think we're in need of some garden furniture.' A slat in the wooden bench cracked. 'How about a trip to the garden centre?'

CHAPTER 9

Recovery And Reflection

Peter thought Jon's office smelled of Moroccan tea and noted the remains of a cinnamon and raisin bagel on his desk. It was Monday morning. His office was slowly filling up with people, and the last of the group entered, making a total of twelve, as the clock struck nine. Jon stood up from his desk and walked over to close the heavy dark wooden door. He opened up a sliding wall to reveal a table complete with a ship not dissimilar to the one in his house and a wall with a series of drawers with dates on each written in gold script.

'Please be seated, everyone. Firstly, I hope you enjoyed our little summer party. And well done to everyone in relation to our little foray into the past. A particularly big welcome to our four newcomers to our merry band. You might like to know that all our journeys are not as adrenalin-fired as the one you experienced.'

There was laughter from the others in the group, but not from Peter and the other three, who were at the forefront of the events.

'I would like to give particular recognition to Peter and Jadie, as they both played their parts well in recovering from the actions of a sailor who unfortunately spotted movement in the cabin from the quayside. Don't get me wrong, any of you – both George and Dianne also played as important a part in saving the day. Jadie and Dianne, I am aware, provided particularly, er, moving distractions or attractions in the prison, which helped allow the escape without injury.' More subdued laughter came from the floor and both Jadie and Dianne blushed. 'I also hope that you do not have to do that again. Unless of course it involves a life-or-death situation. But without it you could all have still been there, dead or alive.'

Peter was now reflecting on the high-risk nature of their work and beginning to understand why the sometimes diverse training they had been undertaking these last couple of months had been so intense at times. He was sure that Dianne, Jadie, and George felt the same.

'I can see by the looks in your eyes that you are probably wondering what, how and other such things … and I'm sure your thoughts include appropriate expletives thrown in for effect. Well. All four of you passed and will each now have a team allocated that will work with you. Henry will do the honours and organise introductions with you later this morning.'

Jon walked around the room inspecting his 'troops'. 'We are a secret organisation and although called the CPS, we are hidden behind the title and offices of the Crown Prosecution Service. Our full and correct title is the Crown Protection Service. Yes. And for those of you new to us, our secret organisation has been in existence since 1575, when the *Golden Hinde* was constructed, to protect the Crown at all times and at all costs.' Jon turned away from his audience for a short while appearing deep in thought. After a pause, he turned back to continue. 'Yes, and our recent excursion was successful and you experienced some of the risks involved with our work. I might add that we don't always return with a full complement of personnel. We have had our casualties.'

'So how,' said George. 'How—'

'George, thank you. Let me explain further.'

Jon walked around the room again as he was speaking, stopping in turn at each of the new team leaders.

'With our knowledge and now considerable experience of sixteenth-century history, which we now know to be fact, the Crown was a particularly precarious seat to occupy. After the death of Henry VIII there followed five years of Queen Mary. These were dark, difficult times. The country was very unsettled and contentious issues surrounded the nature of Mary's reign. During this time accusations were thrown at our then Princess Elizabeth and we almost lost her to the Tower of London. Accusations around her loyalty to Mary and a close relationship with a male companion. So, it was decided by a number of skilled craftsmen in alchemy and witchcraft to form a group of people that would protect the Crown and its immediate heirs at all times to the best of their ability, even if it meant the ultimate sacrifice. Whilst constructing the ship, which you might wish to note was originally called the *Pelican*, named after a bird seen on a voyage, they created, by a mixture of skill and good fortune, and luck, I might add, a time portal through which you all travelled on Saturday, taking us back to a relatively stable moment in time in Queen Elizabeth I's reign.'

Jon paused and took a sip of his tea and looked toward the ship on the table, sweeping his hand over the drawers dated with every year since 1558, the year Queen Elizabeth I came to the throne.

'The portal, when used correctly, will take you back to the same time as here but to the chosen year. It also has the reliability of taking us to within fifty metres or so of the Crown, wherever he or she is. We have had, as you can imagine, some interesting arrivals in the past, and I've no doubt you will come to hear about them in time.'

'The Royal Baths in Bath, for example,' said Henry with laughter in his voice.

'Yes,' replied Jon with a smirk. 'A little embarrassing for all of us. Let us continue. We at CPS have worked meticulously and visited every day in every year since Queen Elizabeth I was crowned in order to ensure the Crown and the heirs to the Crown are protected and that history doesn't change regarding the death of the monarch before their allotted time. Even before March 1603, when Queen Elizabeth I passed away, she and we were preparing for the succession. It was decided primarily by the Queen, long before her death, that James I would or should be the rightful heir to the throne, assuming of course that he outlived our Elizabeth. And James being from Scotland brought together two countries in strength against our enemies. England had many enemies in Elizabeth's reign, brought about through religion, greed, the lust for power and the discovery of lands throughout the world. France and Spain were especially our fierce rivals for discovering the New World.'

There was continued silence in the room whilst Jon was speaking.

'During her years on the throne, the Queen, or the Virgin Queen as she is sometimes known because she never married, wanted to show the strength of England as well as her own. This strength that she showed, although some people considered it power, was reflected in her desire to regain the seas. The French and Spanish referred to her as the Pirate Queen, because she had set about challenging their superiority on the seas and around the world. No doubt you all have heard of Sir Francis Drake. We still experience the lasting effects today of his three-year voyage to circumnavigate the world from 1577 to 1580. The sinking of the Spanish Armada under astonishingly short odds in 1588 propelled Drake and Elizabeth, as well as England, as a nation to be respected and feared. I'm sorry if I'm digressing a little but I felt you needed to understand some of the history.' Jon paused, went to sit down at his desk, and took another sip of his tea.

'We protect the Crown.' His fist hit the table and Peter could sense the passion and responsibility that sat on his shoulders.

'Yes. There have been instances when matters of life or death have arisen, very sad in all the cases, some unlucky and others …' He paused. 'Others through the call of duty. But a necessary sacrifice, bearing in mind the extreme importance of our work.

'Right. Enough of my lecturing. Let us now review the good, the bad, and the not so good of our sixteenth-century visit. Each of you in turn, please. I'm sure you have all been reflecting on your own experiences and I hope you managed to get some sleep over the weekend.' Jon laughed.

'Newcomers first. George, your thoughts, please.'

George cleared his throat. 'Well. On the bad points, I think I, or we, should have listened to you when you said to keep away from the window, because being observed was our downfall.'

'Correct,' replied Jon, 'and a good starting point.' He reminded them all that the visit for the four newcomers with the team was to observe only and not to interfere. George continued. 'I think we worked well as a team, not just the four of us but as a collective group of people working together.'

Jon nodded and looked contemplative. 'Dianne, your review of events please.'

'I agree with George, although we felt exposed as women to the risk of violence and abuse and feel that we should at least carry a weapon to protect ourselves and others.'

'Interesting point and well made,' replied Jon. 'Jadie.'

'Yes. I agree with Dianne, and George also, and realised that in this instance twenty-first-century underwear possibly saved the day. I know I should have changed to local costume requirements.'

'Good, and yes, you are right, we have had incidents in the past that are concerning and we do our best to avoid them.'

'Such as?' asked George.

'To take the point of wearing twenty-first-century underwear in the sixteenth century: fortunately it would be mainly hidden from the naked eye, but a pair of Gucci glasses,or designer clothes would cause a big issue and put you and your colleagues in danger, hence our costume and make-up departments. We have had incidents that have actually been recorded in history, much to our embarrassment, although most have been resolved. At this point, I'll pass over to Henry who has better recall. We often refer to it as the "Hooch in hand" incident.'

'Thank you, Jon. Have any of you heard of the artist Pieter de Hooch? I expect not. He was a Dutch artist in the seventeenth century. We sent a reconnaissance team to Amsterdam in the 1670's to recover information concerning King Charles II and, how should i put it, a particular liaison with a certain lady in the aristocracy, to determine implications for the royal bloodline. The CPS representative took his iPhone with him and it appears from a painting by Pieter de Hooch that he was using it whilst he posed for the painter. He was seriously reprimanded and subsequently sacked because he did the same on a trip into Victorian times in 1860 where an artist painted a portrait called 'The Expected One', which again shows someone holding a mobile telephone. The member of staff, or should I say 'Ex' member of staff, now spends his life isolated on a Scottish island.'

'Thank you, Henry.' Peter, your reflection on our journey.'

'There was a camaraderie and collective teamwork which amazed me.' Peter didn't say any more, which led to a murmur from everyone until Jon continued.

'Yes. Thank you. I agree with all of your sentiments. It is difficult to plan for all eventualities, so you must be agile and awake and aware at all times and act flexibly with your skills and ability to address each situation. Thank you. Henry and the rest of the group, any further comments?'

'I think that we should have left someone with the newcomers on the ship.'

'Possibly. Although in this instance it may have caused a bigger problem. The four's naiveté probably saved the day,' said Jon. 'Right, yes. Let's ensure that a managed plan of action is in place next time and be prepared. Again, well done to all of you. I have a briefing meeting with a minister shortly and have papers to sort out, so go and enjoy the rest of your day.' He looked down at his disorganised desk and shuffled files and papers around.

'Thanks, Jon.'

'See you later, sir.'

After the collective acknowledgement from the group they left Jon to his paperwork, which Peter knew from an earlier conversation was not his favourite pastime.

'Jadie, Dianne, Peter and George,' said Henry as they left Jon's office. 'I'll meet you all in the third-floor breakout area at eleven o'clock and we can start to make the introductions to your teams.'

CHAPTER 10

Job Description

Three of them sat in the refectory waiting for Henry, who arrived shortly before eleven o'clock. 'Hello, everyone … there's someone missing?'

'Oh. Yes,' said Dianne. 'George, he said he had to deal with something urgently before he joined us.'

'Okay. Well, I will only be dealing with you one at a time anyway, so perhaps we will start with you, Dianne, alphabetical order and all that. If you guys can wait there, I will return for George, assuming he's decided to join us.'

Peter was left with Jadie in the breakout area as Dianne and Henry made their way towards the big arched double swing doors. As they reached them, Peter saw George charging through the doors like a bull, narrowly missing Dianne's face and Henry's foot with the door. He stopped abruptly in the doorway.

'Oops, er … Sorry about that. Just a little domestic issue I had to sort out.'

'You're late,' said Henry. 'It's not good enough. Go and sit down with the others. I will return for you shortly.'

George slumped down on a chair at Jadie's and Peter's table.

'Coffee, George?' asked Jadie.

'Please, and make it strong, no milk or sugar, thanks.'

George looked at his phone and then placed it on the table. He leant back in his chair trying to catch his breath. 'Shit. I hate the stock market. One minute you're up and the next down, and if you don't keep tabs on it—'

'Tell me about it,' Peter interrupted.

'I invested in a three-times copper leverage on the back of the news over the weekend of the biggest copper mine in South

America having a collapse and stopping production. So I put a good amount down and it shoots up fifteen per cent before the meeting with Jon. Happy days. And then after the meeting, it's down twenty-five per cent because of some rogue trade, and I've been trying to recover the position.'

'The secret is not to invest or gamble any more than you're prepared to lose.'

'I can't lose it,' said George rather harshly and looked away from Peter.

'Then why did you put money on it?'

'It was a dead cert, and ...'

'Hedge your bets, cover your positions,' said Peter.

'And what do you know about it?' was the stroppy reply.

'You should have considered buying an option on a downward slide. Yea, it would have cost you maybe ten per cent of the value at the time, but you would have protected your position.'

'How do you know all this stuff?' George was calming down a little. He seemed to be of his depth.

'It was my "real" job until four months ago,' Peter said.

'I used to be a Chartered Building Surveyor. You know, buildings and all that kind of stuff. Had a good steady job until this happened. They said that I was chosen from thousands, goodness knows why. I blame the media and all that, who are forever after a story to sell to the public and then sensationalise it. Why? I'm just an ordinary bloke. Until now. Well, you must have been chosen for a reason. And now all this stocks and shares stuff is freaking me out.' George's voice became more and more desperate.

'Look,' Peter said, 'send me over your share positions after the interviews and I will see if I can put them right.'

Jadie's return to the table with George's coffee was perfectly timed, just as Henry came back into the breakout space.

'George. Glad you could make the time to join us. This way, and bring your drink with you,' said Henry, not even reaching the table they were sitting at. He held open the door for George to follow him.

'Wish me luck,' said George. Neither Jadie nor Peter replied, other than nodding to George. Peter realised that George was treading on thin ice. To be late was inexcusable, as was to be 'betting', as the lecturer in the finance training had explained to all of them. 'If you compromise your position financially, it will take your mind off your job.' That was why they were paid such a good salary, to keep focused on CPS duties. It was a sackable offence.

'George alright?' asked Jadie, holding her cup in both hands.

'Yeah. Just a little stretched on his finances, nothing that can't sort itself out. I'll help him out later and that should at least resolve his current problem, but by the way he was talking there are other issues plaguing him at the moment.'

'Such as?'

'He didn't say. It's just I felt he wanted to tell me more. He was speaking about how he got the job and why him. But …'

'Hey. I never quite thanked you for saving my life back there.' She reached across the table and put her hand on Peter's. 'I was seriously worried.'

'So was I,' admitted Peter. 'But you and Dianne picked up the brief communication we had in the cells and then worked well as a team to give us the time to get everything in place down in the dungeon to escape.'

'I wonder if those men have been let loose yet?' said Jadie with a huge laugh.

'I suspect they would be left to rot if the local magistrate had anything to do with it – all that work running out the door like that. Quite funny on reflection,' said Peter sitting back on his chair.

'Anyway, thanks again. Jon's place is big and it makes me very envious,' she said.

'I'm surprised to hear you say that. Your husband-to-be is a lawyer in the City, isn't he? Haven't you got a big pad down in Sevenoaks?'

Jadie went on to say that their house was listed and that they couldn't do much alteration work to it. They had spent ages and a lot of money just trying to replace a dilapidated conservatory, and the neighbours kicked up at anything that was not in 'their' best interest, even though they happily built extensions when they pleased. Jadie was getting herself into a stew about it. Peter suggested that she has a word with George because he was a surveyor and may be able to help. Jadie thanked him for the advice – she was in charge of the maintenance of the house.

The double doors to the café swung open and Jadie immediately stood up and made her way to Henry standing at the doors.

'Catch you later, Peter.'

'Yeah, sure.' Peter was left with his thoughts. The assistant came round to collect the cups and wipe the table. He looked at her and vice versa and they both did a double take.

'Didn't you used to work at the Old Mitre with …'

'Yeah. You've got a good memory.'

'What you doing here?'

'Been working here now for about three months. Got a job offer I couldn't refuse.'

The double doors opened again and Peter turned expecting to see Henry, but it was Jon. He walked quickly over to him.

'Thank you, Irene,' said Jon. 'I just need a moment or two with Peter here if you don't mind.'

'Oh, don't mind me, sir.'

Jon sat down at the table and Irene moved on. 'Peter, something has come up that needs, how can I say it … an intelligent person's input to support and you did extremely well over the weekend. It's that sort of approach and attitude that makes this organisation a success.'

'I haven't seen Henry yet.'

'Oh, don't worry about that, it will be fine. It's only the three senior members of your team that he's introducing you to – it shouldn't take long. Peter, as you know, I was preparing papers for the minister and have now spoken with him. He's advised that intelligence has uncovered a threat to the future of the Crown.'

The double doors swung open and Henry appeared. He stopped when he saw Jon talking to Peter.

'Once Henry has introduced you to your team, would you please come to my office immediately.'

'Certainly, Jon.' Peter stood up and left Jon sitting at the table by himself, deep in thought. Peter glanced behind him and the cleaning lady had returned to the table and was speaking with Jon.

Once out of the breakout space and through the double doors, Henry asked Peter if everything was okay. Peter responded by saying that Jon had said an issue had arisen that needed to be sorted out, but he didn't know what it was. They continued chatting as they walked along the corridor and after dropping two flights of stairs they entered a small meeting room.

Three people sat at the table. They had their backs to them as they entered the room, almost like an interview situation, thought Peter. Henry and Peter walked around to the other side of the desk and sat down.

Peter looked up. He couldn't believe his eyes. It was Bigsey from Goldson's. 'What the hell are you doing here?' said Peter, slowly breaking into a big smile.

'I was going to ask you the same question.' They both stood up and shook hands vigorously. Peter had been so focused on the surprise and delight at seeing an old friend and colleague he didn't see the other two people. To Bigsey's left was Isabelle, his old team secretary; he gave her a welcoming hug.

'Wow, what a surprise, what a great surprise,' he said with even greater enthusiasm.

To her left was someone he didn't know. Peter apologised to her. She stood up and shook hands with him across the table.

'Hi. I'm Carole, with an e. Glad to meet you.' She had a distinctly southern hemisphere accent. Peter didn't want to guess which country because he knew that if he guessed wrong it wouldn't go down very well.

'Okay, you guys, sit yourselves down please,' said Henry. 'Looks like we're not going to need many more introductions,' he said, smiling at the faces around the table. 'I'll let you get to know Carole a bit better and then we can meet up after lunch in my office.' Henry got up and left them alone in the room.

'Well, well, well, I am flabbergasted. How? What? Sorry, Carole, we all used to know each other and work together in a previous life here in London. I've been here for just over four months. Bigsey here, or you can call him Martin, Carole, and Isabelle, when did you join the CPS?'

'Must have been about three weeks ago now,' Bigsey said looking towards Isabelle.

'We've only come into head office today. This is our first time in London – we've been at training courses in Salisbury for the last three weeks. We met Carole down there and we were told that we would be working together but we didn't know it would be you. It's really good and reassuring,' said Isabelle.

'I'm not sure how far you've all been briefed on matters, so I'd better find out what you have been told first, please, and then I can help put the jigsaw together. Bigsey, what have you been told your role is?'

'Supporting the team leader in any assignment big or small and whatever time of day.'

'So that's the same as before,' said Peter. They all laughed.

'Isabelle, and yours?'

'Basically the same as Bigsey but dealing with female matters and situations that might involve a gentler approach.'

'Not so sure about that,' said Bigsey with a smile. Isabelle pushed him on the shoulder and laughed.

'Carole, and yours,' asked Peter.

'Well, I was recruited about two months ago down under, and asked to work with you guys. I've been with the NZ SAS for seven years, no attachments, and felt that when the approach was made by these two guys, one with an odd green eye, they said I had no option but to accept, I felt it was an opportunity not to be missed. I have relatives in Wales but had never been to good old Britain and have always wanted to do some travelling.'

'Did they say how much travelling?' asked Peter.

'No.'

'Nor to us either,' added Bigsey and Isabelle.

'Bigsey. I was going to ask you earlier. How did Old Barrel Face take it when the two of you handed in your notice? He must have had kittens.'

'He was unconcerned. I think Sir John had already briefed him and they had replacements lined up for us. We both saw Sir John before we left and he was very good about us leaving. He even looked proud.'

Peter was sure they were being watched - there was a large and very reflective window on one of the inside walls. He wondered if the others had noticed. However, it wasn't going to stop his teams introductions and briefing.

There was a knock on the door. Peter turned and Henry entered the meeting room, followed by a tall colourfully dressed black man with dreadlocks – a spitting image of Bob Marley.

'May I introduce you to the fifth member of your team. Conrad, this is Peter, your team leader, Martin, or Bigsey as he seems to prefer to be called, Carole, and Isabelle.'

'Pleased to meet you.'

'Conrad here is from South London but was born on the Caribbean island of Antigua. I will leave you all to get acquainted.' Peter stood up and shook Conrad's hand, as did the others.

'Not sure why you would want to come to live in London. I'd be happier in the Caribbean considering the weather over here,' said Peter. They all laughed and that seemed to help with the introductions. Conrad joined them at the table.

Bigsey explained that he and Isabelle had been having a beer at Ye Olde Mitre and were approached by two men who came and sat down with them. One with a beard and …

'The other had a funny eye,' said Peter.

'Yes, that's them,' said Isabelle, and asked how Peter knew. He explained that they were the two who had approached him on the Underground. 'They later described themselves to me as from "the CPS recruitment agency".'

'Yeah,' added Isabelle. Bigsey sat back and let her explain. 'They said that if we applied we would both get the job at an increased salary and all the perks that we already had. They said we would meet people we knew. So here we are. It took me a while to decide to accept,' said Isabelle. 'I had been with Goldson's for over ten years, and you know that gets certain privileges.'

'What about you, Bigsey?' asked Peter, realising that he needed to add his side of the story.

'Well, with you gone I must admit I felt rather lost and that a part of me was missing. I needed a change, even though I was given no option. But seeing you here now is just great.'

'Sorry, Conrad, Carole. We didn't mean to leave you out. I just thought I'd get the easy ones out of the way first so you can see where we fit in. Carole, do you want to continue from where you left off before Conrad joined us.'

Conrad nodded and smiled; he seemed to be in a good place.

'That's fine, I'm used to it. I'll give you my story,' she said, sounding excited. 'I'm twenty-eight years old, and lost both my parents when I was in my late teens – they were killed when an earthquake struck the region of Christchurch, as I said earlier, no attachments. I was approached whilst climbing, would you believe, on Mount Cook on the South Island. I was on annual leave and joined an organised group of climbers on a ten-day hike out of Christchurch. And, you know what? You mentioned the guy with the beard – he also had a distinctive gold tooth here at the front of his mouth – and another guy with a strange-coloured eye, well, they were both there. After a couple of days walking they started chatting with me, and they convinced me that I should come up to see my relatives in lovely Great Britain. Not that I've got many here in London, they mostly hang out in South Wales, Burry Port near Llanelli. Do you know it?'

They all shook their heads. *What is it about people coming to GB? They think you know places four to five hours away in the middle of nowhere.*

'Anyhow, I'm always up for an adventure and a challenge and they said that this job would be interesting and varied and that I would be working with a nice group of people. Like they said to you guys, I had already got the job.'

'Thank you, Carole. If my recent few months here are anything to go by, varied and challenging is an understatement,' said Peter. 'Conrad. Welcome. I'm sorry, we hadn't meant to keep you out of the conversation, but you've been listening to each of our stories. Bigsey, Isabelle and I used to work for the same company, but we've got here via different routes. Carole here is from New Zealand. How did you get to be cajoled into joining the CPS?'

'Well, man. Thank you, Peter. When I was younger, in my teens, I'd not been as good as I am now and had a few instances of facing the CPS. You know when you're younger you haven't got the direction that perhaps you should have. My father left me and my mum and my two sisters when I was six years old, so it's been a long journey to get here. After some time behind bars. I cleared my head and decided I was going to make it and to go straight – no drugs, no booze. After my last stint in Wormwood Scrubs, I got me a job as an apprentice bricklayer on a building site in Brixton. Got myself some qualifications in bricklaying and then started my own business. I was asked to build a few extensions and that led me on to managing the projects. I became a qualified project manager last year. But I got a lot of abuse from the tradesmen and the building companies, and then unfair squeezing of the subcontractors and suppliers, you know what I mean. Like the cheque is in the post, and you've not cleaned up properly so we's not paying you the full amount of your contract. All greedy excuses to not pay, so it made me think really hard again about work. So I left the building industry and decided that I would go and stay a while with my mama and youngest sister who had moved back to Antigua. And there I was sitting on the plane minding my own business, you know, and these two guys sat either side of me on the plane and started to talk to me and tell me about a good job that I could get. I thought these guys were into drugs, you know. Yep, you know who I mean – the guy with the eyeball and the golden-tooth man as I called him. He didn't mind. Yeah, he's kind of weird but in a funny nice way.'

'Really?' said Isabelle. 'I'd say he was rather persuasive. I was very reluctant to answer any of his questions. It wasn't until Bigsey and I met again at work the following day that we both had had similar experiences a second time on the way home – a newspaper thrown at us and an advert circled and telling me to apply for it.'

Although he had almost finished, Conrad's story was interrupted by Henry. Peter was called away, and he left them chatting and getting to know each other better. Other than Bigsey and Isabelle, they had not met each other on any of the training courses at CPS.

'Looks like you have a nice balance with your team, Peter, and they seem to be getting on,' said Henry as they walked along the corridor.

'Yes, early days yet but I agree with you. A nice group of people from very diverse backgrounds.'

Henry opened a door at the top of the set of spiral stairs into a room Peter had never seen before. It was a very old library, filled top to bottom and wall to wall with books of all shapes and sizes, all with a coating of dust. Sitting around the central table were George, Jadie, and Dianne.

'What kept you, Peter? We've been waiting ages for you,' said George jokingly as he joined them at the table.

'Right, you four, you now have your deputy leaders and they will be your key support in your teams. Behind each of them, sit groups of people, experts in all walks of life. Key to your and our successful operation will be your research and logistics teams. Wherever you are sent will involve a full understanding of the locality before you leave. That way we reduce the risk of losing someone in the field, so to speak, or putting at risk the people that we are required to protect.'

A door hidden at the back of the library wall slid open. Jon appeared through it and joined them at the table. 'I trust that Henry has introduced you to your teams and that you are now fully acquainted with them?' They all nodded.

Jon was not one for pleasantries when it came to CPS business, and immediately continued speaking. 'George, your initial job description, and I must stress this is initial – you will understand better a little later.' Jon put his hand up to stop George from interrupting him. 'Your job will be to protect the two boys, Princes George and Louis, and also Princess Charlotte for a while. Don't look so astonished. You will have some help. You will be doing this with Dianne. This will be up to the age of eleven for George, after which we will reappraise the requirements. Yes, George, your namesake, which we thought would go down well with all concerned.'

Dianne's eyes grew very large.

'Jadie, your job will be to look after Prince Harry. Unfortunately this will take you away from home from time to time, but, as you have already experienced, the return journey can be quite quick with not too much travel sickness, I hope.'

'No. Thank you, Jon, all fully recovered.'

'Peter, your job will be to look after Prince William … you could say the jewel in the crown after Charles. I always like that expression "the jewel in the crown" – it reminds me of that film …'

'William?' asked Peter, astonished.

'Yes. William as in Prince. You're close in age and have similar interests so it was decided that this would be your initial appointment.'

'So what about the King and other senior members of the royal family—' asked George.

'That, as you should have already realised, George, was taken care of years ago. And remember, our role is to protect the Crown. As much as we all loved Prince Philip and his speeches and support the Queen Consort , they are not blood relations and are of secondary if not tertiary importance. We also have to bear in mind that this is driven by available resources, hence the prioritisation.'

'Is that why Princess Diana died?' asked Jadie.

They all looked at Jon. He hesitated with his response. 'This,' he paused again, 'this was a very delicate matter at the time. We had been pressing for greater protection for immediate relatives of those in line for the Crown, but …'

Henry answered for Jon after the two of them briefly looked at each other and Jon nodded, Peter could see from the way the two of them were reacting that they must have been asked this question many times before but not so abruptly. Henry thought carefully before responding. 'I think the simple answer is *yes*. The protection she had was more on a personal basis rather than organised protection from us at CPS.'

'So, in a nutshell,' added Jon, 'I will give you an example. If Catherine the Princess of Wales or the Queen Consort were in danger, our priority would always be William and Charles, regardless of the circumstances, before considering their predicament.'

'And what about a situation where you had to make the choice between King Charles and Prince William?' asked Peter.

'It would be Charles as priority, because he is on the throne,' said Henry.

'So the King's other child, Harry, doesn't matter then?' asked George.

'Oh, he does matter, he matters a great deal, but it's all about the Crown and prioritising the resources we have available. If we had a threat to some of the lesser members of the royal family, that would be addressed, but not to the detriment of the key lineage,' said Jon.

'Why haven't Prince William and his children been protected before?' asked Peter.

Jon and Henry looked at each other and Jon nodded to Henry.

'They have. But we have had to instigate a wholesale change because it was found that our organisation in protecting them had been compromised by what I suppose you would call outside forces.'

'What do you mean?' asked Jadie.

Henry and Jon looked at each other again with a degree of angst apparent.

'Working against the Crown,' said Jon abruptly, and turned away from Jadie.

'What do you mean – against the Crown?' added Dianne, frowning.

'As I said, outside influences, detrimental to the Crown.' Jon turned back to his audience.

'So where are those people now that we're doing the job for CPS?' asked George.

'One has been pensioned off and the other … the other died in service.'

'How?' Peter asked, now taking a considerable interest at this point in the conversation.

'Let's just say that it was necessary,' replied Jon.

'But why?' Peter insisted.

'He was in communication with another country to undermine the Crown and with that, the country.' replied Jon sharply.

Peter sat silently for a while with everyone else, all reflecting no doubt that they were now in deep espionage country, and there was no going back with the knowledge they had.

Jon eventually broke the silence. 'I trust that you all now understand the importance of your roles. You may find from time to time in your duties that you come across one another. You must use your intelligence as to how appropriate it is to be speaking to that person and the level of conversation.'

'Why are George and Dianne working together?' asked Jadie.

'There're three children, and they will from time to time be attending separate events or parties that the children attend, hence the two jobs.'

Henry lifted his bag onto the table and pulled out four packs of papers. He gave each of them a bundle.

'These are sensitive, and as you know, papers or laptops are not, I repeat not allowed out of the building under any circumstances.'

They each opened up their packs. Inside there were papers on the history of each royal, and how the CPS support teams would assist with any issues or situations that arose.

'Read these papers thoroughly, then read them again and again until you know them inside out. Return the full pack to me here this time next week. There are dates of events, official openings, birthdays, and the like. You must know everyone and as a continuous rolling calendar as new events are added. You will be tested, so make sure you pick up every detail in the packs. In the meantime, get to know your team and how they are going to fit into your responsibilities. Some team-building exercises will be useful, to bring out their strengths and weaknesses. This is a very time-sensitive period at the moment. As you would have gathered from what we have told you, the Crown's position below Charles is not protected as fully as it should be and needs to be promptly addressed for obvious reasons.'

CHAPTER 11

Lilibet And Sarah

The week after the summer party at Jon's flew by for Peter. He had his research and bundle of papers concerning William to read and study. Both he and Sally were looking forward to seeing Peter's parents, who they hadn't seen since moving-in day. They were due over on Saturday morning for breakfast and his dad was to start building the wardrobes. They still had clothes in removal boxes, in various piles, and strewn around the house. To keep things simple, Peter had his clothes and boxes in one of the spare rooms and Sally in another, but it did make the upstairs of the house look absolute chaos.

Peter's parents arrived in their estate car at eight thirty. The car was loaded up with timber and sheet panelling on the roof rack and boxes of tools in the boot. This was only the third time they had visited the house, the first being in an evening before the purchase and the second, the moving-in day. They sat at the rickety old timber table on the patio in the back garden. Peter's father duly made a note of it in his work notebook; the list was getting longer each time he looked around the property, but he enjoyed being creative and making things. Breakfast was extended with conversations about the garden and what they were hoping to do with it. After a full English breakfast, Peter and his father decided that they had better get started so they'd get something done before lunchtime.

Sally showed Vi, Peter's mother, around the garden, whilst Peter and his dad unloaded the materials and tools from the car into the house. Peter's dad, Keith, set about measuring the recess next to the fireplace in the master bedroom and commenced cutting the timbers; it was going to be noisy and dusty for a while.

As Peter continued to offload the last of the panels from the roof rack of his dad's car, he heard a car pulling up on the gravel drive. It stopped outside the front door. He looked across and recognised the people in the front seats. The car doors opened.

'I hope you don't mind, Peter. It's such a glorious day, and we thought we would come over and visit as we were … sort of passing,' said Jon taking off his sunglasses.

'He just wanted a free cup of tea,' added Jemima, getting out of the car. Jon and he shook hands and Jemima kissed Peter on both checks. One of the rear doors to the car opened. Josie, their eldest daughter stepped out.

'Hi, Peter, nice to see you again.' Smiling, she swept her hair away from her face.

'And you, Josie,' said Peter. 'Sorry about the state of me in these rough clothes, but we have my parents over and are making a start on the wardrobes.'

'Oh, how excellent. I've not seen Keith for goodness knows how long,' said Jon, who had already made his own way into the house.

'He's upstairs, Jon,' shouted Peter, looking back at the two ladies.

'Oh, don't worry, Peter, he'll find him. Actually,' said Jemima, 'Jon just wanted another nose around your house, as did I.'

Peter chuckled and led Jemima and Josie into the house. Finding no one about, they walked out of the dining room doors and into the garden. Vi and Sally were at the back of the garden looking at shrubs.

'Hi, Sal, Mum,' Peter called out and waved at them. 'We've got some more visitors.' Sally waved back and they slowly made her way over to them. Peter made the introductions for the benefit of his mother and then said that he would leave them to amuse themselves whilst he went to help his dad.

'What would you like to drink? I'll bring it up,' Sally asked.

Peter turned. 'Just a decaf coffee for me and Dad, no sugar in either. Thanks.'

Their conversation drifted after Peter as he made his way inside the house.

'Okay, on its way. Sorry, Jemima, Josie. What would you like to drink?'

'I'll have the same, please,' replied Jemima, following Peter into the house. 'Your house is lovely, Peter, and these stairs are very grand,' she said, running her hand up the handrail as they made their way upstairs. Peter could hear the men's voices laughing and talking, the noise level getting louder as they approached the bedroom.

As they entered, the talking stopped briefly and Peter sensed a sudden issue.

'Hello, Keith, how are you?' said Jemima. 'Haven't seen you for, wow, must be twenty years or so.' Her face turned pink as she spoke. Jon quietly and discreetly left the room.

'No,' Keith replied. 'It must be that and more,' he added with excitement in his voice.

'How's your leg been?'

'Gosh. That was years ago, Jemima, and it's fine, thank you.'

'What are you doing here?'

'Building a wardrobe for Peter and Sally. They've so much to do I thought I would help out.'

'Jon was never much good at woodwork.'

'Peter. Peter.' Sally's voice came from downstairs. 'Can you come and help me with the drinks please?'

Peter left the room leaving Jemima and Keith talking. As he walked down the stairs, he looked out of the landing window into the garden. Jon and his mother were hugging. Peter stopped. It seemed a rather long hug. *Oh well, they haven't seen each other for a while.* Peter almost bumped into Sally coming out of the kitchen.

Peter, could you take those drinks out onto the patio please for your mum and Josie? Thanks. Jon's is there as well – I'll join you in a minute. I must get some of those biscuits out – you know, the ones your dad likes oat and ginger.'

'Okay, Sal.' Peter looked out of the kitchen window. Jon and his mother were still close to each other, but making their way back to the others on the patio. Peter stopped staring, got the biscuits and took the drinks out to the others now sitting at the table on the patio. Peter noticed a sparkle in his mum's eyes that he hadn't seen for a long time. *I wonder,* he thought.

'Peter,' said Jon. 'I was just recalling the last time I saw Vi. It must have been shortly after Keith's accident in the early nineties and we were at a ball after Keith had convalesced and recuperated. It was his first big outing out. He couldn't dance, of course, so I did the honours. It was constant dancing for me between your mother and Jemima. I remember it well and was exhausted, even the following day!'

Sally joined them at the table. She had a strange expression on her face; Peter thought she looked as if she had seen a ghost and was in shock.

'Sally, I was just telling Peter here that his parents, Jemima and I last met whilst dancing the night away, it must have been well over twenty years ago.'

'Lovely,' Sally replied politely. ' I've never been to a ball.' Sally looked at Peter thoughtfully.

'Oh well. That can soon be arranged,' replied Jon jovially. 'Lovely tea. Thank you, Sally. Do you have any lemon?'

'Yeah …'

'It's okay, I'll get it,' said Vi. She got up from the table almost with relief, Peter thought. Josie was still at the back of the garden pacing out an area for a pool. Apparently she, Vi and Sally had been discussing the best location.

Jon got up from the table. 'I just need to find a washroom…'

'It's at the back, next to—' Sally pointed towards the house.

'Oh, don't worry yourself, Sally, I'll find it.' As Jon disappeared into the house, Sally became very animated and excitable.

'Peter. I don't think you're going to like this but … I just saw your dad hugging and kissing Jemima upstairs.' She looked at Peter with amazement.

'What? You've gotta be kidding me. Jon and my mum were in the back garden earlier—' Josie joined them on the patio, followed shortly after by Jon and Vi.

'What a glorious morning,' said Jon.

'Did you find the bathroom, Jon?'

'Oh … yes … eventually.' He glanced at Vi.

Keith and Jemima appeared out of the house, both looking rather flushed, and joined them outside with their drinks.

'Josie,' said Jon, 'do you mind awfully going to the car to fetch the presents? They're in the green holdalls in the boot.'

'Sure, Dad,' she replied and ran off through the house to the car.

'I see that Josie has been measuring up for your pool.'

'Yes,' replied Sally. 'She's very good, isn't she.'

'Yes, she should be, she's studying to be a landscape architect and is still playing around with our gardens at home. Loves the outdoor life.' He took a sip of tea.

Josie returned with two bags and placed them on the table.

Jon stood up. 'Right let's see what we have here. Thank you, dear. This is for you, Sally – I know from what Peter has said that you are a garden enthusiast. There're also two ceramic garden pots out the front, but they are heavy. And here, Peter, a bottle of my favourite port.'

Peter looked into the bag. In fact there was half a case. 'You shouldn't have, Jon, Jemima, thank you both.'

'Right, we've overstayed our welcome and have other things to attend to, as I can see you have.'

Peter and Sally saw Jon and Jemima off and returned to the patio.

'Peter. You are probably wondering why perhaps we …'

'Yes, I spotted that,' said Peter.

'Well. I was first engaged to Jemima and Jon was enthralled with Vi, but your mother only had eyes for me as I did for her. We later found out that Jon and Jemima had been seeing each other on the quiet. To cut a long story short, we were both content with the change. It was Mum's and my choice – we wanted to be together. That's why Jon and Jemima are still fond of both of us. Jon in particular is embarrassed. I think he never likes not to get what he wants, but it was a long time ago. But even now, as you've seen, we still hold each other in close affection, nothing else.'

'Jemima and Jon are well suited to each as are your father and I,' added Vi happily.

Peter heard a car pulling up in the drive followed shortly afterwards by a knocking on the door. He got up.

It was Jon. 'Hi, we've forgotten something ...' He walked through the house and out onto the patio and shouted, 'Josie. We're off.'

She had been sitting on the rickety old wooden bench looking at the view across to the downs. The sun on her face, relaxed, she must not have realised that her parents were leaving. Peter thought that in fact her parents had forgotten, their minds on past ventures. He realised that both Jon and Jemima still had a fondness for his parents after all these years. *Maybe that's why Jon and Jemima never married,* he thought.

Nothing more was said over the weekend because Keith and Peter were concentrating on the four wardrobes that were needed whilst Vi and Sally sorted out boxes from the move on the patio and discussed some of the garden design ideas raised by Josie.

Peter had not spoken to or even seen Jon at work since the weekend some two weeks before that Jon and Jemima made a surprise visit to their house. Peter had been locked in his office from eight till five every day, fully engaged in reading and rereading the pack of information given to him by Henry. It was proving difficult. Anything to do with figures he was way ahead of everyone else, but he struggled with reading text and in particular history and the like. He'd had the same problem at school. He remembered with a chuckle the time he had written dates on his arm to try to help in a history test. He scored nineteen out of a hundred before and then twenty out of a hundred after cheating! So he knew that it would take him dedicated time to memorise the information about William and drum it into his skull.

Peter looked up from his desk at the clock on the wall above the door to his office. Twelve fifteen. *God, the morning has dragged.* The door to his office burst open.

'Peter,' said Jon. 'Good to see you – and how are you?'

'Jon. Hi. Yes, I'm well, and you?'

'Busy, busy, busy as always … you know what paperwork is like. We have a mission that needs to be undertaken. Two o'clock in my office, please.' The door closed as abruptly as it was opened. It opened again and Jon's head reappeared. 'If you would like a spot of luncheon, I will be at the Westminster at twelve thirty. See you there.' The door slammed shut.

Failure to attend an invitation to lunch with the boss was potentially a sacking offence at Goldson's. He knew here that it would not be an issue if he didn't turn up, but he was still struggling with memorising information and didn't really have the time to lose an afternoon with beer in his head.

Peter joined Jon in the Westminster 'alehouse' and as required there was no work talk; it was mainly around the summer party and works that Peter had in mind for his house. Peter remembered Sally asking who Jon had got to install their swimming pools and jacuzzi. Jon called Jemima there and then, whilst it was fresh in his mind. He said he was in danger of forgetting when he was in work mode. Jemima had the information to hand and Jon passed it over to Peter.

'Remember to haggle with him over prices that he quotes. If he sees a big house he will think of big money and that's not always the case, as I appreciate in your instance. But we like him. He maintains our pool and equipment and he's reliable.'

They had an enjoyable lunch. Jon talked about his croquet exploits; he had travelled throughout the country to play and had on one occasion been chosen to play for the British team in New Zealand. Peter managed to restrict himself to just one beer. They made their way back to the office.

Jon was in good spirits, not just because of a hearty and liquid lunch. For the first time, Peter was invited to follow Jon through his special door off the street. The 'bricked up door' opened automatically on Jon stepping onto the first of three stone steps. The two of them stood in the lobby whilst the door closed behind them. The inner door followed the outer, clicked and automatically opened inwards. It was dark and steps turned through 180 degrees to a further door which slid silently open and they were immediately in Jon's office.

'Peter, I trust you, that's all you need to know.' There was a knock on the internal door to Jon's office. The door they had come through was still sliding to close, camouflaged by the appearance of a bookshelf, and clicked shut. Jon waited.

'Come in,' he called out. In walked Henry followed by Jadie, George and Conrad, together with a few people that Peter had not seen before.

'Thank you all for joining me. Please sit down. You all know each other? David, do you know Peter here and Jadie?'

'Ah yes, I've heard about your exploits,' said David.

'And Conrad,' said Jon. 'I realise you are the newest to the team and haven't experienced anything like this, but you should find it well organised, as Henry here will explain to you later. He will look after you.' Introductions over, Jon continued. 'The journey we are planning shortly is very straightforward and a good test of what you have learnt so far. There are minimal risks provided you remain alert. You may recall, those of you who were part of the team last month, that we needed to focus on areas and aspects that would be of benefit in the future, not just the sixteenth-century Crown, but on future journeys. In every … yes, David.' The tone of Jon's voice had made it clear he was not to be interrupted.

'Jon, this would be my third mission or adventure and I must admit I did get panicky about the risk we put ourselves through. To be honest with you I have no desire to die in the sixteenth century. I have a wife and a second child on the way.'

'Well. Maybe this work isn't for you?' was Jon's snapped reply.

Jon's sharp response surprised Peter and the general excitement in the room turned serious.

'Death,' said Jon. 'It happens all the time. It's part of life and if you do die whilst on duty to protect the Crown, it is something you should be proud of, serving your country.' Jon was breathing deeply, reflecting, and it must have been a full minute before he continued. 'Yes, it does sadly happen. But, bearing in mind the number of journeys undertaken, and our …' Jon stopped again in thought.

'Interventions?'

'Thank you, Henry. Yes, interventions.' Jon paused and looked away from his people. 'During the dark years of Oliver Cromwell we suffered a considerable number of casualties, but in more recent times we have had very few. In the last seventy-five years, to my knowledge we have had six deaths, four male and two female, and in proportion to the number of people that die in car accidents every year, we are way below average by many percentage points.'

'So how did these people die?' asked David. Everyone looked across at Jon. Peter could see that he was struggling to decide how to respond. It was obviously a very delicate and sensitive subject and was taxing Jon's mind to summon up a response.

'Sorry, I needed to think.' He turned away from his audience who were eager to hear what he had to say. He turned back to face them.' Back with you all now. To answer your question, David. Most of our losses have occurred during our country's darkest hours. In times of war.' Jon sighed and sat down on his high-back leather chair and swivelled around, carefully taking a mouthful of Moroccan tea. 'In early 1941 we sadly lost a male colleague through no fault of his own. He was working as a driver for the king and his family at Sandringham in Norfolk.' Peter listened intently and wondered if this might be his grandfather that Jon had mentioned, and his dad had referred to when they were speaking at the weekend.

Jon elaborated. 'In the early part of 1941, Britain was at the mercy of the German forces. It was decided to take the royal family whenever they could away from London, which was Hitler's prime target to capture. But the king still wanted to be seen in London and would often travel alone leaving his wife and the two princesses in the countryside estate at Sandringham. Hitler had men and women, I might add, that were very capable. He caught us out and we vowed that this would never happen again. A fishing boat left Rotterdam in the Netherlands on a bitterly cold misty February afternoon, not only with nets with a deadly cargo: two men tasked with destroying the monarchy. As dusk fell they arrived close to the Norfolk coast and dropped a dinghy into the sea. The two men rowed the final mile to the shore, undetected. On landing they set up camp in the sand dunes with a view to using the dinghy on their escape.

'The Germans had been told of the king's journey plans from sources inside Buckingham Palace. They were to carry out a reconnaissance expedition and, if the opportunity arose, dispose of the king and princesses. Yes, the coastline was patrolled but they set themselves well in the sand dunes, camouflaging themselves and were initially undetected. I'll come to the detection bit later,' said Jon with a chuckle, which lightened the mood of the room. 'They walked to and around the outskirts of Sandringham daily for over a week trying to gauge the timing of visits to and from the house. On this particular morning, the two Germans were convinced, and they were right, that the king and princesses would be visiting the local church for Sunday morning service. Fully armed, they positioned themselves at a planned distance either side of the main gate to the estate.

'There were of course police and security personnel, but they didn't expect the Germans to be so close. They had cleverly stationed themselves such that one of them could see the gravel driveway from the house and would signal to the other when the royal car was on its way. The signal was given, and as the car approached the opening gates and passed through, there was a barrage of machine-gunfire into the vehicle.

'The vehicle was stopped in its tracks, the driver killed instantly, and there was no movement from the back of the car. The two Germans fled the scene and made their way back to their dinghy in the sand dunes.

'We and the royal party were lucky, very lucky. There were three cars on the gravel in front of the house that morning. As the vehicle with the royal family moved off, the Germans thought that they had struck gold. But the Queen had forgotten something and asked the driver to stop. One of the other vehicles overtook and headed to the station to pick up visitors. The driver never knew what had happened. The barrage of gunfire was deafening. So we had the Germans thinking they had been successful and escaping. Their dinghy, however, was not going to help them. We found out later, through CPS "return" visits and research, that a local had been walking along the shoreline and dunes with his dog, a beagle called Poppy, and that the dog had disappeared into the dunes. You know how desperate beagles are when it comes to food? Well, they are. She had sniffed out a chocolate bar in the pocket of the dinghy and sunk her teeth into the skin of the boat whilst desperately trying to retrieve the bar of chocolate.

'The Germans were caught and arrested a hundred yards out to sea as their dinghy took in water and sank.

'The Germans failed in that attempt. But as we all know, they are strong-willed and very much driven by their Prussian ancestry. There was a second attempt. This time the Nazis sent two pairs of men, Hitler probably reeling from the earlier failure. But with the experience of the first failed attempt, boy, we were waiting for them. They thought they had a cast-iron plan designed to be successful. Am I boring any of you with all this?'

A lot of heads shook. Everyone was listening intently.

Jon continued. 'On this occasion the German assassins were delivered by submarine on a moonless night off the Aberdeenshire coast in the spring of 1943. Their target was Balmoral. Their intelligence had picked up that a full royal party would be in attendance for a celebration. The Nazis decided to pounce.

'The U-boat picked the Germans up from Cuxhaven, north of Hamburg. The journey across the North Sea was quick and undetected. The U-boat sat off the Scottish coast until they received a signal from the German observers in Scotland that the royal party had arrived. Eight men disembarked the U-boat into dinghies. The additional men in the boat were to row the dinghies back once the four assassins had reached land. The U-boat would wait quietly underwater for their return. The four men knew exactly the location they had to head for. They had visited three weeks before to ensure that there would be no mistakes this time.

'The evening of the royal gathering involved a considerable number of cars delivering guests to the house. The Germans were quickly and efficiently in their positions, camouflaged in the grounds around the house ready for the attack. The Nazi plan was to use a combination of mortar and machine-gunfire into the dining area whilst the royal family and their guests were having dinner. The Germans didn't want to miss their target this time – they were fully aware of the consequences if they did.

'We however had already planned for a situation like this and there was no one in the dining area when they attacked. We had set the room to make it look like people were sitting talking and musicians playing in the background. Shadows seen moving around on the curtains were created by a record player with chess pieces moving round and round.

'Miraculously there were no deaths on the British side. The commanding officer and two servants were slightly injured and another seriously, but they all recovered. The royal party was actually gathered in a smaller house away from the main building. The Germans, not realising this, had missed their targets for a second time. The king was understandably very appreciative of the foresight and gallantry. King George awarded medals and a Victoria Cross to the commander who faced the enemy outside from the side of the dining room as the Germans sprayed the room with bullets after the mortar fire.

'One of the Germans was killed in the grounds during the gunfight that followed the explosions. The other three, we later found out, had managed to escape from the grounds and return to their dinghy hidden on the coast. Their U-boat completed their escape to the safety of Berlin. But in Berlin they had already heard of the failure of the mission and they met their fate in front of Hitler. They were immediately sent to the Russian front. For propaganda reasons this and the related series of events was kept under wraps, because it would be so demoralising for the population and an already stretched defence that the Germans had succeeded for a second time in penetrating so far into our country, even though they did not succeed and missed their target.'

Jon swung round in his chair and looked at each of their faces and into their eyes. One pair of eyes was not looking his way.

George's head was down, looking at his mobile phone.

'There is one amongst us who thinks he has better things to do.'

George was nudged in the ribs. 'What?' he said, looking up. Everyone was looking at him. He instantly broke into a sweat.

'George, may I ask what you are doing? And have you been paying attention?'

'Jon, yes, I mean, sir, yes … I just had a personal text to send, it's finished now.'

Jon looked away and moved his chair to face the window. 'Can I suggest we break for fifteen minutes.'

They all left the room and made their way to the café and a much-needed comfort break. George was immediately back on his phone and sitting at a table by himself.

Peter went over to him. 'It's your investments again, I can tell.'

George looked up with desperation carved all over his face. He put his phone heavily on the table and looked away from Peter, tears developing in his eyes. Arms folded, he didn't reply.

'Look, I said I would help if I could. Now let me see what I can do.'

George did not reply.

'If you don't want my help, that's fine.'

George still looked away and Peter made to leave the table.

George made a sudden movement with his arm and pushed the phone towards Peter. 'The access code is 4567 G.'

Peter tapped the keypad. The screen showed a graph with a red line diving off a cliff. Peter checked the summary sheet for the next investment and the next. *Shit, no wonder he's perspiring like a pig.* 'You've got a few issues with your investments by the look of things.'

'Issues is an understatement,' said George sharply, looking towards and then away from Peter.

The portfolio summary showed a figure of £58,769 in the red. But it didn't stop there; the figure was continually changing: £ 58,983 … £ 58,984 … £ 58,985 and so on, in the red.

'It's been doing that for the last four hours and getting worse and worse.' George's hands went to his head, which he dropped to the table, distraught.

'Just wait here, George. Don't go away.' Peter got up and left the café and in a few moments he came back in with Bigsey.

'George. George, this is Bigsey.'

'Yea, I know, we've met,' replied George grumpily.

'He's here to help you, George. Now, be of some assistance otherwise your positions will just get worse.'

'What does he know?'

'Bigsey and I used to work together in the City and he will try to sort out the mess. I've got to go back to the meeting now. You stay here with Bigsey.'

'What will you say to Jon?'

'That you've been taken ill, not feeling well and didn't want to disrupt the meeting. He'll appreciate that.'

'Thanks,' said George, recovering a bit of spark. Peter put his hand on Bigsey's shoulder and said, 'Bigsey here is better at it than I am so you're in good hands.'

Peter followed the others out of the canteen back to Jon's office.

'Now, I trust you have all had time to reflect on my two stories and your commitment to the Crown Protection Service?' said Jon once they had all settled in their seats again. He looked around the room. 'There's one person missing. It's that man George again – where is he?'

'He's asked me to apologise and say he's not feeling well, Jon,' replied Peter, 'and said he didn't want to disrupt the meeting by having to leave part way through.' It was as if Jon could read Peter's mind. Peter could also see from Jon's eyes that George had better watch his step or he would be in big trouble.

Jon continued. 'If you thought that the two stories I described to you earlier were above and beyond the call of duty then listen up. Following the VE Day celebrations on 8 May 1945, which continued for days, weeks and months afterwards, it was thought that the war in Europe was over. But our war was not.

'Days before Adolf killed himself in his bunker on 30 April 1945, he and a number of his senior commanders still believed that Germany could win the war. He and his conspirators in crime decided to let a group of henchmen known as the Brandenburgers Abwehr loose – a last throw of the dice for Hitler. This elite force, often also referred to as the Waffen-SS, was like our modern-day SAS or Seals. They were based in Berlin, and worked in small groups. Their motto *Meine Ehre heisst Treue* translated as "My honour is loyalty".

'These men were battle-hardened and experienced in working behind enemy lines and were deeply involved with the fall of Belgium, the Netherlands and Poland to name but a few. They were multilingual and trained in espionage. Their target was to eliminate the king and princesses. Hitler was still convinced that to capture the Crown would be the downfall of the British people. Hitler had already received agreement from the Duke of Windsor, who had abdicated a few years before the war, that as soon as George his brother and the two princesses were killed he would return to Britain to be crowned. With the Crown secured in his hands, it would give Hitler the route to German victory and supremacy in Europe.

'In the event, they failed, because of one person – Sarah Bray. She was a schoolgirl, one year younger but very similar in height and looks to Princess Elizabeth, and she was recruited in 1944, like many during the war, at a very young age. She was sent to join the royal household at both Sandringham and Balmoral and became a close companion to both princesses. At times they would play games with the king to see if he could recognise which one Elizabeth was. Surprisingly, he was often wrong, but that was because he was looking at them from a distance.'

'How do you know all these facts and events?' asked David.

'I, or should I say we, have returned on numerous occasions to check the facts of these examples and many others and it's exactly what happened,' replied Henry, looking across the room to Jon. Jon continued, but Peter could see that he did so with a noticeable solemnity and a tear developing in his right eye.

'On this particular evening of 15 May 1945, the king and queen had retired after dinner for drinks in the drawing room at Buckingham Palace, taking his red box of ministerial papers, work on which could last well into the night. The queen was sitting on a sofa listening to the radio. The princesses were still full of energy and playing hide and seek despite a long day on the streets of London celebrating the victory with the people. Sarah and two of the maids joined in. They charged around the upper floors of the palace for over an hour until they decided enough was enough and fell onto Princess Elizabeth's bed on the second floor.

'Whilst they had been enjoying themselves, neither they, nor any of the palace guards were aware that three pairs of prying eyes had been watching from a courtyard their every movement from room to room for the whole evening to make sure, from the Germans' point of view, that the people they needed to be present were there when they entered the building. They were.

'These three weary bodies, with tired, strained, bloodshot eyes belonged to the remaining members of a group of seven elite soldiers who had set off from Berlin on 27 April 1945. Their route to Blighty, through war-flattened Europe, crossed enemy lines and border controls. Out of Berlin they headed in a northerly direction to the Baltic port of Rostock, catching a fishing boat to Odense and then across Denmark to Esbjerg by bicycle. Their journey was not without incident. They lost two men, shot dead in a gunfight in Rostock as they were challenged and tried to bypass the custom control at the port, and another defected from their group whilst cycling across Denmark.

'From Esbjerg on the ferry, they changed their clothes, names and passports to those of British servicemen returning from the war. They caught the ferry to Immingham near Hull and then the train to London. They were virtually unchallenged on the train journey and arrived at King's Cross.

'The four of them laughed out loud as they walked out of King's Cross Station. It was aptly named for their mission.

'They were aware from seeing newspapers and listening to people talking on the train that Germany had fallen, but was it just German propaganda to fool the British? They were also acutely aware of the instructions from the Fuhrer. They decided the newspapers were just publishing propaganda. The surviving four men had a crucial mission to carry out. They daren't fail.

'On exiting the station, they resolved to walk to the palace. This they felt was safer and they were less likely to be challenged than if they travelled by tram or bus.

'It was pleasing to the eye, from a German perspective, to see London in ruins, but the life and energy of the British people they found difficult to swallow. They were in a celebratory mood.

'Having reached Buckingham Palace they separated to find the easiest way over the palace walls and into the grounds. After their reconnaissance and regrouping and with the light fading they realised the difficulty. They decided that in order to climb the wall surrounding the palace that they would need a ladder or to steal a van and clamber over.

'They chose the latter, and at 8.15 p.m. the van was driven away by one of the Germans leaving three of the men to clamber over the railings without being noticed. They settled into a corner until it was dark, benefiting from clouds scurrying across the sky, covering the opening rays from the moon.

'When an opportunity arose, the three of them scampered silently closer to the palace, avoiding the security patrols. They sat huddled behind a low projecting wall looking up at the movement in the palace."Ja. We are here. But what now, Klaus? Eh? How do we get in? We can see where the people come in and go and we see up in the windows where the people are, so how can we go in?"

'"I think we must wait just a little longer, Fritz, and then we shall climb using the water pipes and then up onto the roof. Can you see?" He pointed up towards an area of a single-storey building against the main palace walls. Above they could still see the princesses running from room to room on the second floor with not a care in the world, the king still working through papers being taken from a red box on his desk on the first.

'"I think we must get into the palace first, and then we create a distraction once we are in, and we meet here after and if not then at the King's Cross."

'The climb up the drainpipe was easy for three men of their ability. The clambering over the slate pitched roof was a slightly more difficult challenge for them, but they reached the next set of pipes and climbed. The sash window they were aiming for wasn't open, but they were lucky. An air-raid siren started to wail and Klaus, realising the opportunity, skilfully levered open the catch on the window and they were in.

"'Fritz and Wilhelm,'" said Klaus. "You will see to the king – remember the room, it is below where we are now, so go quietly down the stairs, and I will deal with the two princesses."

'Klaus was an astute agent, and was already well decorated for his actions and in particular his courage against the Russians. He was clinical in his approach and without mercy. His strategy was surprise and he hoped his colleagues would be able to achieve the same with the king. "There is no way that the British will be expecting this." He sniggered. "We are so far behind enemy lines the Fuhrer will be very pleased. Maybe even an Iron Cross."

'Klaus listened carefully. Looking back down the corridor he saw his two companions moving swiftly and silently over the deep carpets. They turned left, disappearing down a set of stairs.

'Klaus approached the door that he was sure was to the room they had seen from outside where the princesses were playing. He put his hand onto the handle and held it tightly for a short while, putting his ear to the door, and listened. Nothing. He squeezed the handle and the door opened without a noise. Still nothing. The light was dim, and he could see that it was someone's bedroom. "Where are they? Where are my little princesses?"

'A connecting door to the bedroom opened and he heard female voices laughing. He quickly hid under the bed and then the door closed again. He did not know that no one had come in, and he hid under the bed, his heart pounding, his revolver poised.

'There was a loud bang followed by another, then a series of shots.

"'Ach. Fritz and Wilhelm, you are too early for me, you idiots."

'Klaus tried to quickly get himself out from under the bed expecting there to be someone, revolver poised, but there was no one there. He immediately rushed towards the door that had previously opened and said out loud, "Hello, little princesses, where are you? I am here for you." He walked cautiously into the room.

'Sarah, on hearing the shots, had immediately grabbed both of the princesses and hidden them in a wardrobe. She realised that something was amiss and went for safety first.

"'Hello, little princesses. Hello. I am here to see you come out wherever you are, my little pumpkins," said a voice from the other side of the wardrobe doors.

'Elizabeth and Margaret were shaking with fear. Margaret was about to speak, but Sarah immediately shook her head and put her fingers to her lips to keep quiet.

'The man or men were walking around the room. Another series of gunshots spread the fear of god through them, and they cowered in the corner of the cupboard covering themselves with clothes.

'Klaus had heard a rustling noise but couldn't quite work out where it had come from, and intently scanned around the room until he saw the edge of a dress moving discreetly into the wardrobe, being pulled from the inside. He smiled to himself and moved towards the wardrobe and stood adjacent to the wardrobe doors.

"'I know you little princesses are here somewhere, so please come out now." After a moment's pause, he said much louder, "Now please."

'The wardrobe door slowly opened and someone stepped out. It was Sarah.

"'Ah. Elizabeth, and how nice it is that you come to see me. I have been waiting very patiently for you. Now, where is your little sister – I am here to see both of you."

'Sarah did not respond straight away but tried to find a way out of the situation. "Answer me," the German shouted, pointing the gun at her.

"'She is next door," said Sarah with a wave of her hand. "I can get her for you." She moved away from the wardrobe trying to distract the German.

'Sarah tried to make for the door, but the German grabbed her arm and pulled her close to him, his gun to her neck.

'"Little lady. I have just come from in there and there was no one in there but me."

'Sarah had to think quickly. "But I am sure she is, she went to the bathroom," she said. The German paused. "If she's not," added Sarah, "she will be with her mother downstairs."

'"If you trick me, it is the end for you." The gunman held Sarah's arm tightly as they entered the bedroom that the German had been hiding in. They searched around the room, Sarah trying to be as slow as she could to delay the German. There was no one. They checked the bathroom. Again no one.

'"Now I hear some noise behind me," he said, squinting towards Sarah. Elizabeth and Margaret had moved in the wardrobe. Sarah grabbed the German's gun. They struggled but not for very long. She had none of the German's strength. The gun was twisted by the German and turned towards her and fired.

'The noise alerted the palace staff to another intruder – they had dealt with the two gunmen downstairs – and they were quickly up the stairs to the princesses' bedrooms.

'The German was struggling to push Sarah off him. She had held on to the assassin until the last of her energy was spent.

'The German finally pushed her off and tried to get up, but she held on, delaying his escape; he fired again and she fell to the floor.

'There was a distinct sound of whimpering from the other room. He made his way across the bedroom towards the wardrobe where the princesses were hiding. As he did so the door to the bedroom opened and he was shot dead, after having managed to fire a couple of rounds to injure one of the palace guards.

'When the king and queen were allowed by the palace guard into the room, they ran in looking around for the girls. They saw the dead German, blood pouring from bullet wounds to the head and chest. Turning, they saw a body, still on the floor in Margaret's bedroom with blood seeping into the carpet. The queen screamed and ran towards the body.

'Elizabeth and Margaret, hearing their parents' voices and their mothers' screams, emerged from the wardrobe. The queen twisted around to see her two daughters running towards her, alive.

'Elizabeth, having hugged her mother and father, pushed her mother away and ran into Margaret's bedroom to Sarah slumped on the floor, blood seeping from her wounds. She gently lifted Sarah's head onto her lap, Sarah's eyes flickered open momentarily. She saw the princess, gave almost a glimmer of a smile, and shut her eyes forever.

'Sarah Bray was posthumously awarded the Victoria Cross. She was given the highest honour of a burial at Westminster Abbey. Her grave can still be seen today, with the words on her headstone: "For the protection of the Crown, now, and always".

'That, people, is a call of duty to the Crown. The ultimate sacrifice.'

There was quiet in the room, everyone deep in thought. The silence was eventually broken by Peter.

'How come no one has heard of this story?'

'It would have caused panic throughout the country if the people had known that the Germans were still at large behind our lines. So it was decided that the events that took place would be kept a secret, except for those at the very highest levels. To this day there is still a service to commemorate Sarah Bray, which the Queen attended every year until her passing, at the same time and place as a token of her respect and thanks.'

The audience was again silent, reflecting on Jon's words.

'Why don't we take a comfort break and we'll continue in twenty minutes,' said Jon.

CHAPTER 12

The Crown Protection Service

Jon continued his lecture. 'Even before the events during the Second World War that i briefly described earlier, King George V and Edward VIII were much appreciative of our work and support. To commemorate the activities of CPS, in December 1936 George VI confirmed, following the abdication of Edward VIII and his own accession, that the Royal Mint would engrave the Golden Hind on the back of every halfpenny coin. This the Crown did so that everyone would have the opportunity to touch the beautiful ship at some time in their lives. Edward's decision to abdicate was challenged and many people tried to dissuade him. Each monarch has to make that decision to either serve the Crown and the people, or not. Edward chose the latter for the love of one person - Wallace.' Jon expanded further on the history as well as the responsibilities in active service, reminding them all that their appointment was a twenty-four hour, seven days a week responsibility, and of the continuous requirement for it to remain secret. Only at the very most your immediate partner can be aware of your responsibilities that will take you away from your families and loved ones from time to time.

'You all will have come to realise by now that we all play an integral part in this organisation, the pieces fitting nicely into a jigsaw.' The door to the room opened and closed.

'Perfect timing. Please sit down and join us.' Jon beckoned the newcomers in. The group turned around to see who it was. 'And may I remind you all that two people, two very important people, Tom and Will –' (who Peter still thought of as Parka man and Green Eye man) '– will appear, if you will excuse the pun, from time to time during your work here and in your … travels. They are the most experienced of our people in CPS – even more than me – and they are the most important.'

'I didn't know about that,' said Tom to Will with a chuckle.

'Nice to get a compliment every couple of years,' Will replied quietly.

Peter and a number of the newer members of the group turned and saw Parka man grinning at them, with his yellowed teeth and scraggly windswept hair, and Green Eye man searching in his left pocket for something. He pulled out a handkerchief and opened it onto his palm, revealing his green eyeball. Peter remembered the last time he had that look on his face on the Underground during the days he was being recruited, and then at interview. He closed his eyes and turned away whilst Green Eye man returned the eye to its socket. Peter wasn't a particularly squeamish person but when it came to eyes he was particularly aware and sensitive. It made his toes curl with apprehension, imagining the sensation.

Jon continued. 'Thomas and William were part of the original group of people who constructed the ship and with it the portal. Yes, they are both that old, or should I say they are from that age. Their skills, with others at the time of the construction of the Golden Hinde enabled them to create an ability to step back, and yes, you probably realise, go forward in time and meet with us. They may occasionally look like tramps roaming the streets of London, but they have great skill and ability. Don't let their appearance worry you. Have a chat with them – they are as human as you and I, despite the yellowing teeth and different coloured eyes that you might have noticed.'

'Have conversations with them and enjoy their company. They both have a lot of knowledge and I might add wisdom. Knowledge without wisdom and knowing when to use it is useless. You might also like to know that they both have families back in their own time and I am sure in conversation with them they will elaborate further.'

There were a number of open mouths from those seated around the table, notably from Peter, Diane and Jadie. All three turned again to look at the two of them. They looked back, making faces in a jovial manner. Tom poked his tongue out at them and Will made his ears wiggle.

'I can tell you a few stories that will make your eyes pop out of your skull,' Tom said, turning to Green Eye man and nudging him.

'Literally,' said Will.

Tom added, 'As Jon has mentioned, we are the longest-serving still-living members of the CPS. When we were both youngsters, back in 15-something or other, we came to know each other because our parents lived on the same farm and, back then, there was no teaching as such, but a particularly wise old man, who we ended up calling the Master, from our weekly teachings in the village pulled us out of class when we were both eight years old and said that he felt that we could be extremely rich. Not necessarily with money, but with knowledge. At our age we were enticed by these words and would spend hours with him. Our parents weren't bothered as long as we got back at night. The wise old man would take us to ... Sorry, if some of you have heard this before ...'

'Please go on,' said Jon, smiling, and getting his sense of humour back. 'I always like this story.'

Tom continued. 'Well, his house, or hut I suppose you would call it, was set deep in the countryside away from the prying eyes of the establishment. Remember, this is 1545 and there was very little control of people. Death could occur in the blink of an eye.' He winked at William. 'He taught us about herbs, homeopathy in current speech, and country ways that allowed us to gain some of the skills which were then used with our alchemy and levitation lessons that followed.

'He needed other skilled people to help teach us, or learn us as he would say. Some fairie folks used to come and then literally just disappear before our very eyes, a witch skilled in levitation taught us those skills, and another the readings of the Tarot. Some would view the Master as a man dealing in witchcraft, but these were skills and abilities he had been given and he wanted, with the group of men and women, to teach others before they were lost to eternity.

'During these times anyone remotely linked with anything to do with witchcraft would be watched and sometimes not even that. Just taken away and you would never see them again or they would appear on the weekly ducking stool, and may have been lucky to escape with their lives.

'The Master handed these skills and knowledge to us before they were taken away. We learnt that our skills and knowledge would have to be a secret. But there were others that also had abilities and would use them for their advantage rather than as the Master taught us. At sixteen we was working in the fields collecting hay and in regular conversation of an evening drinking mead and cider, as we did most evenings in them days, especially in the summer months, and we was approached by a full-bodied lady who said she felt that we might need help. The other men helping in the field just laughed, thinking it was just a wheeze to get our money, what little we had, for female favours if you know what I mean. Well. We ignored the invitation until a few weeks later when William and I saw her walking towards us carrying bunches of herbs and the like under her arms. She smiled as she approached the two of us and asked us again to join her that evening. She assured us that there would be other people there. We weren't so sure of that and left her be. But Will and I chatted about it for a while and decided that we would meet her where she asked.

'It was almost dusk when we met her on the outskirts of the village. We followed her at a discreet distance. She took us down into a remote part of the forest. She beckoned us to follow her. After a seven-or-eight-hundred-or-so-yard walk, zigzagging through the forest, we reached a clearing. There, we met a dozen or more people and were introduced to each one of them – witches, wizards and fairies – and told of their individual skills. They said that they had been keeping an eye on us and monitored our progress with the Master, and that was why we were chosen.

'After several months of secretly meeting with this group of people and getting to know them and learning their skills, we was discovered. Sadly there was an attack by people in authority. They burned our meeting house, people shouting and screaming, one evening. Both me and William here escaped.' Will pointed to his mobile green eye. 'We knew that a few had been killed but thought that more of the others had escaped. Unfortunately, capture and torture and death followed, sometimes in public view in order to try to teach us a lesson. If anything it strengthened our resolve.

'We returned for the weekly gathering at one of the alternative safe places that had been agreed in case we was found out. Out of the group of twelve plus us there was only three others left. Two women and the old man: the Master.

'He was so thankful and elated that we had survived that he cried, as did the two young women. As did we all. We were not harming anyone and it was with great sadness that we lost so many wonderful people to ignorance and basic savagery. The five of us vowed to keep together and made alternative arrangements to meet and not just on full moons, which was too obvious for the authorities.

'During our continued learning we found out that the two women were sisters and that they worked with their father building boats down on the boatyard at the mouth of the river. They had learnt the skills of woodcraft since being able to walk, collecting pieces of wood for their father and then learning how to cut and treat the wood, making joints in the wood as perfect as a sewing machine of the twenty-first century. They really were that good. You can see where this is leading so I will keep it as short as I can, although I do like to tell a story or two.' Jon nodded back to Tom in agreement.

Tom continued. 'So there we was, the five of us, and we discovered that ancient yew that's over five thousand full moons old, and not just cut down without a care, but caressed and talked to, requests made to the tree to remove a branch or two, resulted in very special powers. There's a saying that there is power in the written word. Well, there is even greater power in the spoken word, and the chanting and meditating that we done. We didn't know fully what it was we had done until after the women had made the model of the *Pelican*, or should I say the renamed *Golden*

Hinde at the request of a local merchant.

'He had said that he needed a ship that could sail across the seas to the New World and come back again, but didn't want to risk spending his well-earned money on a boat that would sink. So he asked for a model to be made, which the two women did. Oh yes,' added Tom with excitement in his voice. 'The two women, Emma and Agnes, despite them both being a few years older than us two, we got wed and as two couples we has eleven children between us and—'

'Thank you, Thomas,' said Jon interrupting.

'Oh yes, yes, sorry, Jon, sorry. Just digressing a little. So we managed, well, the women managed to create a small-sized model boat with care and detail. We tried it on the water and it was perfect and the merchant then commissioned the boatyard, which in those times was like giving a pot of gold to each one of us. We desperately needed work and for the boatyard to be given this commission saved the village from poverty. He asked for a full-size version of the model.

'Down on the river the boat was built in five months. The whole village was involved. A wonderful sight. The model was kept in the boatyard. It was a sight to see and people would come from miles around to look at it.

'The workers would come up to the model before each day's work began to check on the joint detailing, and for some reason they would each touch the model and run their smooth hands over the shape and sails. I think it was a lot to do with the whole village touching the wood every day and the spirit that had been put into the model that gave the portal the travel powers that it has.

'One day in 1577, the owner brought his wife down to see the boat and he and his wife named it the *Pelican* after a bird he had brought back from one of his travels. The old man and the four of us took painstaking measures to make sure that the ship was perfect and safe. They spent time meditating and chanting whilst they built the model and when it came to making the whipstaff, that was the steering mechanism in them days, they were chanting

"Steer safely on its way wherever and whenever you go come back safely. By touching me you go safely and return." They mentioned every year for over a thousand years going forward in their chanting and wishing safe return for the travellers. This in effect was the spell that created the whipstaff and portal link in the model.'

'Nicely summarised, Thomas,' said Jon. 'I thought you might go on for a bit longer. If any of you want to speak to Thomas or William on that matter further, please do so, and I am sure they will be happy to expand on their story and perhaps even some of their travels.'

The new recruits around the table were taken aback and dumbstruck to hear the story. The older members who had heard the story before were happy chatting amongst themselves as they got up from the table and left the room.

'Henry, George, and Dianne,' Jon called as he looked across the room at the people leaving, 'could you please wait behind? Thank you.' Jon then seemed to realise George was still absent. 'And Peter, please could you also go and bring Conrad in.' The others left the room.

'I've called you all here to discuss a mission, as we call them from time to time when we are called upon by … government departments to support them and expedite. Most of our work is undertaken with meticulous planning but this is urgent. This will require—' The door to Jon's office opened and Parka man and Green Eye man entered.

'Perfect timing, you two,' said Jon. 'Come and join us. Tom and Will here will be your dependable assistance in this exercise. You will remember listening to them just now and of course when you were recruited.'

'There is an annual event, you all may have heard of it. The Brixton Carnival. This will be your responsibility, both during the event and for the week before. We need to gauge the atmosphere, the talk in the pubs and clubs, and then finally in the few days afterwards to see if anyone missed doing something and starts talking about it. There will be a lot of shaking hands and merging with the crowd. This isn't a portal exercise, we will only be needing a black cab … and perhaps a car for the journey north … keeping close tabs on them … can't do it with the portal.'

Peter was wondering who Jon was talking about.

'You may have already worked out that with the ability to travel via a portal there are also a number of restrictions. One in particular is that for the year following the present day on a rolling basis you can't travel to a time zone. But, by planning ahead, which our research team have done by … scouting parties…' Jon looked towards Tom and Will, 'we have already determined key events that we need to be present over the coming twelve months, and this is one of them.'

Jon continued and advised that both Tom and Will had already been to this event 'in advance' a year ago. 'We have at CPS reviewed the findings of their visits and so have gleaned from events that actually occurred that we need a presence.

'Tom and Will,' Jon continued. Parka man and Funny eyes, Peter reflected. 'They have already identified persons that need close attention both before and during the carnival and in order to help in this we have needed local knowledge and experience. This is one of the reasons Conrad has been brought in today.' Everyone looked towards Conrad, who gave a confident nod and a smile and lifted his hand in acknowledgement.

'But I must stress he is with us not just for this exercise. He is now a permanent member of CPS with considerable experience in dealing with this type of event and other carnivals, most noticeably the Notting Hill Carnival, while he was working part-time for the Metropolitan Police. As you may have already noticed when watching television, both the Prince and the Princess of Wales have an annoying habit of diverting from routes set by us for their meeting of the public. This is where we struggle to fully protect. They have already been reminded that they should keep to the programme because Tom and Will have discovered a plot to disrupt a senior royal appearance. I will let them explain in more detail later. One advantage we all have is that costumes and make-up are pretty much unnecessary for this one. We can merge in easily as we are.

'The earlier scouting trips have identified people that are looking not to kill, as far as we know, but to discredit and interfere with William and Kate's life to such an extent that the prince gives up the entitlement to the throne after Charles has ... how should I say ... had his turn. Thus the direction of the Crown would turn towards other members of the royal family, perhaps a King Edward IX, King George VII, or even a King Henry IX.'

'You will by now understand that the Crown follows a natural progression, but some people or groups follow the old sage Nostradamus. His predictions which, to be fair, can be interpreted in different ways, as well as the timing of these so called "predicted" events. I will give you an example. You may be aware that his prediction of three monarchs in quick succession has caused a stir following Her Majesty Queen Elizabeth's death, but we should not forget that three monarchs in quick succession has already occurred, in 1936. There will always be members of the public who have a preference for another royal family member rather than the reigning monarch. I suppose it's a bit like supporting your favourite football team who never win any trophies and languish mid-table'. There was laughter from the audience as he looked towards Peter.

'Anyway, I digress. The Germans being the instigators of two world wars are in the eyes of a lot of people, still viewed as a threat to Britain and the Crown. Which is odd isn't it when you think that they have had considerable involvement in our royal family for centuries. Of particular note is George Louis of Hanover and the date 1st August 1714. He was crowned George I and was one hundred percent German. Queen Victoria's husband Prince Albert was from the Saxe-Coburg and Gotha family, he initiated the German custom of christmas trees. Our Edward VIII who abdicated had links with a well known German called Adolf Hitler. In more recent times the husband of our illustrious Queen Elizabeth II, bless her soul, married Prince Philip who had predominantly German ancestry. Let's not forget Prince Andrew who has a strong following after his career in the Navy and fighting in the Falklands War, although he has fewer supporters than he used to. Harry's followers have grown in numbers because of a strong allegiance to him, which developed during his time in Afghanistan. The people supporting Harry have also had a surge in membership since Harry married Meghan. The Americans love royalty. William's supporters are already high because he has a beautiful wife, Catherine, and three lovely children. And believe it or not, the public still holds Princess Diana dear to their hearts and had expectation that she would one day be queen, which makes it unfairly difficult for Charles.' Jon lifted his cup and saucer, took a sip of tea and licked his lips and looked at the faces listening intently. 'Do not sway from your responsibilities because you have read or heard of a particular news article. Charles will deliver and we will support him. The public can be very fickle, and the extent of television and media coverage has significant influence over their views.' Jon paused. Silence ensued from his audience whilst they absorbed his words. Eventually, Jon spoke.

'So, there you have it'.

There was a whistle from a few people.

'Yes. My thoughts precisely. That's a significant number of potential challenges to the rightful head of the Monarchy. And where and who are all these people, anyone?'

'They are all people called Edward, George or Henry!' said Tom flippantly, followed by laughter from everyone, relieved to be able to release the tension in the room.

'So Anne wants to be queen?' added David.

'I didn't say that,' replied Jon sharply. 'Have you been listening to what i've been saying or do i have to send you all back to nursery school?'

'Yes, I know you know the answer, Tom.' Jon looked around the room for some form of response.

'Well? For a country to have a strong link to a king or queen in our country. Think about it for a moment. That would potentially in the eyes of a lot of Americans provide a foothold into Britain for future expansion. This might all sound out of the ordinary, but think of the logic behind—'

'And we,' Tom interrupted, 'have seen it with our own eyes, whatever colour they may be,' he said, turning his head with a laugh at Will. 'So, everyone, the key at the carnival is to suppress any egg throwing or abuse from the crowds. It should be a happy, fun event, but unfortunately there are people as Jon explained that have their own agenda and want to spoil the party.'

'Thank you, Tom. Eloquently put,' said Jon.

'With the carnival in ten days' time you have three days in which to prepare, before living with the community in Brixton. Tom and Will have organised discussions with the police and the royal couple, and the 'official' bodyguards, and these will take place over the next two days.

'Do not miss these briefing sessions under any circumstances. Peter, George – ah, he's not here. I will need to speak with him – and Dianne, you will also be introduced to William and Catherine so that they recognise you. Jadie, and I can't stress this enough, you have as important a role to play in protecting Harry as other members of CPS protecting senior royals. Should you hear or meet people in the presence of Harry and Meghan with any plan in mind to push Harry to the fore, please make sure you inform me or Will, Tom or Henry immediately. Okay, everyone, there it is. Enjoy it.'

'Thank you, Jon.' They all left the room except for Peter and Dianne who were asked to wait behind.

'George is not here. What do you think of him? Can he be trusted? Has he the passion for this work or is he just here for the money?' asked Jon seriously, pacing around the office.

'Dianne answered first. 'I think he's very keen to do well, and we all worked together when we went back to QEI.' She looked at Peter.

'Peter,' said Jon, now calmer and sitting back in his chair.

'Well, he's pretty much of a sound mind when he's focused, but I know at the moment he is distracted by financial issues. Bigsey is helping him out with these as we are speaking.'

'Ah, so he wasn't feeling ill,' said Jon with a smirk.

'I think, Jon, that if you had a financial predicament similar to

George's it would make you feel ill.'

'Very well answered. Thank you both. Ask George and Bigsey to come and see me now. Thank you both. You may go.'

Peter passed the message to George and Bigsey.

About half an hour later Peter was in his office with the pile of papers that Henry had given him regarding Prince William. George and Bigsey knocked on the door.

'Come in! Well, how was it?' asked Peter.

George sat down in front of Peter's desk whilst Bigsey helped himself to some water from a jug on the side.

George took a while to say anything but eventually spoke to Peter.'He basically said that I have some very good and loyal friends here and not to let them down.' Bigsey had explained what he had done to Jon. Jon was impressed. Whilst they were with him they could see the figures reversing very slowly but in the right direction. Bigsey had calculated that George should, depending on which way the dollar swung against the yen over the next few weeks and balanced with the gold price, see things back to zero. But he would have to keep a look at the trend each day to review the risk allocation and he'd told him how to do that.

'Jon's final words,' added Bigsey, 'were, "Do not let this happen again or there will be consequences." He didn't go into any detail.'

'Thank you, Peter, Bigsey. You've saved my job and probably my marriage.'

'The secret, George, is not to gamble unless you are prepared to lose your investment, and to cover your positions. Don't expose yourself to unnecessary risk.'

'Thanks, guys. I had better go now. I've got a parents' evening at school with Marion. See you guys tomorrow.'

'Cheers, George.' The door closed. Peter and Bigsey looked at each other nonplussed.

'He's not gonna make it, is he?' said Bigsey.

'I'm sorry to say, I think you're right.'

The pre-Brixton Electric Carnival week was busy for the CPS core team. They needed to attend official and unofficial events as well as visit bars and clubs.

One of the most important items on the schedule was the visit to Kensington Palace, which Peter was very much looking forward to.

This would be his first visit to a royal palace other than Hampton Court with a school trip many years ago, when half the class couldn't get out of the maze and missed the grand tour around the house.

Kensington Palace was tucked away, yet still very close to the hubbub of the West End of London. The palace retained its quietness, with the benefit of the park so close. Jon had ordered an official CPS car to take them. This was Jon's way; he hated being remotely late for anyone, particularly royalty. This was, he said, to make sure that they were on time.

They were met at the entrance to the palace by the usual security guards tucked away to the side of the gated entrance. From the outside the building didn't appear to be overly extravagant, but on being invited into the house, the immense splendour and history was immediate and mind-blowing.

At the entrance lobby, they were held up whilst their invitation was checked, and were finally led through from one waiting area to another and finally into what must have been a huge ballroom in its time, and perhaps still was, thought Peter.

'Wow, this is something,' said George, gawping at the surroundings.

'Yea,' replied Dianne. 'Our outfits from a few weeks ago for QEI would have looked the part here.' They had glimpses through the tall sash windows, warmed by heavy curtains either side, across to the park.

Jon had said that the introduction to William and Catherine was a well-coordinated affair, even though there was a lot of hanging around; 'And a cuppa tea and a biscuit,' Tom had said, and it would all be over in a jiffy. He was right to a point. But Peter needed to create a close relationship here and put in the effort with questions and talk about circumstances that might arise without worrying William and Catherine unnecessarily.

Local posters to the carnival read that a very special guest would appear at the Brixton Electric Carnival this year. Although this event was mainly taking place inside, the celebrations were clearly everywhere in and around 'Electric' Brixton. It meant a number of late nights for the team, such as clubbing and attending discos and returning home at two or three in the morning.

On the evening of the main event, the special guest appeared on stage, in fact both of them. First Prince William, followed by Catherine. They were thrown a microphone by the DJ and questioned about what they thought about the music, artists and venue. The pair danced for a short while up on stage to the wild screams and cheering of the crowd.

'There.' Peter heard it towards the middle-rear area of the auditorium. There was definitely a sound of discontent and booing, but was this just sarcastic? Or with intent. He looked across and tried to lip-read what they were chanting. 'Have a kin' .... 'Hare of kin' ... 'Hairy fu kin'. He couldn't quite make it out. Peter called Parka man on his walkie-talkie; there was a good excuse for wearing ear protectors when the music was so loud.

They looked across into the packed crowd and saw the group of people, their hands gesturing a stream of expletives in the air. Hands were pointing towards the stage. Peter couldn't hear what they were shouting. He pushed his way through the crowds and got closer to the party animals and as he did so he could make out the words *Hairy King*. There must have been a dozen or so of them, White, Black and Asian and a wide spread of age groups. *What brings people to such a state of animosity and hatred,* thought Peter. Neither Parka man nor Peter went any closer. They saw George dancing with Dianne in the midst of them. *Well,* thought Peter, *good for them as long as they're careful.*

The 'special guests' on stage left to rapturous cheers and applause. Pumped-up music followed. Peter left the dance area and headed for where the Land Rover Defender that was waiting to collect the royal couple. He saw them emerge from a side door. Parka man was already there, overlooking their exit from the building.

'Peter, all okay?' he said over the mic.

'Yes, all good, Tom. George and Dianne are still in the midst of them.'

William and Catherine waved to people standing outside, and for a change got straight into the waiting car.

'That was all straightforward enough,' said Peter over the mic to Parka man. He didn't reply. He was looking around at the surroundings and at people in the crowd and parked vehicles. He nodded at someone standing close to the car.

'Good,' said Parka man into his mic. 'A straightforward event, except for those rowdies in the crowd. There's always someone trying to spoil royal events.'

'Or too much booze,' added Peter.

'Yeah. Now you're talking I could do with a pint,' replied Parka man.

They watched as the official car pulled away, with motorbikes to the front and rear.

'Where now?' said Peter into his mic.

'My guess is Cambridgeshire.'

'Really? At this time of day?'

'Oh yeah, I can see Peter that you haven't read all the contents of the folder Henry gave you.'

'Oh yes, of course, Anmer Hall up on the Sandringham Estate.'

'Ah, so you did read it.' Parka man smiled at Peter from about fifty yards away. The convoy of vehicles disappeared up towards the Elephant and Castle and Waterloo. Peter and Parka man walked towards each other. An out-of-breath voice from Dianne came over the microphone. 'Danger. Stop the cars.'

'What?' said Parka man.

'George and I overheard the group of people we were dancing near saying that it's not a problem that nothing happened here, but that they will scare them in the car on the way home'. There was still a lot of chanting mostly fuelled by excessive alcohol, emanating from the dance floor comprising "Royals stay at home" to "We love you, William and Kate", "Harry for King", and "Send them all to the Tower".

'So that's what it was,' said Peter, reaching Parka man.

Parka man immediately called a number on his phone and was linked to the driver of the leading motorbike. Peter listened intently to the conversation.

'Where are you headed for?'

'Kensington and then up to Amner.'

'Suggest you divert and go straight to Amner, but using a different route from the norm.'

'Why?'

'Don't ask. Now just do it.'

'Roger, will do.' The motorbike driver explained to the driver of the car and he to the royals.

Parka man had been very calm about it all and Peter asked him why the change.

'Well. Our reconnaissance a year ago picked up a potential incident outside Kensington Palace about this sort of time. Now we know where it came from. Peter, we will need to follow the people chanting and screaming abuse on the dance floor earlier and find out who they are. I'm told by the police that the face recognition cameras can't pick up anyone with the strobes and flashing lights and particularly as most of them seem to be wearing make-up.'

It was one twenty in the morning when they were joined by Conrad, George and Dianne, who emerged from the building, perspiration seeping through their shirts.

'Well done, you two,' Parka man said to George and Dianne. 'Did you hear anything else?'

'No. Other than mentioning something to do with falling from a bridge will stop them.'

Parka man immediately called the lead driver of the escort vehicles. There was no reply. Peter was asked to try. Nothing.

'Perhaps they're out of range?'

'That's not possible,' said Parka man sharply.

There was a crackle on Peter's phone.

'I've got a missed call,' he said. Peter returned the call and got through.

'Yes, we were worried, what happened?'

'The usual … the city underpass … Tom told us to make a change in our route so we're varying it.'

Peter relayed the same to Parka man.

'Okay – just get them to be careful when approaching bridges. We have a tip-off from a reliable source that there may be an incident involving bridges en route. Okay, over.'

'There they are. That's them,' said George with a nod, clearly trying to not be too conspicuous as he looked in their direction.

A group of a dozen or so noisy people were crowded together chatting and laughing and slowly splitting up into groups.

Parka man was quick to take charge and separated the CPS team into pairs to follow them as best they could at a discreet distance. He sent George and Dianne off first; they needed to stay together as a couple because they had been seen together at the nightclub and it would be obvious if they were then seen apart. Parka man had already seen who he thought was the ringleader of the group and decided that he and Peter would track him. The group split further, and Parka man sent Henry and David to follow. Conrad joined them with one of his undercover police colleagues and he was then dispatched to follow a group of four.

Peter and Parka man followed their prey. The noise and revelry soon died down to normal street sounds at two o'clock in the morning. Police sirens in the distance. A screechy car engine, a motorbike with a dodgy exhaust and cats racing from hedge to wall and scampering across the road looking for a tasty something.

The three people that George and Dianne had been following split, two and one. Dianne suggested that they should stick together and follow the couple.

A moment later George heard a rustle from behind and Dianne fell to the pavement. A knife was thrust at George's throat.

'What do you want? You've been keeping tabs on us ever since the dance floor. You police? Na, you aren't, are you, you wouldn't be so stupid, and your bitch here, let's see what she has to say about it.' The man dragged George by the collar across to Dianne who was still trying to get up. On falling, Dianne had turned her mic on, connecting to Peter. But she didn't know where they were in Brixton.

The two people they had been following ran back and joined in the scuffle. The mic round Dianne's ear had been pulled away in the struggle as they pulled her up from the pavement, and left on the ground.

The knife now to George's neck had drawn blood as he was pushed back over a wall whilst being frisked and quizzed. The man pulled the earphone out of George's ear and listened to it. Dianne overheard someone talking about bricks from bridges.

'You bastards been tracking us, haven't you?' He dropped the mic to the floor and stamped on it. You. You got one as well?' He stormed towards Dianne, dragging George with him.

'No. No,' replied Dianne desperately with a screech in her voice. The man from the other couple grabbed both her ears.

'Well. We'll show you a lesson or two. Let's take 'em back to the Old Kent Road and we'll dump 'em in the canal. That's an easy way to solve this problem.'

'Yeah, good one man.'

Dianne opened her mouth and was about to say something, but an arm swiped across her face and she fell back to the pavement.

'There was no need for that,' said George.

'What about this then?' The guy pulled a knife out, shoved it up George's nostril, and flicked the blade. George screamed. It cut deeply into his nose and blood poured out.

'Now, you two got the message, behave yourselves before someone gets hurt.' He shoved George along the street.

The woman helped Dianne get up and put her arm around her. 'There was no need to do that,' she said to the ringleader. 'You've had too much to drink.'

He turned sharply round to the girl, menace on his face and in his voice, pushing his face right up to hers.

'What the fuck do you know? These police people are trying to control everything we do and I've had enough of it. Once those bricks are thrown over the bridges that will teach 'em a lesson.'

George was desperately thinking how he could get help and get out of this situation. He decided that as well as he could, he would leave a trail, a trail of blood from his nose.

'There's no response from George or Dianne's walkie-talkies,' said Peter to Parka man.

'Call 123 and ask for the last location of their mics. I think we're going to have to split up if we're going to find them.'

'Okay.'

'Peter, make sure you keep your mic on at all times. We can then listen immediately to what the other of us is doing.'

'East Dulwich Road, along the A2214 at the bridge crossing the railway lines just north of Nunhead station, headed in an easterly direction towards New Cross and Deptford,' came over the mic, and then it went dead.

Peter heard Conrad inform the others that it was potentially a bricks-off-bridge risk, and that he had informed the lead motorbike rider to be particularly vigilant. He told him that it may be annoying for the passengers, but a zigzag route home avoiding bridges would be the safest.

Peter pulled up a map on his phone. Parka man and Peter jogged towards the last known transmission spot on the A2214. They were just two streets away, but that was over five minutes ago. They ran, both mindful that they might run into George and Dianne and their uninvited escort, and then what?

Reaching the spot, they looked around and found the mic crushed into the pavement, and recent bloodstains. They searched further and found more blood, fresh.

'This has got to be them.'

'Seems to me like one of them is giving us a message and leaving a trail.'

But which way from here? They both looked across the street with two routes to choose from, if they were still headed east.

'We got to be careful moving forward now, could be a trap. What do you think, Peter?' said Parka man.

'It seems to me that they might be headed towards Deptford and the canal area,' said Peter.

'Well, you take that road and follow your instincts and I'll take the street opposite.'

They ran across the road and split up.

'I wonder,' said Peter to himself, still with the mic open to Parka man.

He jogged faster and at a turning in the road saw more blood on the kerb, not as profuse as before but definitely fresh, and a bloodied tissue a few metres further on. He knew he was getting closer. His heart was now pounding faster, not just from the late-night exercise but with expectation and adrenaline. He felt that his hunch was right as he ran along the street, now being lit by the moon.

He stopped abruptly and hid behind a parked van. He had seen on the other side of the road a group of people, stationary outside a house.

'That must be them,' Peter whispered, loud enough that his words could be heard through the mic. He glanced past the side of the van, thankful that the wait was giving him time to catch his breath. The front light of the house came on and then turned off. Those still on the pavement moved on and disappeared, turning the corner down an alleyway between darkened sleepy terraced houses.

'Okay, that's good,' said Peter. 'One less. Only two to deal with now.'

'Peter. Where are you?'

'Good question, Tom,' replied Peter, looking around for a street name. 'Not certain but I'm pretty sure I've found them. Looks like there's two of them, and definitely towards the Deptford Creek area.'

'Okay. Will pick you up on the tracker.'

'Where are you?'

'I'm north of Camberwell at the moment,' said Parka man with apprehension in his voice that Peter picked up; he was still quite far away.

Peter took a step out from his camouflage behind the van. As he did so, the front door of the house opened, a light flickered onto the street, then off, and the door shut again with a slam. Peter swiftly stepped back behind the van, hoping he hadn't been seen.

'Damn, back to three again.' He followed the person at a discreet distance. He was carrying a plastic bag and started to jog, presumably to catch up with the others. As the footpath ended there was a bright street light. Peter stopped before it and listened intently before moving forward. He noticed further spots of blood on the pavement to the right.

Parka man interrupted his thoughts as he spoke over the open mic; it wasn't a message for him, but he could listen in. Henry and David had followed two of the group of people when they had split up after the gig and they had tracked them to a house in the Elephant and Castle.

'Any news on George or Dianne.'

'None. What about Peter? Where's his position?'

'He's … way down towards the Deptford canals. I know, thanks. I'm heading in that direction now'

Peter turned the reception of his mic off as it was interfering with his thinking about how to approach the group. He moved once he thought it was safe into the light and carefully followed in the direction of the blood. It gave him some time to think before he caught up with them.

He rounded a corner on the footpath and stopped abruptly. He could see the group in front of him on the footbridge over the canal. They had stuffed material into Dianne's mouth and were tying her hands together. He could hear their voices.

'Bloody police state. I've had enough of you bastards. This will send them all a message and teach a lesson to all of you pigs.' The leader strode towards George with the intention of stopping him from talking.

Peter heard George replying. 'Come on, be sensible, let's talk about this.' Peter saw George being elbowed in the face and punched in the pit of his stomach. George fell to his knees. Dianne whimpered.

The woman with them shouted. 'This has gone far enough, Ed. Come on, just leave 'em and let's get out of 'ere.'

'Don't tell me what to do, bitch. I told you it's about time we made a statement of our intent.' He shoved her away from George who was trying to get up.

'Shit,' said Peter. Realising that he would have to move quickly, he glanced back over his shoulder to see if there was any support, but there was none. He turned quickly on his heels. *This is going to be dangerous.* Peter turned his mic back on and spoke. 'Tom. Anyone. If you're there, I'm at a footbridge in creekside Deptford. Having to go in – they're about to throw George and Dianne into the canal – their hands are being bound together as I speak.'

Parka man responded to Peter. 'We're on our way.'

Peter moved carefully and quietly to start with and then accelerated up the slope of the footbridge. They had seen him and stared, but were dumbstruck.

'Oi – what do you want? What's your game? Piss off?'

Peter charged into the guy like a mad bull, taking him out and at the same time grabbing the other guy's jacket and pulling him over, aware that a weapon was probably open. He got up quickly and charged at the leader again with a neck-high rugby tackle before the guy could lift his knife.

Bodies were strewn all over the footbridge. George and Dianne were lying on the footpath struggling to move let alone stand up as their hands had been tightly bound.

The ringleader was the first to recover. He picked up his knife as Peter aimed a kick at his arm. The knife didn't move out of his hand, and he grimaced back at Peter.

Peter caught a glimpse of Parka man watching the commotion from a distance; he could see that he was tired and had had to stop to catch his breath after the effort he had made. Peter looked up at the man with the knife in front of him and the other two men now closing in on him.

'Come on then,' shouted the knifeman, pointing towards Dianne and kicking George in the groin. Peter was still on the ground but cautiously getting up, keeping a steady eye on the weapon.

'You're another one of these coppers, I bet?' Peter realised that this was an opportunity for negotiation.

'No, nothing to do with me. I just like a fight on my way home whenever I can get one.'

The guy was moving towards Peter but stopped in his tracks. He stood upright, threw the knife up into the air and it spun several times before he skilfully caught it by the handle. *This guy knows how to use a knife.*

'Where you from, mate?'

'What's it to you?' Peter had caught his attention. 'Well, I might like to join you guys.' Peter's left hand gripped his right fist and he cracked his knuckles.

'In what?' the other guy chirped up from the side, also brandishing a weapon, but Peter couldn't see what it was; he was intent on keeping an eye on the knife flashing in front of him. The three people surrounding Peter looked at each other.

'He knows,' said the woman.

'Shut her up,' said the knifeman to his mate.

'I know your game,' said Peter, realising that it was such a broad and elusive question that covered any manner of things. The man thrust the knife towards Peter's chest. He dodged to one side, grabbing the man's forearm with both hands. The man's other hand grasped Peter's ear and neck, tearing back the muscles. Peter elbowed him sharply in the stomach and his grip loosened for a second, but a knee from behind into his coccyx caused Peter to collapse to the ground. The knifeman stood over his prey.

'What are you gonna do?' said the woman. 'He might be what he said he was.'

'He's had it coming to him, this one. I can smell him, he's definitely a copper like the others.'

'Maybe he does just like a fight. He might be useful,' said the other man.

This was playing into Peter's hands, buying some time. Out of the corner of his eye, Peter could see Parka man getting closer, but he seemed apprehensive to intervene. *He must be trying to gauge the situation,* thought Peter.

'I think perhaps a little bit of fun,' said the knifeman, nodding now and pushing Peter away, turning and grinning to his mates, flicking his knife round and round in his hands as he approached George and Dianne lying on the ground.

'Why do you want to hurt William?' Peter called out. The man stopped and looked back at Peter.

'It's not him. Nuffin' to do wiv him. We just want Harry to be king.' He started towards Peter.

'If … if he wanted to be king, he would have stayed in Britain. Surely?' said Peter, slowly gaining his composure.

'Look, mate, you're exactly the sort of person that …' There was a whooshing sound and a thump as the knifeman in front of Peter fell to the ground. Another whooshing in the air, and his mate stumbled and fell to one knee. The woman ran away from the scene, but straight into Parka man as she made her way to escape up the footbridge.

'What happened? One second they're about to dump us, and the next …' said Peter. There was a rock slightly bigger than a cricket ball on the ground next to one of the men that had been felled. Parka man motioned his head towards the figure standing on the other side of the footbridge. It was Conrad. He was making his way over.

'Boy, are we glad to see you two,' said George from the ground. Parka man undid the rope binding Dianne and George together.

'Conrad?' said Peter. 'You threw those?'

'Oh yes, man,' replied Conrad grinning from ear to ear. 'Back in my younger days I used to play for the Antiguan national cricket team under eighteens, and …' He motioned a throwing action to the amusement of Peter.

Henry and David arrived on the scene and secured the two men on the ground. Tom held the woman tight in an arm hold behind her back. A police vehicle pulled up off the road close to the bridge.

The following morning back at Great Smith Street CPS headquarters, Henry shook Peter's hand as he came into the breakout space and they caught up with the events of last night.

Henry informed Peter that the addresses of the people arrested were raided and the names and contacts of the members of the 'pro-Harry and pro-Ann' groups, amongst others, were found on computers and some of the key driving members behind the anti-Monarchy brigade would now be monitored. This would mean immediate work for Peter in preparation for his full-time role.

They both bought a coffee and Peter a cinnamon and raisin bagel and made their way to the debriefing session with Jon in his office.

Jon sat in his leather-backed swivel chair and spoke to the group assembled in his office. *A motley crew*, Peter thought, but there was a feeling of being at one. Parka man smiled back at him as he took a sip of his coffee and then Green eye man tucked his hand into his pocket; Peter knew he was going to do his eyeball trick so he looked away, but Will was only kidding and laughed back. Jadie and Dianne were both there, sitting near to Peter. They had formed a close bond following the training and the experiences of the sixteenth century.

'The events of yesterday and especially last evening were expected, at least to a certain degree, from our earlier tracking, but as you know from experience these can vary somewhat from what is anticipated.'

Parka man stood up and gave credit to each of them directly involved so that Jon understood their bravery.

'We have also had a note directly from the prince's secretary thanking CPS for their intervention.' Apparently two groups of people were seen and apprehended on bridges up towards Cambridge on the royal car's intended route. The realisation that the diversion had prevented an accident involving the royal couple was much appreciated.

George was not present. He had sent Jon an email in the morning saying that he was still in A&E at St Thomas's Hospital having his nose stitched together. But in his email to Jon, he had also informed him that he had had enough of working for the CPS. The two experiences to date had both involved near death and he felt that this was enough for him and he wasn't a cat with nine lives. He had handed in his notice. Jon continued and said George would not, however, be able to leave because he had committed to CPS. 'He will have continued responsibilities but not in the field. He will be allocated work with our wonderful backroom staff, who, I should add, are as important as our frontline representatives. Please none of you forget or ever lose sight of that. Without them, you would be at risk every journey or protection manoeuvre.'

A reduced debriefing session followed with Henry and Jon.

'Peter, you have some catching up to do with the prince. We've arranged for you to have a morning with him over at my place next Wednesday, so I suggest you come over for breakfast at say eight. He's due with us at ten thirty and his day schedule is telling us he will be with us for forty minutes. Have you read the file that Henry gave you?'

'Yes. Henry is due to test all of us over the next two days.'

'Good, so that works out well with his timing for the visit. In broad terms, Peter, you have to become his friend but not his friend. You have to have a constant awareness of his movements 24/7, his whereabouts and who he is with, but you are not to interfere unless there is a perceived risk that you or even he may feel is present. Now then, to get you embedded fully, part of the exercise after meeting with him will be to revisit the past as well as the future so that you know fully what he's like and the people that have influenced him. The file and test is nothing like the real thing, so you will be making regular visits to view his history over the last forty years or so – to 21 June 1982. From the files you have and any other background research you have undertaken can I suggest you list the events when you consider that he is or was at risk and we will go through these with you next Monday. Tom and Will will also be in attendance – not to check on you or anything like that. They have already visited future events for the coming year, and I am sure they will have some key situations that will need your attention and presence going forward.'

'Thanks, Jon, and you, Henry, and particularly Tom. I had better leave you to it and get going with my homework.'

'Oh, and by the way, I'm having some people over this coming

Saturday afternoon around four for tea and cakes. My favourite – Jemima has a schedule of baking – and this weekend is Welsh cakes. You've no need to bring anything.'

Peter thought, *Oh god, not another journey back in time.*

Jon continued. 'You remember when you were at our party and we spoke about the swimming pool? Well, the firm that did ours is doing their annual service so you can meet them and discuss what you had in mind. You must bring Sally, of course, and take photos. I know that Josie has already taken some measurements.'

Sally and Peter had not seen each other for a few days because of the events in Brixton, so that evening they decided that it had to be a takeaway. Neither wanted to cook or do the washing up. When Peter got home there was a message on the answerphone. It was from George, asking Peter to ring him tomorrow, and a recorded message from Sally's parents who were now making their way through Rome.

Over their Thai, Peter explained to Sally that he had been asked by Henry at work to carry out a bit of research on the royal family. She was immediately interested and wanted to help. As well as being involved with teaching some more recent British history at school, she had always been fascinated with royalty in the UK. By the time Peter had finished tidying up the kitchen after their meal she had done his homework for him. Peter did not expand as to what it was for except to say that everyone new at work had to do it and that they all had to know about the history of the royals and that his particular subject was Prince William.

'Well, Peter.' She put her feet up on the sofa as he walked into the living room. 'You asked me to pull together ten or so ideas, and I think you've got to find out some more about each of the following. I've written down the ones that interest me, so there you go.' She handed the sheet of paper over to Peter and snuggled down further into the deep sofa, relaxing into Peter's embrace. Peter looked at the sheet but was really not in the mood.

Sally seemed quite excited about what she had produced for him. 'Okay, do you want me to run through them? Then you can just relax and listen.'

'Yea. sure, why not.' He settled back on the sofa and put his feet up with a full glass of Malbec, grateful to be home, and listened to Sally's voice.

'Question One: William's time at university. What did he study and did he get a degree in anything?'

'That's an interesting one to start with, but most of that is in the papers that Henry gave me to study.'

'Well, Peter, what did he study?'

'It was Art, and majoring in Geography, and yes he received a degree, an upper second.'

'Good for him. Two: his bachelor party before he got married, where was it and who attended?'

'I think you mean his stag do. This one is a bit more sensitive. There's not much detail in the file that I was given to study. But I would guess that Harry would have been there and probably Andrew. But the file did mention that they went to Annabelle's one evening in London to the surprise of a lot of people, particularly the prince, but the formal gathering was at Hartland Abbey in Devon, where guess what?'

'What?'

'They went surfing.'

'That was presumably to recover from the alcohol. Three: William's twenty-first birthday – where was it held, who was invited and more important, did Kate attend?'

'It was a fancy-dress party held at Windsor Castle with a number of uninvited guests that caught security and us on the hop.' Peter realised what he had said, but Sally didn't pick up on it. 'Not sure about Kate. Maybe she dressed up and no one noticed it was her.'

'Four: when he first met Kate Middleton did he like her straight away?'

'Apparently not,' answered Peter. 'They were nine years old at the time and had no idea what the future would hold.' Sally burst into laughter.

'Five: his last conversation with Diana his mother before she died.'

'Interesting, yea. But way too sensitive. I wouldn't have the courage to ask that one.'

'But it would be interesting to know, wouldn't it?'

'I'm not so sure. I don't feel that would be of benefit to anyone.'

'Anyhow, just some ideas. Here's the next one. Six: sport. Does he do any?'

'Ah. That's better. Much more of a reasonable one. Yes, I do know that he has played polo to a reasonable standard and for charities a number of times and that he generally enjoys sport, particularly rugby and football. He's president of England's Football Association and patron of the Welsh Rugby Union.'

'Wow, lucky man – that must keep him busy, plus having to go and see all those games.'

'He won't see all of the games, Sal. Besides, it's still a good point – it does get him out a lot. He also enjoys skiing and tennis.' Peter was pondering his responsibilities and the security issues surrounding each of the sports. *Oh well,* he thought, *it will get me outdoors, much better than a desk job, and hopefully Sal might be allowed to join me on some of my trips abroad.*

'Seven: favourite books or hobbies – does he have any?'

'Again, thank you, Sal. I'm up on this one as well.' Peter reflected on the questions and the completeness of the file that Henry had given him to study with all the facts and figures. 'Riding motorbikes.'

'Really?'

'Yup. Apparently he enjoys the sensation of speed you get on a bike. His grandmother the late Queen Elizabeth was always terrified he'd have an accident. But he has openly admitted that he has toned down his speed when on a bike for both family and Crown issues.'

'Eight: favourite films or series – does he watch soaps?'

'Well, that's got to be the TV series *The Crown,*' said Peter with a chuckle. 'Makes it easy to catch up with family history of sorts. But interestingly enough, they, I mean William and Kate, apparently enjoy a bit of *Game of Thrones.*'

'Nine: his relationship with his father's second wife Camilla and do they get on.'

'Ow, that's another sensitive question and could hurt. But definitely in the top ten. Not sure how that would pan out, but to be fair they have had years getting to know each other.'

'Ten: favourite food … does he like takeaways and where does he get them from?'

'That's tremendous, Sal, thanks, another very good one. I don't think I could have thought of these or any others if I had been thinking about it all day,' said Peter, feeling satisfied that his 'homework' had been completed. 'That wasn't in the file so I don't know the answer to that.'

'Perhaps haggis because they studied together in Scotland.'

'A haggis takeaway?' Peter pulled a face. 'You've got to be joking, definitely not on my list. My feeling is an Indian, particularly because they're both sporty and it's often a meal after a sporting occasion.'

'Actually,' said Sally, 'I've been thinking about it a bit more and I've thought of a few extra ones that you might like to consider. Eleven: William and Kate's favourite holiday destination.'

'Yeah, that's good. I know they both like skiing but also a bit of sunshine particularly in the winter months. The Alps for skiing and the Caribbean for the winter sunshine, both perfect destinations.'

'Twelve: what really caused the upset between him and Harry?'

'Wow, that would be interesting to find out, but I'm not so sure that would be appreciated if the public got hold of it. My guess would be just sibling rivalry.'

'How? What do you mean?'

'Well, it would probably show neither of them in a good light and the media will just make hay.'

'From William's perspective, it's not his fault he's first in line, nor Harry's for being second. But I feel that Harry has a bit of a chip on his shoulder about it, made worse by the media who just want another story about the royals. They both have to live with it and get on with their lives.'

'What if William abdicated, you know like Edward VIII?'

'Woo. He's not even king yet.' Peter's mind started racing with implications and the events at Brixton and the briefing from Jon. Sal must have been able to read his mind.

'Well, I would presume that the Crown would pass to George, his eldest?'

'That's interesting, Sal.' Peter reflected again on his recent experiences in Brixton, and Jadie who was now protecting Harry. 'You can't have any more now, surely?'

'Last one now, Peter, I promise.' Peter tickled her, and she let out a playful scream.

'Thirteen: when does William become king?'

Yikes, thought Peter that's another big one. 'How do you think of all these questions?' Peter was pondering the implications of knowing what the future held and making sure that it didn't get interfered with. *Tricky, very tricky.*

'There you are, something to get your teeth into.' She stretched across from the sofa, put the list of all the questions on the coffee table and lay back down. Peter picked up the list and looked through it in more detail. Sally was actually pretty accurate, particularly with the last two or three on the sort of subjects that he needed to find out about.

But surprisingly, number thirteen was in the future. Does Sally have some telepathic powers or strength that he or she for that matter is not aware of? There was very little extra that he could add to the list.

'Sal, you've done my homework for me. Are you sure you're not telepathic? A lot of these questions are what I would have written.' They settled down for the evening.

The following morning at work, Peter was expecting to see Jon but was called into Henry's office to review the list. He too was impressed with the content and reiterated that the study of a person by a team leader in the Crown Protection Service involved the past, the present and the future. 'Learn from the past, enjoy the events of today, and plan for the future. All these three need your full attention to address your appointment and duty as a protector of the Crown.

'For numbers eleven to thirteen on your list, you will need to review events and situations over the coming year with Tom and Will, because they have undertaken the required research as an advance working party. Commencing your responsibilities, you are in charge of protecting William and of course you will be immediately supported by your team. How your relationship develops with him and Catherine will undoubtedly be challenging as it has been for each of us with our responsibilities, but hopefully you will find it both rewarding and satisfying.

'We all have our own duties, but remember that all senior CPS leaders Jon, Will, Tom and myself will always be available should you need assistance. Good luck.'

CHAPTER 13

Careless

The following couple of months for Peter were littered with all aspects of the research he needed to undertake to further his knowledge of the Prince of Wales – holidays, friends, hobbies, food, time in the services, family relationships, his health, wealth and work commitments, as well as his timetable for travelling.

During this period, the one occasion he was required to formally attend to the prince became a bit of a fiasco. It was at the Royal Bath and West Show. William would be opening the event joined by the Princess of Wales and the children. This meant that Dianne and George's replacement, Chris, would also be there, so he was looking forward to an enjoyable day out, although he did briefly reflect on the last time he and Dianne had worked together in Brixton, and hoped it would not be so challenging.

Peter was given approval to take Sally to the event, provided Peter's parents also attended, thus allowing him time to break away and attend when required to 'The Prince's duties' as he called them. Peter had gradually explained to Sally that his work at CPS revolved primarily around a form of light-touch surveillance and observation role, supported by the police and security services so as not to break the confidences of CPS. He hadn't yet been allowed to inform Sally of the full extent of his commitment.

The instructions Peter was given for the event in Somerset were that he was to be there two days before the official opening to visit local markets, shops and hostelries so as to gauge the mood of the people. They stayed at Longbridge House in Shepton Mallett, which was more of a hotel than a B & B, and just a short distance from the showground. A briefing note the day before advised him to expect a shower or two. This was an understatement.

William and his family duly arrived in their escorted four-by-four and were greeted by a horizontal rainstorm that uprooted a number of trees at the entrance to the showground and shook exhibitors' marquees; in one tent, a group of people had to hold on to the guy ropes until the wind died down to prevent further damage. Understandably, the Royals remained in their vehicle until the wind and rain subsided some forty to fifty minutes later. The formal opening of the show took place in front of a damp and windswept but loyal and contented crowd that had remained close to the Royal party throughout the rainstorm. The Royals subsequently provided them with a welcome intimate walkabout, which kept all of those involved with their well-being on their toes. The delay to the formal opening had unfortunately meant a rushed visit, much to the disappointment of the stallholders and exhibitors, as well as the three children who had wanted to stay longer to see the animals. All in all, Peter reflected, it was uneventful. The family left on time to travel to another engagement later in the morning, not requiring Peter. This provided him with the opportunity to spend the afternoon with Sally and his parents, although it did mean running from marquee to marquee between the showers to see the stalls and exhibits.

Visits from senior members of CPS to Peter during the last couple of months had been few and he was beginning to wonder if they had forgotten about him. He spent a lot of his time getting Bigsey and his senior team members settled in and understanding how they were to interface with others at CPS.

What became more apparent to Peter was that CPS was a very old-fashioned but passionate organisation in its outlook, yet had very sophisticated equipment to carry out its work. The Historical Documents and Peoples department was split into specialist teams for each royal reign. Monarchs with a long reign, for example Queen Victoria and the two Elizabeths, would require more than just one person responsible, due to the workload when dealing with their history. Interesting, Peter thought, how the two longest-serving monarchs were both women, and pondered on this while thinking about Queen Elizabeth II; *I wonder why that is?* he thought, *especially as they had to go through the rigours of childbirth.*

It was a chilly Wednesday at CPS and the heating was barely on, so Peter sat at his desk wearing a scarf. As the morning wore on, it seemed as though it was going to be like any other in recent weeks, until the door to Peter's office was flung open sharply and Henry's face appeared.

'Peter. Morning. Good to see you. We have an issue – one of our units needs assistance and we need extra support. My office, now, please.' The door slammed shut as promptly as it had opened. Peter picked up the urgency in Henry's voice and got ready immediately, clearing his papers away before leaving his office.

There were three others in Henry's office when Peter entered, two of whom he recognised from his various introductory courses, but one, Peter did not immediately recognise. He stood up as Peter entered the room and introduced himself.

'Hello. Peter, isn't it? Good to meet you. I'm Hargreaves.' They shook hands. Hargreaves had a rigorous prolonged handshake to go with his muscular build.

'Hi, good to meet you too,' replied Peter, trying to figure out where he had seen him before. Hargreaves had dark bushy eyebrows to go with his unkempt hair and a yellowed, pitted texture to the skin on his face and hands.

'Do you know Jane and Lesley?' said Hargreaves, introducing the two ladies.

'Yes, we sort of met during the drama classes earlier in the year.'

The two women smiled at Peter and said 'hello'. They were chatting to each other when Henry burst into his office and looked around the room.

'Good. You're all here. I trust that you have had time to introduce yourselves if you haven't met before.' Henry was out of breath and carried under his arm a bulging pink folder that fell open onto his desk as he reached it.

'Sit down all of you, please, and thank you for joining me. For those of you that don't know, Hargreaves here and his team look after Queen Victoria, 1837 to 1901. It's a big period and his team are at full stretch with other matters. We need additional support.' Henry looked at the four of them in front of him, regaining his composure. 'You have all travelled with the *Golden Hinde* so this will be nothing new.

'We have had a request from very high up, and I mean top level, to investigate and provide reassurance that Her Majesty Queen Victoria's will was not … how should I put it … interfered with or altered before her death on the twenty-second of January 1901. An anomaly has been raised recently regarding her estate that claims lands understood to be clearly in the ownership of Victoria and the House of Hanover at the time of her death should be in the ownership of her father, William IV's brother, Ernest Augustus the Duke of Cumberland, and the inheritors of his estate. You might be wondering why has this taken so long to sort out. I agree. The same question went through my head when I was briefed. So we have to check the period during the weeks before her death to ensure that there was no interference.

'You've probably noticed that it can be cold here in October – it will be even colder in Victorian times. Make sure you see Wendy in costumes and make-up and wrap up warm. We already have three people out there keeping an eye out for anyone changing the paperwork. There is a briefing pack on each of your chairs. Read it fully and make a particular note of the photographs of our people because you will be meeting them and being instructed by them as well as Hargreaves here. Contact your other half or partner and inform them that you have been sent on a course to Scotland and won't be back for up to three to four days, and if they need to contact you they're to contact me in the first instance. The four of you will be travelling together – you know the routine.'

Peter's evening with Sally was subdued. She never liked him going away but at such short notice it had meant some rearrangements to their calendar. Fortunately, Sally wasn't overly put out; she had an Ofsted inspection at school which meant she would be kept busy over the next few days.

The following morning in the office was preparation time, with a review of the briefing notes and costumes. Jon's office was set ready with the *Golden Hinde* at the centre of the table when the four of them entered the room after lunch. Henry was pulling out the drawer for 1901 and the tokens for their return were already laid out on the table. There was no sign of Jon.

'Right, let's have a good look at you all and a final inspection of your attire before you set off. Hargreaves. Peter. Jane, and now Lesley.' Henry stood back and took a final look up and down at each of them. 'You all look very Victorian. Remember, the person you are to meet is Edward Beatly. He's a member of the parliamentary constitution legal team – you will have seen his photograph. At this sad time he won't be far from the Queen's side. He is expecting you all this afternoon, and remember your dress and mannerisms – it's nineteenth-century English with a plumb in your mouth. You all got that?' They each nodded.

'Hargreaves, I will leave you to do the honours with the ship and travel arrangements. I'm already running late for a meeting at Clarence House. Good luck.'

'Thank you, Henry,' replied Hargreaves. Henry left the room promptly. The door closed and was locked from the outside.

'Well, we'd better get a move on,' said Hargreaves as he fumbled with the whipstaff on the *Golden Hinde*. He was preparing to insert the date token when Jane said she needed to visit the washrooms. The others also decided to take the opportunity to use the facilities. On Peter's return to the room he asked Hargreaves where they would likely be arriving. He expected it to be somewhere in Osborne House on the Isle of Wight, which was one of Queen Victoria's favourite homes. The Queen and Prince Albert had demolished the old house in 1848 and built a new house using their own finances. It was subsequently given to the public by Edward VII in 1902 because he couldn't afford to maintain such a large estate. Peter now realised that Hargreaves was very knowledgeable about Victorian times.

On the ladies' return to the room the four of them immediately put their hands on each other's left shoulders with their hands touching the ship. Peter noticed that Hargreaves seemed to be particularly nervous through this procedure; he again fumbled with the whipstaff and date token, dropping them both on the table. He retrieved them, put the whipstaff in his inside jacket pocket and inserted the date token into the position where the whipstaff would have been on the ship.

There was an immediate high-pitched sound and swirling and whooshing in Peter's head and body that he felt lasted forever. But the sensation was no longer than his previous journey and he arrived with a thump, his feet landing on sodden ground. A snowflake landed on the cuff of his jacket.

CHAPTER 14
The King's Pleasure

Peter looked at his surroundings through the swirling mist and flurries of snowflakes. They seemed to have arrived in a wooded area close to what looked like a track or road. There were no pavements or street lights. Peter could see each of the others stirring. Hargreaves was trying to disentangle himself from a hawthorn, cloth tearing as he tried to pull himself free. Jane and Lesley were both lying on the ground at the foot of a muddy bank, on the edge of what seemed to be an area of bog.

'This isn't what I was expecting. Get me a nice warm bath,' said Jane with a chuckle.

'Me neither,' replied Lesley. Peter walked over to help both of them out of the mud.

'Quiet,' said Peter, pausing and listening intently 'Hargreaves, I said quiet. I can hear voices.' Hargreaves continued to moan as he remained entangled in the undergrowth. 'Quiet,' said Peter again sharply. Hargreaves stopped moving as if he too could hear the voices.

Peter saw movement up on the track. He motioned to them all to hide behind shrubbery. Hargreaves slid out of his jacket and left it in the hawthorn. They watched from a safe distance as a procession moved slowly past them. Peter couldn't make out what or who it was, but from the sound of dragging feet it sounded like a lot of weary people.

'Halt,' came a loud command from the front.

'Relieve and ten,' came a second command. There followed a lot of muffled sounds of voices and weapons and bags being dropped. Some of the people up on the track began making their way towards them.

Peter signalled for them all to crouch down even further to hide their faces. The sounds that followed were not unfamiliar on a late Friday night. Neither was the smell steaming around them. Peter briefly glanced at the others; they, like him, held their hands and clothing over their mouths.

'How much further do you reckon on, Richard?' said a deep croaky voice.

'I reckons once we's through the hanger and over the river we'll likely set camp. I'd not think the King would want to be travelling at night.' They finished relieving themselves and moved away. Lesley's eyes were popping out of her skull, her face aghast.

A bellowing command of 'Proceed' came from the front of the line of people; men and women returned to the track and recommenced their march.

After a few moments Peter was about to speak when he again had to motion to the others to get down and to keep quiet.

Two men on horseback were at the rear of the procession, presumably a protection guard.

'What's that. There. Can you see it?' said a more sophisticated voice than the ones that they had heard moments earlier. The noise of horses' came closer. One of the riders on a grey was now heading directly towards them. The four of them crouched down hiding their faces from the strangers and waited.

'Adam – look what I have found.' The man wrenched at Hargreaves' jacket and eventually pulled it away from the hawthorn bush with a tear. He brought it to his nose. 'Smells good. Lovely quality.' He stuffed the jacket into his saddlebag and returned to the track on his grey to catch up with his partner. The men rode off.

'Peter … Peter, did you hear that? They said king. Not queen, but king. Oh my god,' said Lesley frantically.

'Yes. I heard it.'

'Where are we? And what are we going to do?'

'Well, this doesn't feel like 1901,' replied Peter. 'Hargreaves, when you took the whipstaff and inserted the date token, did you put it in correctly?'

'Yes, yes of course. Well, if I didn't, then it's … it's …'

There was silence. Panic and anxiety grew among the four of them.

'I make that 1061,' said Jane.

'God. Oh my god. That must have been the King in the procession,' said Lesley with terror in her voice.

'King Edward, also known as Edward the Confessor, if memory serves me right,' added Hargreaves with a smirk.

'Shut it Hargreaves. We need to return immediately and reposition the token, with Edward Beatly expecting us he will be wondering where we have got to and all hell will break loose,' said Peter. 'Hargreaves – the whipstaff, please.'

Hargreaves' hands went to his chest and imaginary pockets, then his eyes turned towards the hawthorn bushes. The others looked at Hargreaves with incredulity.

'It's in your jacket, isn't it? Isn't it?' yelled Lesley at Hargreaves with a squeal of panic in her voice.

'I-I-I …' came Hargreaves' stuttering response.

'That's our ticket home,' added Jane. 'You idiot, Hargreaves. You bloody idiot.'

'I didn't know I was going to get stuck in a hawthorn bush and have my jacket stolen, did I?'

'You're a bloody imbecile. I always knew you were a problem after the incident at the London Eye.' Lesley prodded a finger into Hargreaves' chest and continued until Hargreaves grabbed it and pulled it away.

'Hey, that was not fair. I—'

'Calm down, everyone. Let's get ourselves a plan. Let me think for a moment,' said Peter, separating the two of them, staring towards the two riders at the rear of the procession slowly disappearing from view.

Other than the movement of animals in the woods, perhaps a boar rummaging for worms and birds in song, there was an extended silence. The realisation that the whipstaff was their only way back settled on all of them.

Peter eventually broke the quiet. 'I know it might sound

obvious, but we need to follow those horsemen and somehow retrieve the jacket – and fast.'

They pulled themselves up out of the ditch by the side of the track and tentatively followed the procession, keeping themselves at a respectful distance from the two riders in front of them.

With the light fading, Peter was becoming concerned they would be too far behind to do anything, but thankfully the river that the men had spoken of came into view.

The four of them approached the river and hid behind a rock outcrop that marked the river crossing. They had a good view towards the camp on the opposite side of the river and could see fires being lit and horses led into a paddock. Tents were being erected. A man was on sentry duty, patrolling up and down the river at the crossing point.

'What do we do now?' said Hargreaves. 'We're stuck here, aren't we?'

'Well, what do you suggest? You got us into this fucking mess,' replied Peter sharply, perhaps a little unfairly, but he felt it needed to be said.

Hargreaves did not respond. The look of anguish on both Lesley's and Jane's faces replied for him and mirrored the current sentiment of them all.

Peter was observing the camp layout and the routine of the soldier on patrol. There seemed to be no other guards looking back across the river. To the left of the paddock and the river crossing point there was a shallow indent in the river, which was being used as a latrine and washing area.

The daylight had all but disappeared. Nocturnal animals and birds were waking up. An owl swooped and hooted, a fox barked and bats flittered over the gurgling river.

Peter broke the silence. 'Right, it's now or never. I'm going to cross with Lesley and see if we can find us a tunic or two and get to the paddock and find that grey horse – and if necessary, into camp. We are going to need some local clothing – it's the only way we can get in without being noticed. Jane and Hargreaves, you stay here. Under no circumstances do you move – you got that?'

Hargreaves opened his mouth and was about to protest but said nothing. They both nodded reluctantly with glum expressions on their faces realising that their last hope was for Peter and Lesley to find the jacket and the whipstaff. Peter roughed up his hair and muddied his exposed hands, legs and face, removed his shoes and socks and pulled up his trousers. Lesley did likewise pulling her skirt up.

Holding their shoes and socks above the expected water level, they timed their crossing of the river at the point when the guard reached the first of the campfires up on the right, and as he paused. A piece of food was handed to him and he strolled back nonchalantly on his patrol, chewing at a piece of meat. It was a cold crossing for Peter and Lesley. They made it across the icy cold waters of the river without incident, dried their legs as best they could and put their shoes and socks back on as they hid behind bullrushes.

'Now what?' whispered Lesley.

'We wait,' replied Peter.

Peter was keeping a close eye on the guard's routine and the people moving to and fro from the camp to the washing area. After a few minutes, Peter saw two men of a similar height and build to the two of them heading towards the washing area.

Peter whispered, "This looks like our chance. Lesley, after I've knocked out the two men, you tie up their feet and their hands behind their backs and stuff whatever you can into their mouths, you got that?'

Lesley nodded. 'But how are you going to …?'

Peter gestured the movements with his hands. A clenched vertical fist and then a   horizontal fist, knuckles protruding. 'Didn't they teach you this in the self-defence lessons? No, from the expression on your face.'

After the two men had walked past. Peter deftly moved behind the last of them and knocked him to the ground. Moving swiftly to the second man he used a judo move before he could raise an alarm. Lesley was quick to act and bind them up with her shoelaces as Peter had asked and stuffed a wet sock into each of their mouths.

'Right, we have limited time here, Lesley. We need to remove their tunics and put them on and make our way up to the paddock. Let's see if that grey horse has a saddlebag. If not, we're going to have to go into camp and find the rider.'

'But that's not possible, Peter – just look at all the campfires and people. There's hundreds of them.'

'Listen to me, Lesley. There is no other way. Do you want to stay here?' Peter shoved his face up to Lesley and whispered harshly. 'Well I bloody well don't.' The removal of the tunics with both men lying slumped on the ground was difficult, but the two of them worked efficiently removing their clothing before putting on the local attire. Peter found it easy to change with just his trousers to remove but Lesley had to tear away the lower part of her dress before she was able to put on the tunic.

They pulled the two men away from the washing area, covered them as best they could with foliage and carefully made their way towards the paddock, avoiding the attention of people whenever possible.

Peter could see the guard on sentry duty heading back again from the camp with more food in his hands. *Good,* he thought, *he's got his mind on other things.* When they reached the paddock, the horses stirred but not unduly. There was no one else around. Peter spied two grey horses among those in the paddock and climbed over the fencing. He approached the first horse – no saddlebag. He walked towards the second grey horse, which kicked up and neighed, just the once. There was a blanket over its back. Peter couldn't see if there was a bag. He needed to get closer. With Lesley's help from the other side of the fence he pulled the blanket off to reveal a saddlebag. Peter carefully approached the horse to calm it down and opened the bag, but there was nothing inside.

'Shit – he must have taken it with him,' said Peter to himself. 'Lesley, we're going to have to go into camp and find him.'

Peter swiftly exited the paddock and joined Lesley. The two of them kept to the outskirts of the camp, bypassing people whenever they could, moving from campfire to campfire. Their outfits were fully in keeping with their surroundings; they were not challenged, although those that did walk past them made a grunted greeting sound, which Peter worked out to be 'evening', and another sounding like 'all's well'. Music, song and jollity spread out from the campfires as did dank smoke, wafting through the woods and stinging Peter's eyes.

A boar was being turned and roasted on a spit over the fourth campfire they came across. There it was – Peter could see the jacket. His heart was suddenly pounding. Hargreaves' jacket was being passed around; the men were inspecting it and smelling it until it was returned to the rider that Peter recognised.

'It's good quality, isn't it?' said the man in a commanding voice. The man rubbed his fingers over the seams. 'So smooth,' he said as he rubbed it over his cheek, 'like the bare skin of my lady wife's backside on a warm summer's evening.' Raucous laughter erupted from all the men.

'It's a great shame it's torn. The stitching is so fine – I have never seen anything like it.'

Peter realising that this was his opportunity, removed his jacket from under his tunic and stepped into the arena, leaving Lesley on the outskirts of the camp. 'Here, try this, sir,' said Peter, moving into the ring of people sitting around the fire. 'It's untorn ... sir. And I am happy to exchange it with you for the torn jacket.' Peter held out the jacket.

'What is it to you? Who are you?' The calmness and jollity around the campfire subsided as their leader spoke. A number of the men stood up, hands reaching for the hilts of their swords.

'I'm Robert, sir, from over the far side of camp close to the river. I saw you speaking of the tear and thought it would be better, sir, for you to have the untorn jacket than I, I being not so senior as you, sir.' Peter looking around at the men, heart pounding.

'He talks with a strange tongue, my Lord.'

'I don't knows him or trusts him, my Lord,' said another of the men next to the leader, who started towards Peter with a vicious snarl on his face, a dagger in his hand.

'He has no weapon on him, leave him be. He is one of us here,' said the leader. The man reluctantly withdrew as commanded.

Peter realised that he had to think quickly or else the four of them were finished. 'The jacket I can mend, sir. I make these jackets for many a year now.' Peter held out the jacket towards the leader, who took it willingly. Peter hoped that the torn one would come back his way.

'It's a joy,' said the leader. 'The King must see this. Come. Come, Robert, we go now to see him.' The leader put an arm around Peter's shoulder and another man pushed a mug of warmed ale towards him, which Peter took.

Peter glanced back over his shoulder to see Lesley standing in the shadows, clearly not knowing how to help or what to do.

Escorted by three men. Peter was perspiring profusely, his heart continued thumping as they made their way towards a central camp fire. His tunic being passed between all the men commenting on its feel and quality of stitching. He had to think straight and get this right or all was lost. As they approached the camp, Peter could see a man and women surrounding him wearing clothing far superior to anything else he had seen. That must be the king, he thought on entering the ring.

'Sire, forgive me for intruding on your evening, but we have discovered in our mists craftsmanship of the highest quality and skill.' He handed the jacket to the King.

The King remained seated and rubbed his fingers over the cloth. One of the women next to him touched a sleeve with her hand and then lifted the material to her cheek. 'It is indeed very fine Sire.' She and the King looked up towards Peter through the smoke of the fire.

'This Sire, is Robert. He has the skill to make this clothing. It is of exceptional quality as you can see.'

'Is this true?' asked the king. 'Yes, Sire. It is a skill I have learnt.' Peter swallowed and paused momentarily thinking how to reply. 'From my father and, he his father.' replied Peter in the hope that he would be believed. The King lifted his head and motioned to one of his men who instantly sauntered towards Peter gripping a large flagon in his hand and poured the liquid into a mug and handed it to Peter. The King stood and walked towards Peter. 'Let us drink and take meat together, we have much to discuss.' Their mugs clicked together. Peter drank and coughed after he swallowed. He guessed that it was probably a strong mead. 'I would like threescore jackets for my men and ladies. When can they be made ready?' Peter couldn't reply immediately as he was lost in his thoughts. What was threescore? One of the king's men then used his foot in the earth, showing the figure sixty. 'Sire this is a considerable order and I should be able to tell you once I have finished measuring. I can start in the morning'. Peter desperately trying to buy some time. The King's hand rested on Peter's shoulder. 'The morning it is then' replied the King who turned away from Peter to join the group of women by the fire. More mead was poured into Peter's mug.

Half an hour had passed before Peter and the party returned to the camp. They were a jovial group on their return, and the men either side of him had an arm over his shoulders. Peter held the torn jacket tightly in one hand that he had said he would mend, and in the other an empty mug that was instantly filled this time with warm ale by one of the men. As they reached the fire, Peter stumbled and the ale spilled over the lip of his mug.

'You will be a legend, Robert, that's for sure.' The leader stretched his hand over the fire to the spit and tore off a piece of meat from the shoulder, giving half to Peter.

'Thank you. By your leave, my Lord, I must excuse myself for a short while from this celebration and feast,' said Peter after taking another mouthful of ale. 'I must piss. You know?' Peter made the action and the men all burst into laughter shouting out loud 'Piss, piss!'

Peter put his mug down on a bench and headed away from the campfire towards the river, trying desperately not to run.

He managed to maintain his composure until out of view and earshot and started to walk faster. He thought all was well until a hand slapped him on the shoulder. He swiftly turned, making ready to fight.

'Peter, Peter, it's me. Lesley.' Lesley stepped back – Peter had lifted his arm and was about to flatten her.

'Good God. You made me jump. Now let's get out of here, fast.'

'You got it then?'

Peter showed her. Lesley sighed in relief and gave Peter a hug. Peter stuffed the jacket into his tunic.

Peter and Lesley headed towards the river crossing, but had forgotten about the sentry.

They were abruptly stopped in their tracks and challenged. 'Where's you two a-goin' at this hour of night, ey?'

'Home,' replied Peter flippantly with a smile as Lesley clouted the man on the back of his head with a piece of wood. He fell unconscious to the ground. She looked down at him worried as to what she had done.

'Come on, leave him, Lesley, he'll be fine. Let's get over the river.' Their crossing was swift, desperate to reach their companions. A head appeared around the edge of the outcrop of rock as they made their way back.

As Peter and Lesley got to the otherside they were greeted by a mightily relieved Jane.

'Where's Hargreaves?' said Lesley looking around.

'Hargreaves left me here. He crossed the river a few minutes ago. He's gone to look for you both as you had been gone for such a long time. I was about to follow and cross the river when I saw the sentry apprehend some people, I realised it was the two of you. I thought you were caught so I hid behind the rock not knowing what to do. Next thing I hear is splashing and the two of you running across the river' said Jane, relieved to see them both. A renewed sound of water splashing, and the three of them turned anxiously. Hargreaves was scampering to get to the safety of his companions.

'Have you got the jacket?' said Hargreaves with desperation in his voice. Peter pulled it out from under his tunic. It was then that Peter had a flashback. An image of Jon in the market as seen from the ship window, the first time he had used the portal, and, behind Jon he saw a face, it was Hargreaves, his face suddenly turning and making his way through the crowds away from Jon. Peter stared at Hargreaves momentarily wondering what he was doing there.

'Jane, Hargreaves, here, take some of this and let's get out of here.'

'What is it?' asked Jane.

'Wild boar. Organic, no preservatives or additives, no plastic wrapping. It's good for you,' replied Lesley.

Peter searched through the pockets of the jacket but couldn't find the whipstaff. He gave the jacket to Hargreaves and asked him to find it as he looked anxiously across the river. They hadn't yet been rumbled.

Hargreaves checked all the pockets, and then again. 'Nothing.'

'What?' said Peter incredulously.

'There's nothing here – it's empty.'

'But I've been holding the jacket tightly ever since I was given it back by the king. Nothing fell out.'

'Oh god, I can't take any more of this,' said Jane, her face dropping into her hands, her whole body rocking forwards and backwards followed by her head swaying from side to side.

Peter looked over his shoulder across the river; there was still no movement to concern him. 'Are you sure you put it in your jacket, Hargreaves?'

'Yes, yes, and yes – in the lower inside pocket on the left-hand side, and I buttoned the pocket closed. Look.' Hargreaves frantically checked and rechecked.

Peter snatched the jacket back and checked the pockets for himself in disbelief. The button to the pocket was still fastened. Hargreaves was adamant that he had put the token in. Peter's fingers searched and found the problem – a tear in the lining of the jacket had opened up the base of the pocket. 'It must have dropped out when your jacket was wrenched from the hawthorn back there,' said Peter, motioning with his head to the place where they had arrived.

'Look,' said Lesley with urgency in her voice. 'We've got some company.'

Peter turned to look back across the river. They all did.

'They've found the guard. We've been discovered,' said Peter.

'Run. Run as fast as your legs can carry you down the track back to where we arrived, and don't look back.'

The moonlit night helped the four contenders for the four hundred metres in the next Olympics. Peter reached the area of woodland and hedges first where they landed some eight hours before, exhausted. He recognised the area immediately by the gut-wrenching smell of urine and human excrement. Hargreaves followed a few seconds behind Peter. A short while later both Lesley and Jane arrived, both bending down double trying to gather some breath.

'Well done both of you. Lesley. You keep watch up on the track. Hargreaves and Jane, when you've recovered let's find that whipstaff.'

The three of them commenced the search, diving into the bushes, ignoring the needles from the hawthorn and the bramble thorns tearing at their arms and scratching their bodies as they frantically searched in the mud.

'I can hear voices in the distance but I can't see anyone. Hurry up and find it, will you,' yelled Lesley.

The search continued.

'Come on, find it,' Lesley yelled again desperately. The three of them continued their desperate search for their passage home.

'Got it. Got it. I've got it,' Hargreaves shouted moments later with joy and relief in his voice, and with a beaming smile. He was covered with bloodstains and shit. He kissed and hugged the whipstaff.

'Lesley, get down here,' said Peter, 'let's get the hell out.'

'They're charging down the track now towards us,' she called out, an arrow whistled in the air and brushed past her arm, followed by another that embedded itself in a tree. She joined the others. Peter stood up and looked briefly down the track – men, soldiers, hundreds of them with lanterns, flaming torches and tapers, reflections of the flames flickering off their weapons. A series of arrows whistled past, one landed ominously close to Peter.

'Left hand on shoulders,' called Peter. 'Token in the middle and touch the whipstaff.'

'Wait,' said Jane frantically, 'I need to find my token.' Her hand grasped at her jacket and then at her bosom searching for her hidden token that she remembered, she had tucked away inside the cup of her brasserie.

Relief on Jane's face, followed by her hand coming out of the top of her dress, holding a token between her fingers, just as the first of the soldiers reached the other side of the hedge. Another arrow whistled in the air and embedded itself with a sickening thump. 'Arrh'.

Jane touched the whipstaff and they disappeared.

There was quite a collection of people in Jon's office when they returned.

'Well, well, well. What have we here?' said Tom looking at the bloodied group.

'Have you been visiting a sewage farm? You darn well smell like it,' added Will. He grimaced and turned away.

'Henry, Hargreaves here needs urgent attention,' yelled Peter when he woke. The ominous thump of an arrow that Peter had heard, had sunk into Hargreaves' right thigh.

Henry immediately stepped towards Hargreaves to inspect the damage. Very little blood. Hargreaves' head swayed from side to side. 'Mary. Get him to St.Thomas's Hospital straight away. If they ask how he got the injury, tell them it was a stray arrow during archery practice.' Tom took a closer look at the arrow. 'Good quality hazel'. He snapped it easily in his hand to reduce the arrows' length, Hargreaves groaned with pain. He was helped up by Mary and Will.

Henry had called in Tom and Will with a view to sending them to look for the four of them after Edward Beatly had informed them that Hargreaves and the others had still not arrived.

'How did you know what happened or where we were?' asked Peter.

'After speaking with Edward, who had checked in and around Osbourne House for you, we then found that the date token had been inserted upside down. That told us immediately where you had gone. This has happened before, but not always with the best end results. Our problem was that we couldn't follow and expect to find you straight away. As you know, the *Golden Hinde* takes you to within fifty to a hundred metres of the crown, and in four hours the Crown or you could have moved miles away,' said Henry.

'Tell me, Peter, what was it like meeting the king?' asked Tom, sounding a little envious.

'Well it was no different really from speaking as we are now except I, and I'm sure Jane and Lesley here will be happy to tell you more, but I would rather get showered first and have our cuts cleaned up and changed out of these clothes.' Tom smiled and acknowledged Peter's request and patted him on the shoulder, then wished he hadn't with the smell and brown staining on his hand.

An hour later three clean twenty-first-century people emerged back into Jon's office. Henry listened intently to their story and didn't say a word about Hargreaves' injury or his mishaps; this was something Peter was sure that Jon would deal with. Henry was more intent on listening to how the four of them had dealt with the situation. Will was eager to find out what they ate and drank, Tom about the language, clothing and food and what the people were like. Henry about leadership and decision making.

'Henry, any news on Hargreaves?' asked Peter.

'He's undergoing surgery to remove the arrow as we speak. He will be fine.' Lesley and Jane continued to describe their experiences of the adventure. Peter listened to them for a while and asked to speak to Henry privately. The two of them moved to a corner of the room away from the excited voices of Lesley recalling the visit into camp and Jane the river crossing and being pursued.

'Henry. Does Hargreaves have any other responsibilities other than Queen Victoria?' Henry contemplated his response for a moment.

'None, that's his baby. Strange. Why do you ask?'

'It's. Well it's just that. Well, how can I put this, perhaps I didn't see him, but when we went back to Elizabethan times at the summer party, you remember, my first journey on the Golden Hinde, I think I saw Hargreaves from the ship.'

Henry was motionless for a few seconds, the expression on his face slowly changing from thankful they were back safely to serious. He replied.

'Are you sure?' he looked up at Peter who detected the concerned look on his face.

'I think so. He was about three or four rows behind Jon in the market area and he seemed to suddenly turn away when he realised that Jon was present in front of him.'

'Well, well.' replied Henry. 'That might explain a number of things. We couldn't work out how you were discovered on the ship so quickly. Why would he do that? Maybe he? He's got a lot of explaining to do.'

'Explain what?'

'What he was doing in Elizabethan times when it's not his responsibility. He is, as you know, in charge of 1837 - 1901.'

'But surely he would have been given authority to travel?'

'Yes, you're right. He was reprimanded a few years ago for unauthorised travel, and was grounded. His reason or excuse, was that he collected coins and wanted to complete his collection for the years 1930 - 1940. It sounds like he's starting to take liberties again, when. CPS has put a lot of trust in him. He pushed to be responsible for Victorian times.' Henry rubbed his chin in thought. 'There was a report a few years ago that said he had been seen talking to King Edward VIII, which doesn't on the face of it sound a problem, except, he apparently had Hitler and Martin Bormann standing next to him during the conversation. We sent Tom back to check the validity of the observation, but he didn't find any record of them meeting and it was put down to an incorrect sighting and the matter closed. But this will mean the file will need to be opened again. Hargreaves is a senior employee and has been part of the senior CPS management for a long time.'

'I don't understand. How did he travel without...' Henry held his hand up to prevent Peter talking outloud.

'Peter, you would be told eventually. There are three whipstaffs. The two additional ones made by Tom and William once they realised the power of the portal, in case a problem arose with the original. All are kept in Jon's safe and only removed when required. There are only four key holders.' Henry turned away from Peter looking towards Leslie and Jane and the group of people listening to their recollections. 'Hargreaves must be working on a different agenda than just CPS and his so-called 'coin collection'. Anyway, I can't deal with this matter now. I will need to discuss this with Jon immediately. Thank you Peter.' Henry finished the conversation abruptly and started to make his way towards the door.

'Oh, and Henry?'

'Yes.'

'Henry. I've had enough. I'm leaving. I'm going to head off home to see my wife.'

Henry nodded, then added as Peter stood up, 'Formal debriefing ten o'clock in the morning please, Jon's office. He will need to address the seriousness of this sortie, issues with Hargreaves and, we still have 1901 to sort out.'

Peter left the room astounded as to what he had been told and exhausted.

Peter's responsibilities continue in...
The Secret Journeys of the Golden Hinde . Part 2

EPILOGUE

A secret society, the CPS formed hundreds of years ago still exists today. The original Golden Hinde facilitating the protection of the crown, past, present and future.

The Secret Journeys of the Golden Hinde was originally called 'Sarah Bray'. She is a character in the book who gave her life to save a Princess. The change in title was not to undermine her sacrifice but reflective of the story.

ABOUT THE WRITER

This is Philip's second book. The first, *Time Bomb*, written as an adventure story to help educate/remind people of all ages of the climate challenges we are all facing. Spread the word.

Philips currently working on the second book of this series as well as continuing with Peter's Journey's on the Golden Hinde.

OTHER PUBLICATIONS

Time Bomb (Published Spring 2022)

An environmental adventure story, informing and reminding people of all ages (5 to 105) of the climate disaster in front of us.

The health of our planet is still being ignored. We have the knowledge but are not using our wisdom quickly enough.

This is the first of a series of three books. The second *'Echo Bay'* is set 5 years later. Work in progress.

The Secret Journeys of the Golden Hinde Part 2

Peter continues his work at the Crown Protection Service. Work in progress.

Printed in Great Britain
by Amazon